Benjamin Franklin and a Case of Artful Murder

By Robert Lee Hall:

Exit Sherlock Holmes
The King Edward Plot
Murder at San Simeon
Benjamin Franklin Takes the Case
A Case of Christmas Murder
Murder at Drury Lane
A Case of Artful Murder

A Benjamin Franklin Mystery:

Benjamin Franklin and a Case of Artful Murder

Further Adventures of the American Agent in London

ROBERT LEE HALL

St. Martin's Press
New York

LIBRARY OF CONGRESS CATALOGING-IN-PUBLICATION DATA
Hall, Robert Lee.
    Benjamin Franklin and a case of artful murder / Robert Lee Hall.
        p.   cm.
    "A Thomas Dunne book."
    ISBN 0-312-10936-9
    1. Franklin, Benjamin, 1706-1790—Fiction.   2. Government investigators—England—London—Fiction.   3. Americans—England—London—Fiction.   4. London (England)—Fiction.   I. Title.
PS3558.A3739B43   1994
813'.54—dc20   94-6285
                                                                      CIP

First Edition: August 1994

10 9 8 7 6 5 4 3 2 1

Benjamin Franklin and a Case of Artful Murder

*IN WHICH Mr. Franklin is
importuned by a soul in distress . . .*

Crocuses lifted their yellow heads in Mrs. Margaret Stevenson's tidy backyard, whilst out upon the Thames the great sailing ships that ferried goods from East and West rode at anchor against a cerulean sky.

April had come to Craven Street after a long winter in which Mr. Benjamin Franklin had delivered more than one murderer to justice.

At his desk in his second-story chamber the gentleman busily scribbled letters in Pennsylvania's cause. From the kitchen below arose the aroma of apple pie. A rapping sounded upon the door, and lifting his head Mr. Franklin glanced to where I sat with my Latin by the morning fire. "Polly, eh, Nick?"

"Likely," agreed I, looking up, glad for some respite from Virgil.

His chair creaked as he twisted. "Come, child."

Our landlady's pretty, honey-haired daughter burst in. She was twenty years old. Hurrying to Mr. Franklin's side, she thrust a letter breathlessly into his hand. "Delivered this moment, most mysteriously. Its bearer said you must read it at once."

Mr. Franklin's eyes narrowed. " 'Mysteriously'?"

"He would not say from whom it came."

"You asked?"

Polly wrinkled her nose. "I inquired, he would not answer. Come, your letter."

"But what did you observe of him?"

"That he was a man."

"I dote on particulars."

"He was shaped like a man. Had whiskers like a man. In short, a man."

"But, his features—?"

"A mouth, a nose, two eyes. Dear sir, your letter."

"His clothes?"

"I should have blushed if he were naked!"

Mr. Franklin threw up his hands. "Pah, I begin to think that nothing will make you blush. Do I not teach both you and Nick to report better than this?"

"I will report ev'ry button on his waistcoat if you will tell me what is in his letter."

Mr. Franklin turned to me. "What shall we do with her, Nicolas?"

"Toss her out," said I, laughing.

"Ha, too mild a punishment!"

We were spared deciding her fate by her mother's voice from below: "Polly Stevenson! Come down at once! You know you are to fetch me a joint from the butcher."

The young woman stamped her foot. "O!" She fled the room.

Mr. Franklin leant back. "I like her spirit, Nicolas. Yet do I promote too forward a manner?" He tapped the letter. "To this." Unsealing it, he read with a "Hum," and an "Oho," and when he glanced up his brown-gray eyes were lit with interest. His lids crinkled behind his small round spectacles and his smile curled thoughtfully. "It is provoking, Nicolas, it is indeed. . . ."

Aeneas' quest to found Rome could wait. "Yes, sir?"

But this proved an hour for interruptions, for there came a second rapping at the chamber door, and our landlady entered with rustling skirts. "Sir, a lady to see you."

"Titled?"

Her eyes rounded. "Why, yes, sir. But how—?"

The gentleman waved the letter. "By this. Is she placed in the parlor—the *best* parlor, ma'am?"

Mrs. Stevenson was proud of her huswifery; her breast puffed like a pigeon's. "I know how to treat the quality, sir."

Mr. Franklin smiled. "That is because you are the finest landlady in London." He made a shooing motion. "Down quickly, then, and tell her we are coming."

" 'We'?"

"Nick too, naturally."

Mrs. Stevenson frowned. The dear woman loved me as my mother would have, had she lived, but she disapproved of making a twelve-year-old boy privy to too much.

When she was gone, Mr. Franklin groaned up from his chair. "Pah, Mrs. Gout plagues me this morning. She is as persistent as a woodborer! My stick."

I handed him his bamboo.

"Better." He thrust and parried as if 'twere a sword. "Let us down to slay dragons!"

"Dragons, sir?"

He winked. "O, I hope that there are dragons, Nick."

As we descended, a tall dusky-skinned man passed us going up to his attic room. This was Peter, Mr. Franklin's black-amoor servant whom he had brought with him to London.

Mr. Franklin gave Peter murmured instructions.

3

On the ground floor he led me into the parlor.

This was a pleasant room at the front of the house furnished with a sofa and two straight-backed chairs. A forest of gewgaws which Mrs. Stevenson had acquired in the years since her husband died crowded mantel and shelves, and the walls were hung with embroidered sayings of Poor Richard, stitched by her hand. An eleven A.M. fire burnt in the grate. A woman waited. She gazed out the window upon Craven Street but turned as we entered. Though our landlady hovered in hopes of hearing what passed, Mr. Franklin shut the door.

Stepping forward, he made a small bow. "I am Benjamin Franklin, ma'am. By your letter, you wish to see me regarding a private matter?"

The woman gazed at him. Her eyes were cool umber brown, her chin lifted, yet there seemed some agitation, some ill ease, barely concealed by her manner. I guessed her age at thirty. Her fingers, in fine kid gloves, moved in a ceaseless agitation at her sides.

"Mr. Franklin, of Philadelphia?" said she at last in a low, rich voice.

"The same. Beg pardon, but may I inquire if you are just come from Drury Lane?"

She stiffened. "Why, yes. The playhouse. How did you know?"

"And did some sewing there?"

"You amaze me, sir."

A modest shrug. "A tiny spot of blood upon your glove. You pricked your finger."

She gazed in wonderment at her right glove. "But I might have pricked my finger many ways."

"Nay, some tails of scarlet twist upon your sleeve proclaim you pricked it sewing."

The thread was near invisible. She peered up from it. "Yet how do you know 'twas at Drury Lane?"

"The rouges and powders which actors use. They fly everywhere. Most vexing. You have got some upon your lace." He pointed. "See?"

Turning her wrist, she discovered a blush of pink which I should never have noted had not the gentleman shown it. Her eyes met his once more. Mine stole a look at him too: a stout, aging fellow a little above middle height dressed in plain worsted breeches and coat, his shoes square-toed and as blunt as his round, open face. He wore no wig but just his longish brown hair, tied back with a simple black ribbon. Fifty or so. You would have passed him on any London street and taken little note unless you were arrested by a quietly amused movement of the mouth or a soft glow of eyes as he turned over in his brain some quiddity of humankind.

Our visitor compressed her lips. "Mrs. Goodbody was right. You see much."

"The wardrobe mistress of Drury Lane. An excellent woman. I merely use my eyes. And my brain. Your father, pray, was in the cloth trade?"

She looked truly alarmed. "Now I know that someone has told you about me."

"No one."

"But—"

"You are a lady of quality. Such women—I mean no disrespect—do not sit and sew at Drury Lane. Some special association with the craft drew you to take up the needle as you passed the time."

"You are exceedingly clever."

"London abounds in such men; I hope that I am more than

5

merely clever. Pray, how do you come to know Mrs. Good-body?"

"Her friend was a friend of my husband's."

" 'Friend'? Her former lover, you mean."

"You are frank."

"As you must be if you wish my aid. What led you to seek Mrs. Goodbody today?"

"Her common sense."

"Her discretion too? Come, speak honestly."

Until this moment the woman had contained her agitation. Now, in response to Mr. Franklin's inquiry, her facade cracked and a helpless need split upon her face. She sank onto the sofa. "You are a good man, I see it." An affecting wail: "O, please help me, Mr. Franklin."

He stirred. "Dear me, I shall, all I can. You have but to say how."

She glanced at me.

Mr. Franklin followed her eyes. "Never let the boy trouble you. Nicolas Handy, my page, my squire, a paragon of discretion. Quite indispensable. He will take notes as you speak, but they will remain secret, as will all which passes in this chamber. You may trust him completely."

She searched my face.

I nodded to assure her.

"Then—" She sighed. Whilst she dabbed the corners of her eyes, I pulled from my coat pocket the duodecimo book I always carried. My pencil too. Mr. Franklin took the seat opposite her and I drew up the wooden chair by his side. For a moment, framed by the half-drawn velvet curtains of the room, she did not speak, and I studied her. She was slender, dressed very fine in purple satin with gold buttons and tiny ribbons. She wore upon her head a small hat, like a boat upon the waves of her rich brown hair, artfully curled. Her fingers sported rings, her throat softly glistening pearls. The fur of her long black cloak, which she had tossed carelessly upon the sofa, was the finest ermine. Her face showed breeding—yet it was breeding acquired rather than born to, I thought. One thing was certain: the woman was beautiful in an un-English way. Of Latin blood? She had olive skin, large, deep brown eyes, full lips. My hand longed to draw her, but I restrained it.

She began to speak, tremblingly:

"Have you heard, sir, of the Shenstone Diamond?"

"No."

"But it is famous."

"Forgive me, I do not know it."

"I am Vanessa Chetwynd, Lady Shenstone."

"The diamond, then, is yours?"

"My husband's. It has been in his family many years."

"I see."

Her fingers worked in her lap. "It has been stolen. That is . . . I do not know if truly stolen." Her eyes lifted in despair. "But it is surely missing."

A clopping of hooves rose from the street. The cry of an oyster seller. "You wish me to help you to recover it, then?" inquired Mr. Franklin gently.

She bent forward in a hope so pathetic that my scribbling fingers were stilled. "Would you? I can pay you to do so."

'Twas a painful moment. Mr. Franklin lifted a hand. "Tut, let us not speak of payment—not now, for I can promise nothing. I have business in London, but it goes exceedingly slow. As I fret at inaction, I shall hear your tale. There may prove some ready solution. You say you do not know if the diamond is truly stolen?" Settling back, he laced his fingers in his lap. "Begin at the beginning: tell the history of this famous gem."

And so she did.

❧ 2 ❧

*IN WHICH we learn of a famous gem
and an infamous loss . . .*

The murmur of London served as background to Lady Shenstone's tale. She took a tremulous breath:

"The diamond's birth to human eyes is lost—that is, who dug it out of the earth and cut it in the shape it has today. What is known is that it came from the East. It was in Europe by 1550, arriving first in Venice, where the doge placed it in his collection. His lady wore it; its reputation grew. But, finding himself in need of money, he sold it. It went to Spain and from thence to a small but wealthy German duchy. Later it spent some years in the hands of a Parisian noble, where it drew envious looks on his lady's bosom in His Majesty's court at Versailles. (You may see it in a portrait of Madame Gascoigne by Hyacinth Rigaud.) It has been worn by wives and mistresses. It has been coveted by scoundrels and lords. Rumor whispers that three men died in attempts to place their hands on it, and women have spent storms of tears for want of it."

"Is it so very beautiful?"

"And terrible."

"How came your husband to possess it?"

"The Shenstones are an old family; they trace their lineage

back to Alfred the Great and are proud of an intermingling of highborn Norman blood. They own great estates—that is, they did. But at the height of their power, in Queen Anne's reign, my husband's grandfather bought the diamond. His lady was a great beauty, vain. Having heard the gem made any woman who wore it the envy of all others, she begged him for it. It proved for sale, and uxorious old Shenstone encumbered himself with crushing debt to possess it. The irony is that his willful wife lived but three months after it came into in her hands. She is why the cursed thing arrived in England."

"Plainly you hate it. Why?"

"Because it means so much to my husband. In his eyes it *is* the Shenstone name; it is his one great treasure. People say, 'There goes Shenstone; *he* owns the diamond.' "

"And because he values it more than you?"

A tremor shook her ladyship.

"And it is *you* who have lost the gem?"

The woman palely nodded.

"Tell how."

She took breath. " 'Tis all because of a picture, would to God it had never been proposed. My husband must have a portrait of me, to hang in our London house. He knows much of art—he is a connoisseur and collector—and so took the choice of painter upon himself. This fell to James Cavitty, of Cranbourne Street. My husband met with him, a pose and background were settled upon, and the thing was begun.

"I sat three times, but only for my face and hands. When I asked why my figure was not done, Cavitty said 'twas the custom: I would deliver the gown which had been chosen, and it would be draped upon a lay figure to spare me standing in it. This pleased me, for I had developed a dislike for Cavitty. But his next news made me frown. My lord had insisted the Shenstone Diamond be in the picture, prominently upon my bosom. 'You will deliver that as well, ma'am,' said the artist, as cool as if he asked the time o' day. 'So valuable a thing?' I protested, but he answered with wheedling assurance that that too was the custom, and he promised he would watch over the gem as if 'twere his life: ' 'Twill take but one day to limn it. No harm can come in a day.' O, how I have learnt the lie in that!"

"All of us must learn it. Go on."

Her hands twisted. "My husband had left town—some business at his estate; I could not ask him what to do. I debated. Had he not insisted the gem be in the picture? Too, Cavitty made me feel I should displease my lord if I did not act. In short, I removed the diamond from safekeeping and delivered it, taking two strong manservants with me to protect against robbery—how wise in precautions I thought myself, how proud!—but 'twas not in the streets of London that the gem slipped from my hands.

"I was to leave it with Cavitty and retrieve it the following afternoon. I did not sleep well after I let it go; forebodings wracked me—why had I not waited for my husband's counsel?—yet I awoke to sunny skies, no dark clouds. I shopped in the Strand, I made some calls. Yet still I felt ill-ease. Promptly at four I presented myself at Cavitty's door in Cranbourne Street, for I longed for heart's ease.

"An old manservant brought me to the studio. I saw at once by the artist's face that something was amiss.

" 'Well?' says I, breathless.

" ' 'Tis gone,' says he.

"He might as well have struck me. 'The diamond?' says I.

" 'I cannot find it,' says he.

" 'But you *must*,' says I.

" 'O, I shall.' He wore a terrible smile; I did not know what to make of it. 'It has been . . . misplaced, but I shall find it.'

"I could only stare. 'Misplaced where?'

"He grew insolent. 'If I knew that, ma'am, I should lay hands on it now.'

"I rushed to him. 'Come, sir, you *must* lay your hands on it. Otherwise I shall call a constable.' I had never liked him, Mr. Franklin. He had been haughty when painting me, ordering me to sit still or hold my head just so. Now he bent into my face.

" 'Call the constable if you please, ma'am,' says he. 'Then your husband must learn of the affair.'

" 'Of course my husband must learn of what you have done.'

" 'Of what *you* have done, I say. Did not *you* give me the gem?'

"I gaped, yet I saw with a terrible sinking where he led.

"He sneered. 'Was't not foolish to let the diamond out of your possession?'

" 'But you assured me—'

" 'Assured? Could you not have stayed with the gem whilst I painted it? I said that you should.'

" 'Why, you did not.'

" 'I say I did. And who is to say I did not return it and you lost it through some carelessness?' " Lady Shenstone passed a trembling hand over her brow. "How despairing I felt. It was as if a pit had opened at my feet, and I tumbled in. The man was right, I should never have given him the gem. A thing so important to my husband? Yet I had never believed it could be lost. The worst of it was I did not know what *lost* meant.

" 'You say the diamond is only misplaced—?' I pressed him.

" 'I may recover it,' was all he would reply.

" 'But how long until you do so?'

"He treated me as if I were some importuning beggar: 'That is for me to know. Go home. I shall send to you when I discover further.'

"I begged him, but he had become stone. I was but a

11

woman, his manner seemed to say; I must put things in his hands. He took my elbow, he steered me to the door. 'I have sittings to attend to.' With this he thrust me out.

"At first I was outraged. I should put my husband on him! I should have him whipped! But then I thought: if I did so, my lord should learn of my folly in giving up that which was so dear to him. Cavitty had read me well. Why had I not used more sense, told the man he must come to our house to paint the gem? Was he not in our employ? Should he not do as I commanded? Yet I had let him lure me by false assurances and now found myself in his hands. Riding back through London, I reflected harder than I have ever done in my life. What to do? At last I decided I had time, I would wait. Cavitty might recover the gem. Surely he would!—had he not all but promised? Anything to prevent my husband learning the truth.

"And so I returned home and struggled to be of good cheer. I played with little Toby—Tobias, our dear son—but all that had given me joy tasted of brass. I began to see that my hopes were built on sand. Cavitty might be only falsely assuring me. For all I knew he had the diamond and meant to sell it to his profit. Had he planned this all along?"

Mr. Franklin had sat very still. "Very troublesome indeed," said he at last. "How long since you learnt the diamond was missing?"

"On Tuesday. Wednesday and Thursday—this very morn— I applied to Cranbourne Street. Yesterday Cavitty snarled that he had no word. Today he would not even see me but bade some manservant tell me he was busy. I have been tormented, Mr. Franklin; I cannot sleep. My husband returns in a fortnight."

"Thus you come to me." The gentleman held his hands in his lap, his black buckled shoes together before him. He gazed at his visitor, yet I thought he saw, too, reflections in some

12

deep pool. He rubbed the knee of his breeches as he pondered her tale.

For my part I longed to thrash the impudent Cavitty.

The fire crackled. Mr. Franklin stirred. "If I am to recover this famous diamond (I make no promises), I must know what it looks like. Nick is adept at drawing. Describe it to him, ma'am."

Lady Shenstone looked doubtful. "Very well." Turning a page, I poised my pencil as she began to speak. Her voice came low and urgent, its words conveying both the gem's beauty and her hatred of her husband's love of it. She described with great precision; yet struggle as I might, I could not limn that which I did not have before me.

Mr. Franklin made a gesture. "Might he sit next you, ma'am, so you may guide his hand?"

She nodded, and I rose to join her, traversing to a realm of sweet, subtle scent, she sliding so near that I could feel the small urgent movements of her person and hear the soft creak of her stays. Her gloved hand with its little spot of blood guided mine. "You are expert indeed." Her warm breath ruffled my hair. "Yes, yes, that is it . . . no, more facets, so . . . and the setting . . . wrought like this—"

When I was done I departed my lady's heady sphere, back to the chair beside Mr. Franklin. Together he and I looked at my drawing. The diamond was magnificent: large and oval-shaped, set in a filigree of gold. This was but pencil on paper; the real thing must take one's breath away, and I recalled how only months ago four splendid emeralds had played their role in a perilous adventure.

"Your boy has done well," said Lady Shenstone.

"Nick is a fellow of parts. So this is the Shenstone Diamond, beautiful indeed; I see why it is coveted. How many times did you say you sat for James Cavitty?"

"Three."

"For how long each sitting?"

"An hour."

"You delivered your dress to be painted the same day you delivered the gem?"

"I did."

"What did Cavitty do with the dress?"

"My manservants carried it in, wrapped to protect it against the dust of the town. Cavitty told them to place it upon a chair in his painting room."

"You saw this done?"

"I did."

"And the diamond?"

"It is kept in a small rosewood box with a silver clasp and purple velvet cushion, on which the gem rests. This box I gave to Cavitty. He must have read my misgiving, for he repeated in his rude way that I need not fear: I might pick it up from him tomorrow, for he meant to work on it that very afternoon. He has a sort of artist's desk against one wall of his studio, cunningly designed, with many compartments that fold out and open up. After first looking into the box, he placed it in the large center drawer of this desk. He closed the drawer. That is the last I saw of the Shenstone Diamond."

"Not the last forever, let us hope. What was his expression when he first glimpsed the gem?"

"Why . . . he lifted the lid, he looked. Perhaps his fingers tightened a little on the box, I do not recall."

"And so you left and returned home?"

"I did."

"Who else knew you gave the diamond to Cavitty?"

"No one."

"The manservants who accompanied you?"

"I sent them out to my chair before I took the box from my cloak."

"Yet might someone in the artist's studio have heard him tell you that you must bring it?"

"There were many people about: his sister, an assistant, an apprentice, servants. And, now I think, there were two doors to the painting room; neither may've been completely shut. And the screen behind which Cavitty paints—it was pulled out; someone might have stood in back of it, I suppose."

"Whilst he painted, did you converse?"

"A little."

"On what subjects?"

"He hoped to move to larger quarters, he said. He hoped to employ another apprentice."

"He is ambitious, then. And what did you tell him?"

"Nothing. I found the man too haughty, as I said."

"Now, ma'am, I should like to know more of you."

"If you believe it will help."

"A brief history?"

She smoothed the satin of her bodice. "As I told you, Papa was a cloth merchant. He began in a small way but is clever and strong-willed and did well, so that by the time I was twelve we had a fine house in London and a coach and servants and went about in society. I was educated at home; my brother went to Oxford."

"How did you come to marry Lord Shenstone?"

A wry smile. "Money is in want of a title. Titles are in want of money. I had a large dowry. Lord Shenstone had his name. And so—" She lifted her hands.

Mr. Franklin peered. "Was it so very much a matter of buy-and-sell?"

"No, I do not mean to mislead you. There was strong feeling

on both sides. I loved my husband—love him still—and he loves me. I only meant to say how we were brought together. My father never wished to marry me to a man I did not care for. On the other hand he was no fool; 'twould be no bad thing if the man I loved possessed a title. Lord Shenstone looked for a wife with a considerable dowry. (I have never faulted him for living by the way of the world.) Learning of this, my father approached him. They met, they parleyed. The upshot was a dinner at our home to which a number of people were invited, though only one was allowed to find himself alone with me as if by chance. For propriety's sake this first meeting lasted but ten minutes, yet it was enough for me to begin to see my lord's good qualities. We were married eight months later."

"And that event occurred—?"

"Five years ago."

"Your husband's need of money grew out of his grandfather's beggaring himself over the Shenstone Diamond, you say?"

"And out of his father's attempts to recoup the loss. His father only made things worse, for he was near ruined by the South Sea Bubble."

"I see. Yet your husband still possessed the diamond. He might have sold it—others had done so before him. Why did he not?"

Bitterness returned to her tone. "Pride. The thing had become an emblem. Losing it was—is—in his mind like losing his name."

"But your dowry turned matters around?"

"For a time; for two years we were well off. Yet we came gradually to live in more and more straitened circumstances. My husband games. Too, he keeps a fine equipage; he is accustomed to a grand style of living. Thus debts arise, bills come due. But happily that is over; we have for the past six months had plenty of money."

"O? Indeed, I am glad to hear it. Pray, what brought about the change?"

"Luck at gaming."

"That is what he told you?"

A small frown. "I have no reason to doubt him. Now we are out of the woods, he promises to go no more to the tables."

"So, if this affair of the 'misplaced' diamond were resolved, you would be thoroughly content?"

Her eyes saucered. "O, yes, Mr. Franklin! Can you help me?"

He brooded. "Your habits with the diamond—how often do you wear it?"

"Not often. To parties, balls, oratorios of Handel; my husband likes to see it upon my breast on such occasions."

"Otherwise—?"

"It is kept under lock and key, in a strongbox in a room off our bedchamber. The strongbox is cunningly disguised; it seems but a dressing table. No servant ever sees us open it."

"The key?"

"There are two. One is hid in our chamber; not the slyest felon could find it. My husband keeps the other."

"You said you were glad to learn you need not sit more for the artist. Was it so unpleasant?"

Her lips compressed. "I do not know if you will understand, but there were . . . currents of unhappiness there."

He tilted his head. "I do not entirely understand. But I mean to if I am to help. Where precisely is your husband's estate?"

"Oxfordshire."

"Not so very far from London, then. And he returns in a

fortnight? That adds pepper to the pot." Mr. Franklin rose. "We must dish you up resolution before the dish grows too hot. Dear lady—" He held out a hand, which she took as she stood, he brushing her glove with his lips. "—I have much to think on. Where may I find you if I must know more?"

She gave an address in St. James's Street. Then, with effusions of deep gratitude, she was gone.

Mr. Franklin's gaze met mine. "Not exactly dragons, Nick. But a mystery to solve— 'Twill do!"

✥ 3 ✥

*IN WHICH a young man has a
birthday and proposes a plan . . .*

Mounting to Mr. Franklin's second-floor chamber, we
entered just as noontime bells pealed over London.
The fire had long since died, but the sun shone
bright, and Mr. Franklin flung wide the casements of his bow
window. There stood Northumberland House, Westminster
Bridge; there stretched the long, mighty reach of the Thames.
He gazed out whilst I stood by his chair. Though the city
spewed coal smoke, the air was infused with Spring, and the
wavelets of the great river sparkled as it curved south. Bird-
song twittered above a thousand close-packed rooftops.

Mr. Franklin had chosen this lodging for its proximity to the
seat of power. Near ten months in London, he still waited
upon the obstinate Richard and Thomas Penn, whose defeat
was the main object of his sailing. He had naught but praise for
their father, who had founded the Pennsylvania colony, but he
had conceived a great contempt for the sons, inheritors of the
proprietorship, who lolled in their fine London houses and
would not allow their lands to be taxed.

'Twas to petition the Crown to force 'em to pay that

Benjamin Franklin had been sent to these shores by the Pennsylvania Assembly.

But that business was not on his mind as he turned with a lively look. "And so, Nick, what do you make of our visitor?"

"I think you begin to get a name as a rescuer of souls in distress, sir," said I.

He smiled. "Speak more to the point."

"Well, then, Lady Shenstone—" I faltered.

He tilted his head. "Is beautiful?"

"Yes."

"With a sweet scent about her? Fetching ways? A winning figure?"

"All of that."

"You begin to note the ladies, then." His warm brown eyes measured me. "You are growing, Nicolas. Why, you are an inch taller than when you first crossed our landlady's threshold! Hum, we must think on your future. But to the business at hand: what make you of our visitor's story?"

"Very affecting, sir. I despise this Cavitty."

"Truly a blackguard—by her telling."

"He might not be so?"

"Coins have two sides. What is *his*, I wonder? Think you, how strange—the diamond *misplaced*. I do not know how to take it. And the man assuring her he can recover it, though he seems not to be sure where it has gone?—I have not heard such a tale. And then, her husband: his family, his gaming, his debts, his pride in the gem which bears his name . . . How many crimes are committed in the name of Name! Does my lady tell all? Half the truth may be a great lie. Indeed, the affair shows much that wants development and may divert us as we wait upon the Penns. Dear me!" Glancing at his pocket watch, he propelled himself toward his wardrobe. "I shall be tardy joining Straney at the George and Vulture." He pulled forth a blue coat with bright brass buttons. "Whilst I am out, Nick, your Virgil. You may practice your drawing too."

"I shall, sir," said I.

Much as I longed to accompany Benjamin Franklin on his peregrinations about the city—to clubs where he enjoyed the conversation of learned men, to philosophical societies, to Westminster itself—so pleasant was Craven Street after the bruised life I had led at Inch, Printer, from which I had been rescued just months ago, that I rarely regretted being left at home. When Mr. Franklin was gone, my gaze encircled the familiar room: the oaken door; the fireplace faced by his comfortable chair; the small side table, whereon rested today's *London Chronicle*, which his friend William Strahan—Straney—published; the bow window; the broad desk littered with foolscap; the bookcase spilling with titles, from Locke to his own scientific essays; the dresser with the painting of his little son, Francis, who had died of smallpox before he was five; the featherbed; the wardrobe. A modest room for so remarkable a man.

Would he recover the Shenstone Diamond? I thought on that as I sank into his chair with my Virgil, frowning over Aeneas. But my mind refused to transform the Latin to English, and I snatched up my notebook. There, unbeknownst to Mr. Franklin, I had sketched Lady Shenstone. I squinted at my effort. Though I wanted instruction in the finer points of art, I believed I had improved. Had I not captured much of the woman, her character as well as her look? Her firm shoulders and strong chin showed she had spirit; otherwise she would never have sought Mr. Franklin. Was she as helpless as she made out?

But it was less her character than her feminine nature that held my eyes. Mr. Franklin was right; I grew, in more ways than one, and I began to feel tormenting promptings that made me toss at night and burn by day. How I had been stirred by sitting next our beautiful visitor. How pretty I began to find Polly. How I noted the soft cheek and rounded figure of many a maid we saw in the Strand. Further, I was tumbled into confusion by the changes about my person, feeling my face hourly to see if the soft fuzz upon my jaw grew to a manly beard. As for my voice, it had begun to creak and crack like an old floor.

I made my way back to Aeneas but was glad when after half an hour I could with good conscience leave him to go fetch water for Mrs. Stevenson from the pump at the top of the street. There I hung about awhile listening to the tittle-tattle of the neighborhood. Back at number 17, having delivered my pail, I was entrapped by Polly on the stairs, she begging me to tell her what had been in Mr. Franklin's letter. "And who was the lady who called soon after? What did she want?" Polly purred. She petted my arm, she called me Sweet Boy, her milk-warm breath transfixing me. 'Twas delicious importunity, but I held out against it (Mr. Franklin liked to keep his business to himself), and her honey ringlets tossed as she flounced off in defeat. Dressed very fine, Mr. Franklin's son, William, came in at four from the Middle Temple, sniffing as he passed me as if to say, O, *you*, as he mounted to his chamber. There was no love lost betwixt us.

Wishing to be alone, I crept out to the embankment at the foot of Craven Street, on the way stopping by Mr. Tisdale's printing shop to smell the ink, which I loved as much as Mr. Franklin did. By the lapping Thames, perched on a piling, I drew three ragged boys flinging dead mice at gulls. How good it felt to be outdoors after long Winter, which had nearly froze the river. I gazed out at the broad sweep of the Thames. Might I one day sail to America with Mr. Franklin on one of the tall ships riding in her reaches? I knew he must one day return to his wife and daughter.

Dusk fell. At eight P.M. we gathered for supper in the cosy, stone-flagged room belowstairs, next Mrs. Stevenson's kitchen. Her table was large and round and always set with what Mr. Franklin proclaimed, "the finest fare in London." It was exceedingly fine this eve: a roasted shoulder of mutton and potatoes and peas and a salamagundi, which I had never ate before, and cider and a bottle of port for the gentlemen. We were the usual five: Mr. Franklin, William on one side of him, I on the other, Mrs. Stevenson, and her Polly, rallying William as she often did, though I believed she liked him better than she let on. But there was a sixth, Peter, Mr. Franklin's blackamoor, who sat with us, though he usually ate alone in his room under the eaves. I was puzzled but pleased at his presence, for he had soft eyes that saw keenly whilst his ears understood more than mere words. His gaze met mine; we secretly smiled. Our understanding ran deep, for I too had been a slave in my way; Peter and I were both former slaves.

After the dishes were cleared came an apple pie, oozing sauce. "For you, Nicolas," pronounced Mrs. Stevenson, setting it before me, "as it is your birthday."

My eyes flew to Mr. Franklin. He nodded. "It *is* your birthday, Nick. True, you never knew the day, for no one ever took note of it at that wretched place I saved you from. But before Dora Inch hung at Tyburn I wrung the information from her. You are today, Nicolas Handy, thirteen years old." He wrapped an arm about my shoulders. "Hurrah!"

At this they all beat upon the table with their trenchers, even William, and drank a toast. Tears threatened, my heart was so full, but I swallowed 'em and said I was sure I never deserved such kindness. Then came presents too. Polly gave

23

me a fine linen shirt which she herself had sewed, Mr. Frank-lin a book: *Robinson Crusoe*. William presented a waistcoat which he had had made by "the finest tailor in London," he boasted, which mitigated our quiet enmity. "Thank you, sir, very much," said I. Hanging his head, Peter murmured that he was sorry he had nothing to give, but I reminded him that he had saved me from Mr. Bumpp in the adventure with the em-eralds. "I shall ever be grateful for that."

I cut the pie and we ate—delicious! Afterward Mr. Franklin took up his fiddle and played tunes and sang merry songs, then snatched up Mrs. Stevenson and whirled her in a jig about the room and into the kitchen, from whence we heard a clanging of pots, Mrs. Stevenson laughing and crying, "Nay, sir, but nay!" as they jigged back and struck the table so hard the candles spilt wax. "O, O, O!" sputtered she, rocking on her heels and clutching her breast. "My heart, my heart!"

'Twas amongst such grand frivolity that Nick Handy knew the first true birthday of his life.

Thirteen years old. I thought on this as I mounted the stairs with Mr. Franklin at ten P.M. On the landing William nodded good night and went to his room. I made to enter mine, the tiny chamber opposite Mr. Franklin's, but he beckoned, "A word, Nick," and I followed through his door. His casement was still open, beyond which London lay dark, though I glimpsed bright points of stars in the sleeky black firmament above the angled roofs.

Closing the panes, Mr. Franklin sank into his chair. "Sit you, lad."

I perched on the end of his bed.

He regarded me. "So. You are a young man, now, I see."

"I do not feel a man," answered I.

"Truly, it takes years to form one. I myself am still in the making." He shook his head. "How this affair of the Penns makes me *old*! But 'tis you, Nick, I think on. What am I to do with you?"

I stared. "Do with me, sir?"

"I mean, what shall you do with yourself? Many a boy your age is 'prenticed out, yet I am reluctant to take that step, for I like to have you by my side."

I was moved, for there was much behind these words. I was Benjamin Franklin's natural son, the issue of his liaison with Rose Handy, whom he had loved. Knowing she was with child, she had fled America for London only to fall into the Hexham household, where she was murdered out of spite by the wicked lady of that house. Mr. Franklin had learnt my whereabouts only six months ago, yet though he had rescued me, we never spoke to others of our true relationship. Indeed we rarely spoke of it betwixt ourselves.

"I should not like to leave you, sir," said I.

"Yet something must be done, some course set. Your drawing, I think on that. 'Tis a true talent, and is it not best to seek your life's work in what you love?" I understood this, for he himself had meant at age forty to retire to his beloved scientific pursuits before his colony's call forced him to butt heads with the Penns.

A thought struck me. "Lady Shenstone said the painter, Cavitty, looked for another apprentice. Why cannot I seek that place?"

"What?"

I bent forward. "Think, sir. Did you not say you wished to learn Cavitty's side of the story? If I were in his studio—not truly indentured, only to be tried, perhaps, for a time—I could learn of art and of the whereabouts of the Shenstone Diamond too."

His look said he did not entirely reject the idea, and I hung fire as he sank back rubbing his jaw and glancing at me now and then from under his brows as if I were some new species of boy. "Cavitty would have to agree to this 'trial,'" murmured he at last, gruffly. "I shall think on it. To bed with you, now."

I went light of heart to think that I might help Mr. Franklin in so interesting a way. Yet alone in my chamber I had second thoughts. Might it be perilous? I shivered. What had I proposed?

Only thirteen, I pulled the coverlet over my head as the watchman cried the quarter hour from the cobbles below.

❧ 4 ❧

*IN WHICH we scrutinize satire, stay a
bully, and meet an artist . . .*

Friday dawned grayer than Thursday, with the discommoding fickleness of the English sky. Rolling out of my narrow bed, I gazed out my window as I pulled on shirt, breeches, boots. At seven A.M. soot-dark clouds scudded from the east, and a wind shook the budding branches in Mrs. Stevenson's backyard.

Rain would fall before the half hour.

I went as usual to Mr. Franklin's chamber. His casement stood open, he before it as naked as the day he was born, dipping his round, sturdy body in brisk knee-bends: ". . . eighteen . . . nineteen . . . twenty." Done, he puffed to the basin to slap cold water about his person whilst I drew his maroon dressing gown from the wardrobe.

I handed him the garment.

"Thank you, Nick." He put it on. "Ah, how my air-baths invigorate!" Drawing me to the window, he gazed out with an arm about my shoulders as if he offered the whole grand smoky house for our investigation. He turned. "I have thought on your proposal."

I met his eyes. "Yes?"

" 'Tis an excellent idea, I believe. It depends, of course, upon Cavitty: he must agree to take you on trial, with no indentures (we do not wish to yoke you to him). But if he proves to want an apprentice as Lady Shenstone suggested—and if he agrees to temporary terms—we may learn if the life of the artist suits you."

I felt a smile grow. "Truly?"

"There is much still to be seen to, but it is possible. What say you, Nick? Still game?"

"O, yes!"

He smiled back. "I thought that you would be, in accordance with which, I have sent Peter round to tickle Jimmy Ralph's fancy, for we may need a second actor in our play." He went to his desk. "For now, a fire, eh, whilst I write the latest news to my goodwife, Deborah? Later we shall gad about London."

With mounting excitement—and some trepidation—I blew up a blaze as the first fat droplets of rain scattered down.

By ten we were in Mr. Franklin's coach, Peter our driver. At the top of Craven Street we turned right, into the Strand. The rain had proved fitful, ceasing soon, though shop signs swayed in a gusting wind. A young whore plied her trade amongst greasy puddles at the corner of Northumberland Street, and I gazed at her with a mixture of pity and shameless desire, glad when Mr. Franklin distracted me.

He had got back a note from Mr. Ralph, saying that that gentleman should be happy to meet us today. "But first we shall explore London's world of art." I saw by the way he leant on his bamboo that he was as eager as I. 'Twas like him to leap in feet-first—though with forethought (his mind was both restless and methodical). As we drove east in the direction of St. Paul's, he mused. "An artist may be many things, Nick. He

28

may earn his bread as a coach painter, sign painter or wall painter. If he is more skilled, he may render old-master copies. Or he may become one of those traveling limners who trudge about with his easel on his back in hopes that some tradesman will pay him for a picture of family and dogs."

"May not he become Joshua Reynolds too?"

"You know of Mr. Reynolds? How you come along! But 'tis not talent alone that gains that height. To rise to it a man must be able to say he has been to Italy to commune with the spirit of Raphael. He must also have the wherewithal to set himself up to impress the Quality. And he must be adept at bowing and scraping. (Your bowing and scraping will take you far.)"

Plainly becoming a respected artist was no easy thing. Passing under Temple Bar, we arrived at Carrington Bowles, in St. Paul's Churchyard. This proved a print shop, where some dozen people gawked on the pavement in front. The attraction was the display of prints in the bubbled glass panes, the top row devoted to dour canonical countenances (John Wesley's was prominent). But these were not what drew most eyes. 'Twas those lower down—and in easier view—that caused a stir: wicked satires. "Lud, how he *dares*!" cried one gent. We looked. Some aimed at political targets I knew naught of—but others, jackasses with human faces, made their point even to an ignorant boy. A whole parade of London sin was pilloried: gluttonous lords, licentious ladies, tipsy clergymen, vain actors, rhymeless poets, self-seeking politicians, cheating tradesmen, wanton courtesans. I admired their lively line. Might I do the like someday?

We entered upon more prints, bins of 'em: etchings, engravings, mezzotints, woodcuts. Prints on the walls too, tinted and untinted, framed and unframed. Many were copies: Rubens and Rembrandt, Boucher and Watteau, Grünewald and Dürer, Leonardo, the Bellinis, the Carracci. Most of these names were new to me (my education with Mr. Franklin was aborning), and the gentleman let me view my fill, peering, studying, discovering how much I must learn. Madonnas mourned Christs, Danaës were showered with gold, Venuses rose from the waves, dead hares lay amongst plates of fruit. There were military portraits, portraits of squires, family portraits. One bin was devoted to racehorses, another to hunting dogs. There was even a prize hog, Butcher, who squinted like a cutpurse from his filigreed medallion.

Beckoning the shopman, Mr. Franklin tapped a print in which a well-known member of Parliament took money secretly from French agents. "There is no proof of this crime. May a lord be found guilty by a print shop?"

The man pursed his lips. "His guilt or innocence is nothing to us, sir. Satire is all the rage."

"And no law prevents?"

"None."

Mr. Franklin sighed. "Tell of these, then." He pointed to eight prints handsomely framed, William Hogarth's *The Rake's Progress*. With unsparing scrutiny they depicted folly's descent into ruin.

The shopman's eyes lit. "More to your liking, eh? 'Tis one of many series of prints. You are not a subscriber, then?"

"Pray, what is that?"

"An artist embarking upon a series makes up a ticket, which is a contract with a subscriber to deliver a number of prints as they are done. Thus you might obtain *Views of Rome* or *Squires of Surrey*. Or this. 'Tis unsubscribed, the last available. Should you care to buy?"

Mr. Franklin said no, but as we turned to go our attention was arrested by a print near the door: *Peter Pursestring and the Excise Bill.*

'Twas signed James Cavitty.

We peered at it. 'Twas rectangular, about twelve inches high by eighteen long, not so scurrilous as the print of the gentleman taking money from the French, but an attack nonetheless.

"Many would recognize this 'Peter Pursestring' under a different name," said Mr. Franklin.

"Would they, sir?" I could not help admiring the artist's skill, his venom too. His graver bit like a knife, and I began to see how art could wound.

"He is good, this Cavitty," murmured Mr. Franklin. "You shall learn much of him, perhaps. Let us go." We went out to our coach. "The artists live in Leicester Fields, Shorter's Court, Compton Street, but the great many of 'em inhabit St. Martin's Lane. That is where we shall fly next."

We soon passed St. Clement Danes, I happy to have so fine a guide. As often, Mr. Franklin circled about his subject, moving from far to near, to obtain perspective. The Fleet became the Strand, and we were shortly in St. Martin's Lane, debouching at the corner of Long Acre under the sign of The Maulstick, from which emerged a roistering babble at twelve-thirty, Peter was told he might return to Craven Street. "We shall foot it."

We began to stroll, seemingly at random. London's Capital of Art! The potato-seller pushed his barrow, the beggar boy cadged for coins, a woman in skirts and bonnet peered in shop windows as women did all over London, but this street had a unique flavor. I thought I smelt paint—and did, for in rapid succession we passed three colormen's shops. There were framers too. Dealers. More printsellers, and I noted a rainbow hue on the hands of many of the fellows rushing by: a carmine finger, an ochre, an ultramarine—painters! Eagerly I scanned their faces for some intentness of gaze or particular satisfaction at how they were privileged to earn their bread; but all I noted was that their clothes were almost universally ragtag; indeed they looked more like dogs sniffing for bones than like lords of a higher realm. Had Mr. Franklin brought me here so I might taste reality too?

At the corner of Cranbourne Street came the clamor of an altercation. We turned. A burly black-haired boy some two or three inches taller than I and two or three years older stood over a smaller red-haired boy; he thrust his face furiously into this boy's face. "You stupid, useless mole!" screeched he. "See what you have done. Look at Master's painting. You have struck it and scraped it and paint has come off, and now it must be fixed. What shall I do?" He snatched the red-haired boy— "Bloody titmouse. Bloody *mole!*"—and shook him so hard the boy's teeth rattled.

My hands curled to fists. Having been treated thus often by Buck Duffin at Inch, Printer, I hated bullying, as much when it was practiced on another as on myself, and I felt near to leaping upon black-hair. But the manner of his victim stayed me. The child was flat-faced and ugly, his carrot-colored hair sticking up like a brush, and he had a thin frame and even thinner arms, but he took his punishment with a sneer, as if the worst his enemy could do only proved what a fool that enemy was. I glanced at the painting. It was about four feet high and had been leant against a horse-pole outside a framer's shop, a three-quarters portrait, plainly some newly-rich merchant, handsomely finished but with a faintly mocking air, as if the artist secretly laughed at its subject's pompous pose. It was un-framed, no doubt intended for the very shop outside which it stood, and there was a smear upon the white-wigged burgher's elegantly outthrust elbow. Some inches of bare canvas showed through his scarlet coat.

I turned back. The altercation had drawn more than a dozen onlookers, and black-hair now had the thin boy's ear and was beginning to swing him by it alarmingly, like a child on a maypole. "You ass," squeezed out red-hair's hard little voice as his legs kicked by, " 'twas *you* scraped the picture as we passed that window. *You* carried it. *You* did not see the open casement. Master said not to take it to the framer's before 'twas dry, but you *would* take it, and now see what has happened."

Truth never cures a bully, and this dose only made black-hair swing the harder, so that he seemed near to tearing red-hair's ear quite off (or at least to damaging it significantly), and I felt myself about to spring upon him when a bamboo stick halted me, shooting out and rapping black-hair smartly upon the shoulder.

"Stop it, I say," commanded Benjamin Franklin.

Black-hair started and obeyed but with no very good grace. He did not let go red-hair's ear.

"I think punishment is less called for than rectification in this case, do not you?" said Mr. Franklin.

Black-hair's eyes narrowed hotly. "Here, now, wot business is this of yours?"

"Justice is my business."

A lick of lips. "Justice?" Black-hair jerked red-hair's ear. "This *mole* destroyed property."

"Ow!" protested red-hair.

Mr. Franklin stepped meaningly near. " 'Tis justice to that property of which I speak. Should you not take the painting back and repair it, surely a matter of but a few strokes of a brush, the application of which need not trouble your master?" He poked black-hair with his bamboo. "Eh?"

The crowd watched, very still, whilst the older boy digested this plan. "Um . . . p'rhaps you are right," muttered he, eyeing the stick. Scowling, he cuffed the small boy. "Come along, Biggs, you mole. Walk ahead, where I can see you. And if you see any casements, you must give warnin'!"

Biggs brushed himself off, rubbed his ear as if it were a wound he had proudly got in some war, and swaggered back down Cranbourne Street.

Black-hair loomed before me with the painting. Then he had shouldered me aside and was gone.

An April blue sky had erased all the morning's clouds. The mob dispersed. "Would one of 'em," mused Mr. Franklin, watching 'em resume their former paths, "have lifted a finger to prevent this, had I not?" He pressed a coin into the palm of a blind man huddled on the pavement nearby. "A drop, a drop." He drew me on.

"St. Martin's Lane Academy," said Mr. Franklin ten minutes later, pointing. "Sir James Thornhill, who did the Painted Hall at Greenwich, founded it. William Hogarth has reopened the institution."

If I expected something grand, I was disappointed, for the building which he indicated on the west side of the lane, though broad, was unprepossessing: two stories of soot-smudged yellow brick, a stoop, a fanlight door in want of paint, three windows on either side of it, some greenish copper guttering, a slate roof like a sober cap and two Jacobean chimneys twisted into demon's ears. This was the most important school of art in London?

Notwithstanding its down-at-heels look, my heart beat faster as we drew near. Mounting three shallow stone steps, we entered a bare, gloomy corridor off which several doors gave. As no one prevented, we opened 'em all. One door revealed several men slapping clay on armatures. Another gave onto students drawing folds of cloth with squinting stares. Next proved a room of casts from the antique: Apollos and Athenas, heads, torsos, arms, from which yet more students drew. The fourth room held a congregation of silent, mouthless souls hung on pegs, which startled me 'til I saw that they were life-sized lay figures which might be dressed, and posed, as James Cavitty had dressed his lay-figure in Lady Shenstone's gown.

The last door revealed most of interest: a large, high-ceil-inged chamber, perhaps forty by fifty feet, in which students drew from life. We entered quietly. A great tin lamp hung above. Beneath it fifteen or so men sat in a semicircle on low stools, drawing boards on their laps. Behind 'em, a second semicircle of men drew at desks.

On a raised wooden platform in front of a fireplace stood a naked woman.

Never had I seen a naked woman before, and I stopped and stared. She was young, perhaps twenty, with a pretty yet weary face that said she knew much of life. She had an ample mouth and gazed out of heavily lidded eyes. There was something defiant in her look, but it was not that that I stared at but her body. I traced its shape: the slope of shoulders, the rounded breasts with their rose-brown buds, the narrow waist, the flare of hips, the place where her legs joined. I felt unable to let out breath.

Mr. Franklin squeezed my shoulder. "You learn of more than art here, eh?"

He led me silently round the semicircle. Some men drew well, but I was surprised to see that others did wretchedly. No one spoke, and only the soft scratch of pencils filled the air. Mr. Franklin halted beside an old man whose white hair poked out from under a loose-fitting moleskin cap. At first I could not understand why he had chosen this man. Then I looked at his work, and I could not take my eyes from it. I had long known that to draw as I wished meant more than merely making pictures. Some artists spoke of character. The satirical prints cried out against hypocrisy. Other pictures sang the glory of God, others the power of position. Whatever proved Nick Handy's tune, I longed to sing it half so well as this man. His brisk strokes did not merely copy, they *spoke,* and the model became under his fingers a naked, defiant goddess of the streets, her thick, tangled hair a halo of pride.

The man abruptly turned. "What?" Lined old eyes stirred by a restless energy flashed at me before fixing upon Mr. Franklin. "Why do you bring the boy here? He should not be here."

"He has talent. I thought to show him your school," replied Mr. Franklin

Was this then William Hogarth?

Creaking to his feet, the famous London satirist pushed his drawing into a black leather portfolio and yanked its strings. "This is not a place for boys."

"Nick will not be a boy much longer. If he came to your school, might he be instructed by you?"

"I do not instruct. No more. I have attempted to instruct London by my art, but her folly will not be schooled. Should I teach a bitch dog not to whelp? As for our academy, you have a very imperfect idea of it, for there is no regular course of study. For your fee you may come and draw the model. 'Tis an association of artists more than a school, but it does some good, and one day we may have something better, though I despise the idea of a royal charter." He peered at me. "Talent, eh?" He thrust into my hand the soft lead pencil with which he had drawn. "Show, then." Pulling blank paper from his folder, he slapped it upon the table. "Prove yourself, boy."

I stared. "B-but . . ."

His eyes commanded. "Draw."

My gaze fled to Mr. Franklin. He nodded, and with far different feelings than I had had before—no stirrings of desire, no strange wonderment, only terrified uncertainty—I turned to the model. She stood simply, feet forming a right-angle, one leg stiffly back, the other thrust forward. Her left hand rested on her hip, face turned away from the elbow, chin lifted, hair tied thick about her nape. Where to begin? Plunging in, I thrust the pencil so hard at the paper I almost broke the lead, and drew in a sort of scribbling blindness. I saw the model, and I saw lines appear on the paper, but they seemed to have little relation to one another. Clumsy, clumsy! It was as if I had lost the power to observe, my sight blurred, and I felt flushed and shamed.

An impatient hand gripped mine. "Slower, boy. See?"

Hogarth's hand.

He hovered near, smelling of age, of anger, of genius; and my fingers, under his powerful grasp, sketched a foot which seemed a miracle. From thence we moved to repair an awkward hip, the bend of an arm, the turn of the head. "You have drawn the breasts well. They inspire you, do they?" He helped a moment more before he straightened. "Hum, you are not altogether useless. But you must not go at the paper like a butcher at his beef. Do not hack and saw. Practice the S-curve, see?" He drew graceful snakelike lines. " 'The line of beauty.' You must learn to see it everywhere, in the lark's wing, in the whore's smile. What is your name?"

"Nicolas Handy, sir."

He regarded me a moment more. "Nay, not useless." Snatching his portfolio, William Hogarth strode from the room.

❦ 5 ❦

*IN WHICH we meet a lord and hatch
a plot, and two old enemies cross our
path . . .*

Outside St. Martin's Lane Academy I blinked in the
sunlight that had driven away the morning's gray.

Mr. Franklin smiled. "Not useless, eh? Should the
great Handel pronounce me 'not tuneless,' I would glow with
pride." Clapping my shoulder, he pulled a folded *London
Chronicle* from his coat. "To more business." He pointed to a
rectangle of print. "The painter Augustus Broome keeps his
house open today, so that ladies and gentlemen may view his
collection of Spanish and Italian masters—and some works of
his own, for he seeks patrons. Let us there."

We went to Litchfield Street five minutes away, to number
103, a fine, large three-story house with neat white woodwork.
'Twas hard to set aside the knowledge that only moments ago
William Hogarth had helped me, Nicolas Handy, to draw, and
I was wondering if Hogarth's own house might lie nearby—
when the thought was wrenched from my mind.

A dangerous man waited just ahead.

A man named Bertie Hexham.

I shuddered with both distaste and fear. Whip-thin young
Hexham was as unprincipled as his father, and he had no rea-

son to love us, for Mr. Franklin had been instrumental in bringing his wicked family to justice. What did the young rake here? Glad he seemed not to have seen us (he had just turned his haughty visage in the opposite direction), I was about to tug Mr. Franklin's sleeve to point him out, but the brass knocker of number 103 had already fallen, the door was opened, and a manservant bowed us in.

Smelling the pungent odor of mineral spirits, I forgot Bertie Hexham. An artist's house! We found ourselves in an entryway at the end of which oaken stairs led up. I grew all alert. Where were pictures made? I longed to see.

The manservant gestured us to the door on the right.

"Come, Nick." I followed Mr. Franklin.

We found ourselves in what must once have been the large front parlor of the house but was now the painter's display room. Other folk were already present, some six or eight ladies and gentlemen quizzing the pictures hung on the walls. We had seen gentry very much like 'em at Carrington Bowles; plainly, viewing art had become the fashion.

We walked about too. There were about thirty paintings from small Dutch landscapes to a large *Europa*. I had seen little true art in my life—there were in London few places to look at it save the walls of public buildings—and I breathed in these like a new, headier air. A Ruisdael took me with its gaunt tree and windmill. There was a sparkling little Canaletto of Venice. Some Spanish paintings too: dwarves, dust brown castles and arid plains, exotic to a London-bred boy. Every third painting proved one of Augustus Broome's. They were all portraits, with a fine surface but a dismaying monotony. My lord, or my lord and his family—how alike they were, as if stamped from a mold. Though the features varied, the character of the sitters never changed: the wooden stare that proclaimed, *I have a name*, the gesture that said, *This house, this tree, this dog is mine.*

We came to the *Europa*, handsomely framed in plaster gilt. 'Twas a grand work, six by eight feet, taking up most of one wall. Affixed to the frame was a shiny brass plaque: *Painted by Titian.*

A well-dressed gentleman stood in front of the painting, laughing softly.

His was so jolly a jest, some secret betwixt him and himself, that I could not help smiling too. His left hand supported his right elbow, whilst his right hand stroked his jaw as he chuckled. He was lean, with handsome, sharp features and a small, well-formed mouth topped by a soft moustache. A glow of intelligence shone in his light-gray eyes. In his crisp blue velvet suit and polished black boots, he had a confident air.

Turning, he lifted a brow at Mr. Franklin. "Never a Titian, sir, eh? Never a Titian."

"No?" queried Mr. Franklin.

The gray eyes saucered. "What? You do not see it?"

Mr. Franklin turned to me. "Do you see it, Nick?"

"Why—" I was startled to discover that I did.

Before I could say so, Mr. Franklin turned back. "Teach us, sir, if you please."

"Happy to do so. Titian never painted such a . . . *thing.* 'Twas produced by some faker in Venice, for Broome says he got it in Venice—though as to that it might as well have been turned out in Westminster. Chameleons toil in Westminster: Raphael at midnight, Rembrandt in the morn. I have seen 'em at work—wonderful! Masters in their way."

"Forgers, you mean?"

"What else? I have seen 'em in Siena as well, Florence, Rome, where they cook a painting in an oven to age it, an old Italian recipe." He winked.

"But how do you know that this is one?"

"By my eye, man! 'Tis a *pastiche* of Titian's style, but it lacks the master's hand. See you?" He proceeded to trace the painting's faults: the stiff poses, awkward drapery, weak coloring, faulty composition. I felt a small glow of pride as he did so, for at my first glimpse of the painting I had seen the wrongness of it. "The drawing is decent," proclaimed the man, "workmanlike. But the eye is confused by chaotic design. The paint is decently applied, but it has no dash."

"And that cupid . . ." murmured I.

The man regarded me.

I flushed. "By that tree. Beg pardon, but it has two left feet."

Both men looked. Mr. Franklin laughed. "Why, so it does."

The other man peered. "You have an eye." He pursed his lips at Mr. Franklin. "The boy has an eye."

A small smile. "He is not entirely useless."

The man folded his arms. "What do you think of your 'Titian' now? I hope you are not too disappointed to be disabused."

"O, I hope always to be disabused."

"Truly? Then I am glad to oblige." He made a brisk bow. "I must be off. Good day." He was quickly gone.

Mr. Franklin gazed at the painting. "A forgery, eh? I hear there are many in London." As we made to go, he stopped the manservant in the entryway. "By the by, the gentleman just departed, do you know his name?"

"Lord Shenstone, sir."

Mr. Franklin blinked. "But my lord is out of town."

The servant politely shook his head. "Begging your pardon, but he is not, for that was my lord, and no mistake. I know his phiz well; he is a patron of art. You will find his card upon the tray."

We looked but did not find it.

The manservant searched too. "Dear me, I wonder he did not leave his card. A gentleman always leaves his card."

"I, too, wonder why he did not leave a card," said Mr. Franklin, leading me out the door. On the cobbles we looked about for the peer, but the man was nowhere in Litchfield Street, nor was hide nor hair of him to be discovered in St. Martin's Lane when we walked there. Mr. Franklin halted, frowning. "How remarkable that we should encounter him thus. Yet not so remarkable, if he is a patron of the arts. But what is he doing in town? Did not his wife say he would be away a fortnight? Poor woman. What if he discovers that his precious diamond is missing? That would put us out, eh, Nicolas? All our plans in vain?" He squinted into the sky, where clouds formed a flotilla of white in an azure sea. "Yet we shall go ahead with 'em for now. *Semper paratus.* Come, or we shall be late joining Jimmy Ralph at the Devil's Foot."

The Devil's Foot proved a chophouse frequented by artists, a broad, low-ceilinged, noisy room with the customary deep fireplace and oddments of tables and chairs and a withered, cloven foot nailed to a moth-eaten green baize cloth by the door. This bore a strong resemblance to a ram's hind leg but we were assured by our grizzled host that it had been cut from the devil himself: "Chopped it off with my own hands when old Nick would not pay for his porter."

We found James Ralph at a table tucked up against a smoke-blackened wall.

"Ben!" cried the old fellow, leaping up—or would've leapt up if his bulk had let him, for he was as broken-winded and hugely sagging as when he had aided Mr. Franklin in resolving the murders at Drury Lane.

"Jimmy!" responded Mr. Franklin, wringing the out-stretched hand. For a moment, linked, the two men smiled into one another's crinkled eyes. The old friends had come to London in their twenties, and though they had had a falling out over a woman, Mr. Ralph remaining on these shores whilst Mr. Franklin sailed back to America, Mr. Ralph had been one of the first to greet Mr. Franklin on his return thirty years later, all bad feeling forgot. I looked at 'em now, Mr. Franklin in his neat brown suit of clothes, Mr. Ralph in mismatched odd-ments: dirty ribbons, patched breeches, old yellow waistcoat bespattered with port. Though Mr. Franklin had had great success in public life, Mr. Ralph remained a threadbare poet, trotting about Grub Street to scribble scandal to earn him his crust of bread. Yet there was a spirit to both men, and for a moment I could imagine 'em young, arm in arm, pens at the ready, to bring London to bay.

Mr. Ralph slapped at his grimy wig to right it. "Sit you, Ben. Hallo, Nick." He beat my shoulder in greeting, then bellowed to the serving girl to deliver salvation: ale for him and Mr. Franklin and a sillabub for me. The drinks before us, he leant across the table as well as his belly would let him, his voice a yeasty growl. "Now, Ben, your proposal."

Mr. Franklin leant forward too. Quickly he told all: of Lady Shenstone, the missing diamond, our idea that I might be tried out at Cavitty's to learn of art—and to learn of the missing gem too, if I could. "I should like you to play Nick's guardian or some such, to propose him to the artist."

"But why not yourself?"

"I wish to pursue this by other means, and for Nick to do well he must not be seen to know me. You write plays, Jimmy. Are an actor too. Will you do it?"

The man slapped the table. "I'm your man. But who shall I be? Ha, Sir Bartleby Bart!—just the thing. I shall have me some land in Norfolk, some business about town. I shall be a merchant, importing sugar from Barbados, silks from Cathay. Why, I am already very nearly the fellow." He plucked at his dingy coatsleeve. "Of course I must be made to *look* the part."

"We will fit you out."

"Excellent!"

This settled, we turned our attention to the room, a babble of talk: what artist seduced what model, whose portrait had been rejected by Lord What's-his-name because the nose was too big, who was in, who out. Mr. Ralph wrote for the newspapers; he knew all well. "There are not only artists but color-men, framers, glaziers, dealers, auction-men, agents who seek out art in Paris and Rome." Pointing out how the Italians, French, and Dutch sat apart, he grumbled at their prosperity. "See 'em? Cannot we English make good pictures? Yet 'tis an article of faith of our gentry that if you are duPrez or Vanderdonck or Mercatini you must paint well, but if you are goodman Carter, born o' Surrey you cannot. And so the foreigners come and set up their studios where they turn out pictures no better than ours. Yet if they are signed by Signor Signatelli, who says he was suckled by the she-wolf in Rome, the lords and ladies genuflect like Catholics. Pah!"

I had pulled out my pocket sketchbook. I drew the denizens of this *milieu*: a scabrous old artist, a trio of Dutchmen drinking gin, the crippled potboy who limped from table to table collecting emptied pewter pints. I had filled several such books in which I also wrote of my days with Mr. Franklin in the shorthand he had taught me, so that a page might have both pictures and words in a scribbled design. They were meant for just my eyes, and it pleased me to take 'em out and remember what had chanced on such and such a day.

And this day? Was it settled that I should be a spy in James Cavitty's house?

*   *   *

'Twas near four P.M. when we departed the Devil's Foot, James Ralph trundling off slashing the air with his stick. Mr. Franklin walked a little ahead whilst I paused under the chop-house sign to fit my cap on my head.

Looking up, I discovered another face I knew.

Yet this one puzzled me as Bertie Hexham's had not, for at first I could not understand how I knew it. It belonged to a man just stepping into a sleek black carriage in a mews across the way. He wore a dark swirling cloak. Shutting the door behind him, he peered intently back in Mr. Franklin's direction, only part of his face showing beyond the window edge, and he seemed to hide himself, so that I could glimpse only the fringes of an iron-gray wig, a velvet-banded tricorn hat pulled low, a long nose, glittering eyes.

A chill swept over me, for those eyes were lit by a brooding glow. Bespeaking no good, they fixed upon Mr. Franklin. Mr. Franklin did not see his observer; indeed he had not yet noted that I remained rooted by the Devil's Foot, and I was about to rush to him to point out what I saw, when I felt the stranger's eyes discover me. Plainly they had not known I watched, and a fury came into 'em, cold and malevolent, as if I trespassed upon forbidden ground. In the same instant I knew their possessor, and my heart seemed to stop. Memory of being jerked from my feet by the collar took my breath. Memory of a black-cloaked figure racing to escape pursuit in the rain. A story Mr. Franklin had told, of gaming at the Hazard and nearly being murdered for his reward.

Quimp.

The eyes narrowed. They said: *I know you, boy.*

The coach was harnessed to two inky mares that looked like they could race the wind. Quimp's head vanished. Some signal must have been given, for the coach abruptly set out, careering at Mr. Franklin's back.

"Mr. Franklin!" cried I. "Take care!"

He turned, saw, leapt. Agile for a man who neared fifty-two, he tumbled and rolled.

Whirring coach wheels barely missed his head as the black coach spun by.

I raced to help him up. "Are you well, sir?"

He dusted his breeches. "Tolerably."

"Quimp, sir. 'Twas Quimp."

He squinted after the vanishing coach. "Truly?"

"I believe so."

He was grim. "My enemy, then, keeps watch."

I thought on Quimp as I walked beside Mr. Franklin, shivering. We knew him as little more than the five letters of his name, yet they were enough to send goosebumps up my spine. Mr. Franklin had encountered him when he looked into the murder of Ebenezer Inch, and again when he discovered the truth behind Roderick Fairbrass's poisoning. Justice John Fielding had told us of him: "He is behind much of London's crime, dealing in thievery, gaming, whoremastery, murder. Anything for profit." It was said he kept a stranglehold on his minions—he had frozen a man to death for failing him—but few knew his face, and I shuddered to think I was one of those, for he had once threatened me not twenty yards from number 7 Craven Street, though he had been in disguise.

"So you believe the man was Quimp?" said Mr. Franklin when we were safe in his chamber. "If so, if he truly meant me harm, 'tis unlikely he would fail. Does he toy with me, then? Or does his presence have aught to do with the Shenstone affair? It seems it could not, and yet—"

I told him about Bertie Hexham.

"Hexham too?—remarkable. How does he fill his plate now his wicked father and wickeder mother are no more? Quimp, and he in proximity—what may it mean?"

A knock sounded. Mrs. Stevenson delivered a letter, "Just come," said she.

When she was gone Mr. Franklin broke the seal and read aloud:

> To: Mr. Benjamin Franklin
> Sir:
>
> I have had the greatest fright—my husband returned to town last night. As you know I did not expect him for many days. I was in agonies. What should I do if he asked to see his precious diamond? He did not, thank God, and has gone off again, but his return sorely tried my nerves; I could not sleep. Have you any news? I have none—Cavitty keeps as mute as stone.
>
> Thank you for all you do.
>> Yours in deepest gratitude, etc.
>> Vanessa Chetwynd, Lady Shenstone

Mr. Franklin frowned. "My lord did no business at Broome's, so why did he come? What did you make of him, Nick?"

"Very knowledgable about art."

"And forgery. I am not especially fond of gemstones—they are no reflecting glass for truth—yet this missing one begins to fascinate." Calling Peter, he sent him to Cavitty's with a note saying that Sir Bartleby Bart wished to call. He then retired to his desk, where his quill commenced its soft, steady scratch, his buckled shoes hooked round his chair like a schoolboy's, whilst his tongue tested his lips as he searched for words. His steel-rimmed spectacles rested by his inkpot, and he emitted a disgruntled "Pah!" or a pleased "Aha!" as his pen made its point.

I was moved. *Do not harm him, Quimp*, thought I.

He had saved the drawing I had done for Hogarth and, at loose ends, I unrolled it upon the bed where he had dropped it. The model stood out in lines that were economical and sure where Hogarth had guided me and awkward where he had not. Yet I had not entirely done ill. Some of my execution was decent: the hair at the nape of the neck, the defiant eyes. Did I show promise? Yet such was my new nature that the woman's nakedness was no mere arrangement of planes and curves. Her breasts and her thighs seemed to pulse with blood, and my own blood grew warm wondering what it would be like to trace the lines of her body with my hand.

Peter returned at six. James Cavitty had said, yes, he would see Sir Bartleby Bart tomorrow.

"Aha!" cried Mr. Franklin, rubbing his hands. "We must inform Jimmy Ralph."

"Yes, sir," said I. What would our plan bring?

6

IN WHICH I meet an artist and am tested once more . . .

By Saturday morning winter's deep chill was thoroughly gone, little flowers—red, yellow, blue—sprouting in unlikely spots everywhere: upon eaves, at the corners of gutters, betwixt the cobbles and stoops of Craven Street by the Thames.

James Ralph swaggered in at eleven; we met him in the front parlor. His transformation was amazing. Though he could not alter his red, veined nose nor his rheumy eyes, he had become in all other respects Sir Bartleby Bart. Outfitted by a shop in the Strand, he wore handsome dark breeches and a deep blue velvet coat with grandly ruffled lace at the wrists. His brass buttons shone, his black shoes gleamed, and he had turned his customary bibulous slouch into an imperious swagger.

He made a flourishing bow. "At your service, good sir, young gentleman," and plucked snuff from a silver box.

"Ha!" Mr. Franklin clapped him on the shoulder. "I would believe you to reside in some grand house in the best part of town."

"Why, I do, sir! At number 6 Grosvenor Square, the

fashionable side, with ten servants, three brats, my bitch-dog and a wife." He winked.

Mr. Franklin laughed. "I deliver Nick into your hands."

From somewhere Mr. Franklin had obtained a fine coach with an ornate *B* blazoned on its door, pulled by handsome roan mares. Before we left he leant in the window. "If this proves not to your liking, Nick, say so and it shall end."

"Yes, sir." I wished the butterflies would make less flutter in my gut.

We set out. Patting his finery and nodding like a lord to one and all, Mr. Ralph played his part as London passed outside our windows. Capons hung by poultry shops, knife-grinders showered sparks, soot-garbed urchins played leapfrog whilst they spied for likely bits of lace, and ev'rywhere whores strutted, cutpurses crept, and fine ladies and gentlemen made their way.

Cavitty's demesne proved off St. Martin's Lane, in Cranbourne Street where we had seen the black-haired boy bully red-hair. Our coach drew up as noon bells clamored. I squinted at the house, number 23. It was sturdy and large, two stories of red brick; yet it was not so fine as Augustus Broome's. Too, it seemed to want care, as if not enough coin was spent—or at hand—for its upkeep, and for the first time I wondered why Lord Shenstone had chosen Cavitty.

A wind swept along the street as we got down. A brass plaque on the wide white door announced *James Cavitty, Painter*.

With a flourish Mr. Ralph rapped the knocker. "Look sharp, Nick. Stand straight." He prepared himself to play his part.

We were greeted by an old, bent manservant in rather worn livery. Following Mr. Ralph in, I smelt again the pungent odor of varnishes and oils. The entryway looked much like Augustus Broome's, with doors to right and left and a stairway leading up.

Mr. Ralph sighted along his nose as if 'twere a pistol. "Sir Bartleby Bart. Your master expects me."

"He is with a sitter now," the old servant's voice quavered, "but will be with you shortly. Will you wait in the display room?"

"Hem, ah, if we must."

We were led to the door on the left. Just before we walked through I was startled by a small, thin face peering through the stair rails. A child? A dwarf? Abruptly the face vanished as if it never had been, and we walked into a large parlor whose windows looked out upon Cranbourne Street. There was a fireplace, but little furniture: two chairs and a small round table on which rested a marble hand that looked to've been broken from some statue. The walls were a pale color and hung with art as had been the walls of Augustus Broome's, though the London *ton* was nowhere here. Had James Cavitty not yet made his name? The door closed. We were left alone, and I heard muffled sounds from both street and house: footsteps, faint voices. As we went round to survey the paintings, Mr. Ralph kept Sir Bartleby's strut, now and again taking snuff. Though there were a few samples of continental art (I admired a Rosso Fiorentino of Actaeon), most pictures were signed James Cavitty: *The Manse at Fontwell*, *Miss Burridge as Hebe*, *Powdershot*—a stallion who had won at Newmarket. Many were portraits. "The English gentry allow English artists to excel only at portraits," muttered Mr. Ralph. "We cannot paint history or myth, they proclaim." I looked close at Cavitty's work. He might not have the reputation of Augustus Broome, but he was a better artist, I thought. He made each of his portraits an individual rather than one more dog in a pack; there was wit in 'em too. Verging upon satire? Nonetheless I admired his skill.

I was disappointed not to discover the portrait of Lady Shenstone.

Abruptly the door swung open, and the artist himself strode in—yet I hardly had time to observe him before he wheeled round to fling out sharply, "I hear you, sir," in prickly perturbation.

A man stood in the entryway behind him. "I hope you do." Red-faced, in short tie-wig and sturdy boots, he looked to be a newly-rich merchant come to anchor his toehold in society with a portrait. "I tell you again, it will not do! I appear . . . you have made me seem . . . 'Twill not do, I say."

"You wish to look like a lord." Cavitty's voice was a mocking purr. "Very well, I shall make you look like a lord."

"Do, sir, or I draw my pursestrings against you." The man stomped out.

Cavitty slammed the door after him. "I shall change your face to a monkey's and parade it through the Strand, that is what I shall do!" said he to the oak. He whirled round. "What do you want?"

Took aback, Sir Bartleby did not speak at once, and I spent the time examining James Cavitty. He was a smallish man, no more than five and a half feet, but of a formidable mein. Dressed for work, he wore an apron smeared with paint, his shirtsleeves rolled up. His bare forearms showed sinewy and strong, and his long feet in sturdy black shoes were kept square apart as if he preferred trading blows to talk. His head was large, with a bulging brow and eyes outstarting like a hare's. He wore no wig, his brown hair tied straight back. His brows were fierce black lines, his nose flat and truculent, his mouth thin-lipped with a bitter twist. His hands were long-fingered, with large, white knuckles.

"Hem, ah, I am Sir Bartleby Bart," Mr. Ralph found his voice, "and I am come to pay you to take this boy. Pay you, I say."

Cavitty wiped his hands upon his apron. "So your servant said yesterday." He shot a glance at me before peering again at Sir Bartleby. "Why do you choose me?"

"We have sought a place for the boy a good while. There was some rumor you looked for a second 'prentice, and—"

"Damn rumor."

"At any rate, here is the boy." Sir Bartleby gave me a nudge.

Mr. Franklin had advised that I dress in my best breeches and coat (I had but two of each), so I wore gray velvet, and a newly pressed shirt and shoes with polished buckles.

I felt like some pirate's victim set out on the plank.

"How do you d-do, sir?" faltered I.

Cavitty snorted. " 'Tis not for you to ask me how I do, but for me to ask you. You have been represented as a boy who might be apprenticed to an artist. You scribble, I hear. Show me." Snatching paper from a quire in the table drawer, he cleared a space by tossing the marble hand upon a chair. He pulled a shaved pencil from his apron pocket. "Draw."

I took the pencil. "Draw what, if you please?"

"That." He pointed to the marble hand.

I looked where it lay on the cushion. Though broken off just above the wrist, it beckoned gracefully. Aphrodite's? From some age-old temple? Feeling a tightness in my throat, I moved to the table, stared at the blank paper, the hand, the paper.

As yesterday, I must try.

I drew fitfully at first, for I could not seem to get a proper start. How did the wrist curve? How were the fingers bent? Then seeming to catch the way of it—I drew more rapidly and for a while forgot that two pairs of eyes besides my own kept watch. I fashioned the turn of the wrist, the fold of the palm, the twist of the thumb. I must have spent ten minutes at the thing, though the time seemed pass in a puff of air. "There, sir," said I when I had done all I could.

Cavitty kept his knotty arms folded as he stared at the drawing whilst I waited.

Not entirely useless?

At last he growled, "You have been taught."

"No, sir."

"Damn you, you lie."

"I d-do not," stammered I.

His terrible scrutiny seemed to root around in my soul. Then with a curt nod he turned to Sir Bartleby. "The boy may suit." He gave a suspicious squint. "But your terms—why do you refuse to apprentice him at once?"

"Because of his mother, sir, my sister," came the prepared answer. "The boy is her natural child. (His father fled to India years ago, good riddance to him.) The boy was brought up in our household and must now have a trade. He likes to draw, and so we thought to place him here. O, if 'twere up to me I should sign the papers at once and be done with it, but his mother dotes on him and must know he is at something which she thinks 'truly suits.' I hate such fiddle-faddle! But my sister is a woman who . . . hem . . . well, I must please her. She asks: can the boy be a boy of work for a time, to see if he takes to the artist's life?"

"I do not like it," growled Cavitty. " 'Tis not customary."

"No, indeed. But as I have said, we will pay—not a great deal, for you will have him to work for you, but . . . something."

"How long a trial do you propose?"

"A month."

Cavitty brooded. "That is not so very long." His gaze measured me. "Time for you to see if you like it, I suppose. What is your name?"

"Nicolas, sir."

"You understand that you must do as I say? I will be your master?"

"O, yes, sir."

He turned back to Mr. Ralph. "A day-boy only, that must be understood. We cannot lodge a boy who is not 'prenticed."

"My sister wishes just that, so she may have him home of an eve."

"She has not spoiled him?"

"Nay, you will not find him spoilt."

"Very well, done—so long as he is here by seven each morning and does not expect to leave before six."

"He will arrive at seven sharp."

The door had half-opened, and I glimpsed the hem of a pale green dress in the entryway. "As to terms—" Sir Bartleby named a figure. Cavitty acceded to it, and the green dress whisked out of view.

The artist turned to me once more. "Today is Saturday. You shall start o' Monday, hear?" said he.

"Monday, sir. Thank you."

A maidservant hurried in, her little cap askew. "Beg pardon, but Miss Bowker is here to be painted."

Cavitty made a disgrunted sound. "I must see to her. Tell your sister how we have settled this business, Sir Bartleby. But make it plain that in a month's time I must have the boy or let him go. A decision must be made."

"O, you shall know in a month."

As we moved toward the door, I glanced at the maid. Barely my height, she appeared a few years older, no more than fifteen, plump and pretty. Meeting my eyes from under half-lowered lashes, she gave a wan smile, at which I smiled back; then we were in the entryway once more. I had thought green-dress gone, but she stood behind Cavitty, and I saw by a similarity of lineament that they were related. She was thin and severe, and her sharp look seemed to measure to a farthing the size of Sir Bartleby's purse.

"You have concluded your business?" inquired she in a high, dry voice.

Cavitty made an introductory gesture. "My sister, Mrs. Fanny Bone. Sir Bartleby Bart."

Sir Bartleby bobbed his head. "Pleased, mum."

"My pleasure, sir." Her voice was hard as metal. "I could not help overhearing some of your converse. You will have my brother to teach the boy? It is proper that you pay for that, for my brother will be at some pains. But, beg pardon, should not you lay down somewhat in advance? For the service which we—which my brother—performs?"

Cavitty reddened. "My sister—"

Sir Bartleby tutted. "I understand sisters. A week's pay, eh?" He jingled coins, it being Mrs. Bone's hand that darted out to receive 'em. Sir Bartleby puffed his chest. "Come, Nicolas, we must be off." He tapped his large, red nose. "Seven sharp, Monday. Let us go."

I was about to follow, for I had had enough for today—when the door burst open and a small boy scrambled in.

Red hair. A flat, ugly face. Biggs, the boy whose ear had been pinched by the bully.

Of course!—the damaged portrait had come from Cranbourne Street; why should it not come from number 23?

And then black-hair was there too, his belligerent face rising up before mine before he pushed past in pursuit of Biggs.

He was pulled up short by Cavitty's scowl. Snatching off his cap, he hung his head. "Beg pardon, sir, but I sought t' catch Biggs. He has been up to mischief again, the mole."

"I never!" shot back Biggs by the stairs. "He's alyin' about me, like always."

Black-hair leapt for him. "You—!"

"Leave be!" The warning in Cavitty's voice made even me start.

Black-hair halted, biting his lip.

"For shame!" snapped Mrs. Bone, rigid with fury.

Sir Bartleby put a hand on my shoulder to guide me out, of which I was glad, for I had caught a narrow-eyed look from black-hair. Did he recognize me? My last glimpse before the door closed was of the strange face peering through the stair rails. Then we were out upon the street.

In our coach Mr. Ralph toyed with his ribbons. "Did I not do well? O, I am sorry the play is done."

Done for him, but not for me. As we headed back through London I sat sunk in uncertainty. What part did Biggs and black-hair play in the Cavitty household? Would they prevent me playing mine?

⚜ 7 ⚜

*IN WHICH we call on a Jew, a blind
man, and an engraver . . .*

We were in Craven Street in a quarter of an hour. Mr.
Ralph had a pressing engagement with some cro-
nies at the Shakespeare's Head, and so 'twas left to
me to relate our adventure. Leading me to his chamber, Mr.
Franklin sank into his chair and laced his fingers over his
waistcoat. "Tell all that transpired."

Duly, I described ev'rything: the house, the entryway, the
old manservant, the face on the stairs, the painting room, the
angry patron, Cavitty, my drawing, the greedy sister, the pretty
maid, the surprise of Biggs and black-hair.

Mr. Franklin's mild look altered. "I am sorry to learn Biggs
and black-hair are amongst the *ménage,* yet they do not raise
any great obstacle. One or the other may recall your face, but
you were a boy in the street, that is all, with no connection to
me. 'Tis Cavitty I wish to hear more on. A good painter, you
say?"

"I thought so, sir."

"But does not know how to flatter?"

"He paints men and women as they are."

"O, a very great sin! But how did you like him, Nick?"

A ship's bell clanged out upon the Thames. I chose my words carefully. "I did not dislike him. He quarreled with a man—but may be for good reason. And though he is stern, he tested me fairly. His eyes quizzed me hard, but . . . well, so do yours, sir, at times, begging your pardon."

"And will never cease doing so whilst I breathe! By your reckoning Cavitty may prove a decent fellow, eh? What then of the diamond?" Mr. Franklin rose. "All for now, Nick; our landlady calls upon you to polish her spoons. When you are done, write down all which occurred this afternoon; I wish to peruse it at my leisure. One matter more: I should be pleased if you would draw a likeness of James Cavitty, so I may study his face."

I completed the polishing by four, the writing by five. Alone in Mr. Franklin's chamber (he had gone out) I struggled over the drawing 'til six. 'Twas hard without its subject before me, yet I got Cavitty tolerably well: the small but powerful body, the bulging eyes, the restless, pugnacious spirit.

Mr. Franklin had almost as many friends in London as enemies, and was frequently out, with the Royal Society, the Masons, the Honest Whigs, or with his friends, John Fothergill, Peter Collinson, and William Strahan, the publisher of the *London Chronicle*. Mrs. Stevenson, Polly, and William Franklin and I therefore supped without him at eight. Candlelight flickered whilst a small joint steamed beside a pudding and carrots.

Polly had barely seated herself before she flew at me: "Why does Mr. Franklin always do so much for *you*, Nick?"

William sat to her right. He dabbed his lips. "Indeed, Father does far more than he ought for a mere boy of work." With a small smile that said I was worth no more discussion he thrust a fork of beef into his mouth.

I got little sleep that night but tossed and moaned, dreaming on Quimp, who lurked and crept whilst his face changed form like wax. In fitful waking moments I fretted over what 'twould be like at Cavitty's. Would black-hair harry me?

Rain had again fallen, and mud squelched under our coach wheels as Mr. Franklin and I rode along the Fleet next morn, in the direction of St. Paul's. 'Twas Sunday, the thoroughfares less ajostle than customarily, though a pigman drove three squealing porkers in our way. A spring breeze freshened the air.

Mr. Franklin had determined that today, before I went to Cavitty's, we must call upon men who might help in the matter of the diamond. The first was to be the Portuguese Jew, Joseph de Medina. This was London's most knowledgeable trader in gemstones. (Mr. Franklin had met him when he looked into the poisoning of Roderick Fairbrass.) He resided in Gracechurch Street by Leadenhall Market, at the corner of Bull's Head Passage: the heart of the City, where money was king. His was a modest, narrow brick house, and by ten-thirty we were mounting its high stone steps. Mr. Franklin rapped. The door was fitted with a spyhole, but it opened readily to reveal de Medina himself.

"Mr. Franklin, you are welcome," came his rich, solemn voice. He was tall and somberly dressed in dark red velvet, his thick brown hair hanging loose about his face. About forty, he was swart and powerfully built, with a brooding, face, large strong hands, watchful liquid eyes.

In moments we were seated in plush leather chairs before his broad desk in his finely furnished office.

Whilst Mr. Franklin and our host exchanged pleasantries, I glanced about. I had sat here before; the room had not changed: polished brass, a carpet from some eastern realm, tall windows strongly barred, and, most significantly, a great iron safe the height of a man. In it was a king's ransom in rubies, diamonds and emeralds; thus the barred windows. Too, de Medina kept a loaded pistol in his desk drawer; he was, he assured us, the finest marksman of Portugal.

"Do you know of the Shenstone Diamond?" Mr. Franklin came to the point.

De Medina inclined his handsome head. "One knows the Rakofsky Ruby, the Garamond Emerald. One knows the Shenstone Diamond."

"Famous, then?"

"Infamous. 'Tis all one."

"If it changed hands, would you hear of it?"

"Likely."

"Even if the transaction were secret?"

A small smile. " 'Three may keep a secret if two of them are dead,' as you say, Mr. Franklin. I would learn of it, perhaps not in the day or week—but within the fortnight. A notorious beauty cannot travel even by night without tongues wagging. But why do you inquire about the diamond?"

Mr. Franklin told Lady Shenstone's story. "I trust you will repeat it to no one."

"But, what do you suggest?—that this painter, Cavitty, pretends the Shenstone Diamond is missing so he may secretly sell it?"

Mr. Franklin gazed down, up. "I do not know what I mean." He sent a look across the desk. "But if you hear that some transaction is afoot or has been made—if our beauty creeps by night—will you send word?"

De Medina lifted eloquent hands. "For you, Benjamin Franklin, yes."

"Remarkable, de Medina," said Mr. Franklin when we rode west under Peter's expert handling of the reins.

I agreed.

Our next stop was the Blind Beak of London.

In twenty minutes we were in Bow Street, Peter pulling up before number 4, green-shuttered, on the east side, where the Chief Magistrate for Westminster dealt out judgment; in another moment we were in his inner sanctum, the small, tidy chamber back of the Justice Room, the Blind Beak himself seated like a huge toad, stertorously breathing, behind a desk as free of papers as if a wind had blown 'em away.

Papers were no use, for John Fielding had been sightless from the age of seventeen.

He was a massive man, many-chinned, with ears that showed round the edges of his wig like nobbly growths. Those ears were said to know the voice and footstep of ev'ry cutpurse in London, and his mind was a catalogue of suborners, whores, and receivers of goods.

"The boy is with you?" rumbled he when Mr. Franklin and I were seated before him.

"I am, sir," replied I.

His bulk seemed to creak as he leant toward me. "Yet your voice has altered. You are older. How old, boy?"

"Thirteen, sir."

"An age when sin knocks. You do not sin?"

"I try not, sir."

"You bring him up well, then, Mr. Franklin, would you had charge of ev'ry wicked child in London."

"And money to lift 'em out of poverty?"

"Aye, your poverty is a great inciter to crime."

Liking to hear the latest about criminal catching, Mr. Franklin pressed Fielding, and the magistrate readily obliged, spitting out a tirade against Parliament's "damned obstinacy" in refusing to pay for a force of men which might effectively police the city. "We have too few constables, and our bumbling old Charlies are little help. O, there are 'Mr. Fielding's People,' as they call 'em, but not enough to rein in whoring, gaming and rioting. Counterfeiters too have their ways; coining is a great game these days."

"Counterfeiters of paintings and statues as well?"

"If there is gain to be got. We have our informers—these old ears hear many tales—but when we get word of some plot, more often than not the perpetrators are fled by the time we arrive, as if they have informers of their own."

"Quimp," murmured Mr. Franklin.

Fielding sighed. "Aye, Quimp, damn him. Watch out for Quimp."

Mr. Franklin brought himself to the story he had half an hour ago revealed to Joseph de Medina.

Justice Fielding sniffed. "There is no crime in this. The gem may be returned, as this Cavitty promises."

"Or it may not. I have some doubt."

"You seek help?"

"In a small way. You know of the fencing of things. If you learn that some great gem has been passed in secret, tell me."

A rumbling laugh. "*Quid pro quo*, you must keep me informed of what you learn too."

Mr. Franklin smiled. "I like to trade with you, sir."

We left Bow Street round about one, Mr. Franklin buying a loaf of bread, a wedge of Stilton and two red apples for us to munch as our coach moved along. How I loved to go about with the gentleman, to see the great city! Mansions raised their proud fronts whilst hovels leant against one another like drunken old men at an alehouse. Yet I could not ride entirely free of care, for there seemed more to this affair of the Shenstone Diamond than had first appeared. The glimpse of Bertie Hexham, the encounter with Quimp, my second meeting with the black-haired bully—all unsettled me. I consoled myself with the hope that there could be no danger.

We stopped by St. Bartholomew's Hospital, to see Hogarth's *Pool of Bethesda*. 'Twas large and impressive, Christ ministering to the sick.

I liked Mr. Hogarth's engravings better and said so.

Mr. Franklin clapped an arm round my shoulder. "Then let us see how an engraver works, eh?"

Five minutes delivered us to Charterhouse Street, where above the door of a yellow brick facade hung a signboard—*M. Ravenet, Printmaker*—and in smaller letters: *Engraving, Etching, Mezzotint*. For the third time that day Mr. Franklin rapped a knocker.

"*Entrez*, Monsieur Franklin," said the very thin, small man who opened to us. Though he wore an impeccably powdered wig and a spotless suit of clothes, ink clung to his fingertips and nails, and I smelt ink too, from some other room.

Mr. Franklin made a bow. "I am come, as I sent word. This is my boy, Nicolas. 'Tis kind of you to open your door o' Sunday."

"*Pas du tout*, I am always happy to open my door to a man who seeks knowledge of my craft." He beckoned. "*Suivez-moi, messieurs.*"

Ravenet had thin, arched brows. With a lively waggle of 'em he led us to the back of his house, into a large room looking out upon a tangled garden. Two tall windows let in light. The main furnishings were a long worktable set with unfamiliar tools, and a press unlike the presses I knew, which printed the likes of *Tom Jones,* for this one had a great metal roller in place of a screw. The walls were hung with glazed prints ready for purchase. Some were satirical as we had seen at Carrington Bowles, some portraits, and there were cows in fields and nymphs and shepherds and King George himself, with his

Hanoverian glower. The smell of ink was strong, but there was another sharp smell which I did not know.

Monsieur took keen pleasure in describing his craft. He explained that he rarely printed work of his own making, being too busy printing the work of others. Some of these artists did the engraving themselves, delivering the plates to him. More often he himself engraved pictures for 'em, from their designs. He showed us the smooth, reddish copperplates, of various sizes, which he kept in a cabinet. From thence he led us to his worktable. The design he presently worked on was about fourteen by sixteen inches, a horse and rider. Taking up the graver, a steel rod some five inches long, wedge-shaped, with a slanted, pointed end and short, round wooden handle, he proceeded to cut lines in the metal surface: a beech tree by the horse's flank, some clouds. I watched admiringly, for the tool might have been a part of his hand, so dexterously did he turn it. *"Voilà,* the lines shall be filled with ink, the ink then forced from the plate onto paper in the press." With the triple, fluted blade of a scraper he removed the burr left by the graver.

Mr. Franklin expressed his admiration. "But what if you should make an error in your design?"

"Regardez." Monsieur showed how lines might be removed by harder motions of the scraper or, if the lines were shallow, effaced by a burnisher. He showed us another method, etching, in which the copperplate was covered with a thin layer of a mixture of waxes, gums, and resins: a ground. The drawing was done by cutting lines through this ground with a fine-point etching-needle; then the plate was submerged in a mordant bath, "to bite the lines." This aquafortis was the pungent smell I had detected. Some of the acid lay ready in a wide porcelain tray at the end of the table. My nose wrinkled at the odor, but, at a depth of about half an inch, it looked harmless, like water, and as the Frenchman reached for his copper I

thoughtlessly tried it with my finger. At first there was a coolness, not unpleasant, then a small tingling. Suddenly my finger burned, I cried out, and with an *"Alors!"* Ravenet grasped my hand and thrust it into a basin of water which he kept nearby. This relieved the burning, though my fingertip still stung.

"Goodness, Nick!" cried out Mr. Franklin.

"Niter and calcinated vitriol," said Ravenet, still holding my hand. *"C'est très dangereux.* It can dissolve flesh and bone."

Mr. Franklin peered at my finger. "A lesson learnt. Are you well?"

"I believe so, sir."

"I am glad to hear it." The crisis past, he bade Ravenet proceed, at which the Frenchman diluted the mordant with a precisely measured amount of water and slipped the copperplate into it. The process took my mind off my wound. Little bubbles formed about the lines in the blackish ground as the exposed copper was dissolved by the diluted acid. Ravenet kept his eyes on the process. *"C'est fini,"* said he after two minutes, dexterously lifting out the plate with wooden tongs and rinsing it to stop the acid's action. "I may now wash off the ground and print it, to see the progress of the plate."

"Do you know the painter, James Cavitty?" inquired Mr. Franklin. "Is he one of the artists who comes to you to have his paintings turned to prints?"

"No. But I know of this Cavitty. Why do you ask?"

"An engraving we saw in Carrington Bowles. Excellent work."

"He is an excellent engraver, one of the best in London; his hand is as good as mine."

"Praise, indeed."

"But he employs Phillippe duVerre to print his plates."

"One of your countrymen?"

"I confess it."

"What? Is not duVerre a credit to his craft?"

Ravenet bit his lip. "He is . . . quite good. Quite skilled."

"Yet you hesitate to speak of him. Why?"

"I hear tales about the man."

"Tell one, monsieur."

"It is rumored he left France because . . . but, *non*, I must not spread rumors. And now: mezzotint . . ." Ravenet showed how a toothed rocker was used to roughen a plate so it would print black, then how lighter areas could be burnished away to achieve subtle shades. He showed drypoint and stipple. At Mr. Franklin's request he printed his picture of horse and master, laying on the ink, wiping it from the surface so it remained only in the tiny indentations. "Great pressure is needed to force the ink from the lines onto the paper. Thus: rollers rather than the screw." Dampened paper was placed against the plate and pulled through the press under layers of special blankets.

Mr. Franklin watched. "May the boy try?" asked he.

This was allowed. My finger no longer stinging, I spread ink, wiped the plate with cloth and hand, dampened the paper, fit it onto the plate, laid the blankets, turned the crank.

"He has great dexterity," commented Ravenet when the finished picture was lifted from the plate.

"I should like to purchase the print he has done. What cost, if you please?"

Ravenet protested that it was in an incomplete state, but Mr. Franklin must have it, and did, for a shilling, for Ravenet refused to take more. He also purchased, for three and eight-pence, two small country dances, originally book illustrations, of which printers did many, the Frenchman told us.

By three we were encoached and swaying back to Craven Street. "You knew of engraving before, sir," said I, "though you pretended not to."

"Did I? I confess, then, that I made the first copperplate press in America, and many's the time I have inked a plate and pulled it through. You remembered, eh? But I came to seek information on the custom of artists, James Cavitty in particular. He engraves his own designs . . . interesting." He peered at me as we passed St. Mary le Bow. "You will learn many new things at Cavitty's tomorrow. How is your finger? No great pain, I trust. Be careful what you touch."

❧ 8 ❧

IN WHICH I sweep a floor, draw a picture, and make an enemy . . .

Next morn, the world blue-black and London stirring but fitfully beyond the bow window, I stood in Mr. Franklin's chamber. By candlelight he examined the plain brown suit of clothes I had put on. He gazed soberly into my eyes. "Thirteen. Brave lad." He clapped my shoulder.

And then I was gone.

Peter drove me as the first faint streaks of light spread over the city. I had much to think on. I looked forward to being a student of art—Cavitty might prove a hard master, but if he was fair what mattered stern treatment? Yet I was uncertain of my role: not quite a pupil nor yet an apprentice. How should I play it? I was not the illegitimate son of Sir Bartleby Bart's sister. I must spy out the whereabouts of the Shenstone Diamond. Further there were Biggs and black-hair to contend with. All in all I was in a high state of agitation as we turned from St. Martin's Lane into Cranbourne Street, to number 23, the brass plaque, *James Cavitty, Painter* dully gleaming. The coach halted. I got down. Peter offered an encouraging salute, and I sent back a grateful smile.

As the doddering watchman cried, "Seven o' the morn, and all's well!" I let the knocker fall.

Do not disappoint Mr. Franklin, thought I.

The door opened, and I obeyed the beckoning arm of the wan, pretty maid whom I had seen Saturday. Then the door was closed, and faint smells of paint once more assailed my nose. Gazing about the entryway, I seemed to feel an uneasy air about the house. The echo of my own doubt? The maid peered at me with shy, avid eyes. Her voice betrayed a quaver of eagerness: "You are the new boy."

"I am."

"I am Annie."

"I am Nicolas."

"Nicolas." She tasted the name with her small, pink mouth. "Master is not yet down, though Mrs. Bone is. She is the mistress. Mistress is always up early. Mistress is everywhere." At this she darted a look over her shoulder as if Mrs. Bone might be listening, but not even the thin child's face which I had seen before stared down. Annie regarded me with shy interest. "You are to help Master in his painting?"

"I hope so."

A dreaming smile curved her lips. "I should like to paint. Pretty things. I would paint lapdogs. One day I will have my very own lapdog." Her eyes were a pale, shining blue, as if washed by the sun, and for a brief, hopeful moment they gazed into a future in which she was the mistress of much more than lapdogs, but this only made me sad, for few maids had such dreams answered. "I hope you do, ma'am," said I nonetheless.

Her dream winked out. "O, you need not call me ma'am. I am beneath you, sir. I am beneath ev'ryone. Will you follow me to the painting room?"

I did, noting that her cap was not set straight on her head, and that the ties of her apron were atangle. We entered the room opposite the display parlor: the room in which art was made in Cavitty's house.

My pulse quickened as I stepped through its door, for I had never visited such a realm, and my own dream cried out in my heart: *Nicolas Handy, Painter.* It proved a large room, about twenty feet wide on the side facing the street and forty long, marching back into the house. Some alteration in the original structure must have been made to create this lengthy space, but however it had been achieved, 'twas grand to my eyes. The floors were dark fir planks, the walls white plaster. Windows at both front and back let in light, and a small stove against the west wall glowed against the morning's chill. Farther back, by this same wall, was a dais about six feet square, about a foot off the floor. On it rested an elegant, red-cushioned chair, and I was at first startled by what appeared there, a naked man wantonly sprawled, though in a blink I saw this was one of the hinged lay figures which might be dressed for painting. There were bolts of cloth pinned to the wall behind the mannequin, and, nearby, a half-length plaster column and other odds and ends: a pewter bowl, three candlesticks, a shepherd's staff, two straw baskets, a small harp, a soldier's breastplate, lengths of purple ribbon, a salver, even a dead goose—props for the painter. Before the dais stood an easel, on it blank linen canvas stretched on a frame. Against the wall rested an open-shelved cabinet containing jars and gallipots of color with names that made me long to paint with 'em: flake white, turchino, Naples yellow, gamboge, lake, *terra verte*, Chinese vermilion. There were, too, Venice turpentine, beeswax, Jew's pitch, linseed oil, sugar of lead, mastic, copal—the uses of which I longed to know. Brushes of all sizes poked out of jars, and three well-used palettes lay near a jumble of paint-smeared rags. A workbench sat some feet from the cabinet, where (I was to learn) colors were mixed and driers added and other magic done. Another table stood at the front, with tools such as Monsieur Ravenet had shown—gravers and burnish-

71

ers—along with many copperplates. There was a small copperplate press as well, which surprised me, since we had been led to believe that all Cavitty's engravings were printed by the Frenchman, duVerre. I inhaled the heady smell of mineral spirits as if it were a courtesan's scent.

There were people too, yet I hardly took 'em in, for at that moment my eye discovered the portrait of Lady Shenstone.

It rested on a second easel against the left wall, not ten paces from me. It was large, about four by six feet, a full-length. My lady was depicted in a wood, in a rose pink gown with lace at her wrists and bodice, very elegant, as if she were some fine plant grown in the wild. She wore a plumed hat and carried an ivory fan, and her figure was turned slightly away, though her head on its long neck gazed squarely out. Her face at first appeared serene—but Cavitty had captured some inner agitation, a hint that all was not well: a Diana ill at ease in her wood.

Yet what I stared at most was the gem upon her breast: the Shenstone Diamond. It had been skillfully limned: large, flickering with blue-and-yellow lights, set in the handsome filigree of gold which I had attempted to draw. I saw how poor a thing my rendering had been, lacking color and spirit. The diamond glowed at the very center of the picture and there was a tension between it and Lady Shenstone's face, both oval, both beautiful, yet contrasting—the first a geometry of icy facets whilst the other expressed some suppressed turmoil.

"Is this the boy?" came a deep demand.

I started.

"Yes, sir," said Annie in her little, quavering voice, and I remembered only then that she stood by my side.

A man strode from the central workbench where he had had his back to us. He was of medium height, stocky and robust in his plain workman's garb, about thirty-five, I guessed, with hard knots of muscle in his stockinged calves and a thick mass of dusky brown hair that curled fantastically about his face. His voice revealed an unmistakable foreign accent.

Hands on hips, he regarded me from under brows like jots of charcoal, and there was something burning in his eyes that bespoke a passionate nature. "*Andiamo*, you must be put to work." He jerked his head for me to follow.

Annie darted one last small glance, curtsied, and was gone.

"Cully!" demanded the man.

Black-hair.

He had been sweeping at the far end. Coming with stomping steps, the sullen young man peered at me as if I were something he would prefer to strike rather than greet, and I prayed his eyes recognized me only as the boy who had come with Sir Bartleby Bart.

"I am Signore Amadeo Mazzoni," said the wild-haired man in his accented voice, Italian, I guessed. "What is your name?"

"Nicolas Handy, sir."

The Italian gestured. "This is Cully Stringer, Signore Cavitty's apprentice. I am his assistant. You are to be the—*Dio*, what?—pupil, I am told. *Attenzione*, we all work at many things. We not only draw and paint, we mix colors, we prepare canvases. We also sweep. Hang your coat there." He pointed to a peg by the door, and, obeying, I received in turn a leathern apron which he tossed to me. It was much too large, but by tying it tightly I contrived to make it hang about my hips. Signore Mazzoni took the broom from Stringer's grasp. "You will begin by sweeping." He thrust the broom in my hands.

Thus began my education in James Cavitty's household.

I had swept at Inch, Printer, and I swept now, glad to do so because it gave me opportunity to learn ev'ry inch of the room. By the east wall stood a third easel, whereon rested the picture of the burgher who had demanded that Cavitty portray him better. He was stubborn-jawed and squint-eyed, John Bull to the life. How to put a nobler face on that? I also noted a door toward the rear, on the other side of the dais. Where did it lead? Of most interest was a mahogany artist's cabinet, many-drawered, its lid up to form an easel: surely the same in which Lady Shenstone had watched Cavitty place her husband's precious diamond. It sat near the engraving bench. Out the front window I glimpsed Cranbourne Street, out the back a tidy garden in which Annie hung clothes to dry.

Upon handing me the broom Signore Mazzoni had set Cully Stringer to mixing pigments at the paint table, whilst he himself took up a palette and set to work on the burgher's portrait. Though the brown coat and white cravat and tricorn hat appeared finished, the hands and face were only sketched in, in warm gray tones. Mazzoni began to apply glazes of color to the hands, and I contrived to take my sweeping near so I might watch him. How deft he was! Never had I seen a painter at work, and though he was but an assistant he was skilled. Had he learnt as an apprentice? Why did he not have his own studio?

Glancing up, I discovered Cully Stringer watching, and I averted my eyes. *Be cautious, Nick. Provoke no ire.*

But Stringer proved to need no provocation, for when Signore Mazzoni left the room somewhat later, having finished the hands, the apprentice rushed at me and delivered a thwacking blow upon my shoulder.

"What?" cried I, stumbling back.

He thrust his face into mine. "That's to let you know who's head boy, see?"

My arm ached to the fingertips, but I drew myself up. Stringer was older than I, inches taller, and plainly stronger, but strength did not count for ev'rything, for Mr. Franklin had showed me just where and how to strike a bully to bring him low. Stringer's lips smiled, his mean glare daring me to strike back, and I longed to do so, if only to show him he could not raddle Nick Handy. Dropping the broom, I bunched my fists and felt to my toes the taut, meaning gathering of a blow.

But I unleashed nothing. I must get on here, I must play my role. Most important I must serve Mr. Franklin. And so shame-facedly I forced myself to hang my head and play the sheep.

Stringer snorted. He kicked the broom at me. "So long as that's clear." He grabbed the front of my shirt. "And don't you be goin' to Master, or you'll only get it worse!" He swaggered to the workbench.

Doggedly I picked up the broom.

The master arrived at eight, just as Cranbourne Street began to rumble with wakening commerce. He marched in by the front door, wearing a shirt and breeches, no coat. Pulling from another peg by the door the paint-spotted apron he had worn o' Saturday, he tied it on. Mr. Ralph had told us that many an artist worked in a grand suit of clothes, to impress his patrons, but Cavitty plainly affected no such pretensions. I looked cautiously about. Though Cully Stringer had dawdled at his task, he made a great show of labor the moment the master entered.

With but a glance at him, Cavitty strode straight to me. "Put away that broom."

I leant it against the nearest wall.

"Come." He led me to the mahogany cabinet. From one of its drawers he snatched out my drawing of a hand. This surprised me, for I had thought he had likely thrown it away, but he stood in the light of the front window regarding it, then me, with compressed lips and a look in his bulging eyes that seemed to weigh some vexing matter. As on Saturday his brown hair was pulled tightly back, and he had a restless air, like a high-strung steed primed to gallop. Shoving the drawing

75

back, he felt about in the drawer with a great, scowling thoroughness, and in three others besides, peering under the folding easel to boot. "Damn," muttered he. Did he seek the Shenstone Diamond? Surely he had gone through these drawers before.

His brooding eyes fell on me. "You show some promise. You may be wasted on the broom; we shall see." He led me to the raw, buff-colored canvas on its easel before the dais, about two and a half feet wide by three high. Lifting it by the edges— "Never dig your fingers into a picture, boy!"—he carried it to a small bench in a corner. Nearby sat a pot of a whitish mixture. "A ground," said Cavitty. "Begin by priming the canvas with it. Like this." Dipping in a wide brush, he showed how to apply the medium in even, penetrating strokes, so the canvas was well-sealed.

There came a scrape of wood on wood. "That's *my* job," protested Cully Stringer.

Cavitty sent him a withering look. "More than one can do it. I am master here. Be about your business."

Stringer went back to paint mixing, but I felt a sinking at the resentment this would rouse. "Do as I have shown you," commanded Cavitty. "I shall examine your work when you are done." Striding to the painting of the burgher, he picked up palette and brush and set to work on the face. With a deep breath I glanced at Stringer, whose glare promised retribution. How to placate him? But I could not. Let the reckoning come.

Taking up the brush, I was at once pleased at how the liquid soaked into the canvas. Moments passed, and in spite of Cully Stringer's clenched presence, there grew a companionability of labor in the room: workmen at their tasks, making the small sounds—breaths, scrapings, tiny hums—which said progress went forward. I recalled similar times at Inch, Printer, when I set type or turned the screw of the press or bound books, bliss to a boy who had little in his life save work. Signore Mazzoni returned through the back door carrying a canvas which he placed on the empty easel before clearing the dais of its oddments in readiness for the next sitter. I caught a glimpse of Biggs, who darted in, took orders from Cavitty, darted out. The small child's face which I had seen on the stairs appeared too, round the front doorjamb. It still wore its strange, fey look, but I had no time to reflect on it, for a hand snatched the child back: Mrs. Bone's. Marching in, she squinted round like the captain of a ship. I had a moment to examine her. In spite of her brusque manner and out-starting eyes, she was not an unattractive woman, and her brown hair lay soft about her neck. She and Mazzoni exchanged a glance whose meaning I could not read, but she appeared satisfied to find her brother working dutifully (if not happily) on the burgher's face, and she drew the child out.

I took all this in whilst applying myself to my task. Gradually the canvas turned white under my hand, ready for the artist, and I wondered how one began a painting. Line first? Color? Lord Shenstone had said I had an eye to tell a good picture from a bad, but that was a far cry from painting one, and I hoped if I ever earned the chance I would not be found wanting.

I observed Cavitty to see how he would remake the burgher's features. A lowborn cunning seemed stamped into 'em, but Cavitty lifted the sunken chin, put light in the stubborn eyes and so altered and rearranged brows and nostrils and dewlaps that the bulldog was transformed into a greyhound— amazing. Yet something was lost. A real man no longer stood there, however imperfect, but only a *kind* of man in whose countenance nothing remained but vacuous nobility; the portrait might have been done by Augustus Broome. It should please the burgher but it did not please Cavitty, for his mouth curled in contempt with each brushstroke.

"There, damn you," cried he when he was done, flinging down his brush. "Mazzoni, take this . . . *thing* out of my sight so it may dry." Wiping his hands on his apron, he came to examine my work. "Hum, a decent job. Stringer, show him how to clean my brushes. Be quick about it. I have a sitter soon."

Signore Mazzoni lifted the burgher's painting by its edges, as I had been shown was proper, and carried it through the rear door. Cavitty went out by the front, leaving me alone with Cully Stringer.

With no great joy I approached him at the workbench.

"Wot do *you* want?" demanded he.

"You are to show me how to clean the brushes."

A curl of lips. "You tellin' *me* wot t'do?"

My arm still ached from his blow. "You heard Master. You are to show me how to clean the brushes. You had best do so at once."

I do not know what Stringer would have done in answer (he looked like throttling me), for at that moment Mazzoni returned, and Stringer was forced to obey, though he pinched me hard as he showed how to dip the brushes in spirits and press 'em in cloth to remove the paint. "You must do this sev'ral times, see? Wipe 'em well afterward, and set 'em in their pots by size. Master does not like to look about for his brush." Another pinch for good measure. "Be about it."

I moved to the far end of the bench, out of his reach. The front door had been left ajar, and as I worked, the small fey face peered round it again, then the child entered, a girl, perhaps six, with light brown hair that hung down straight and limp. Her outstarting eyes said she might be Cavitty's daughter. Mrs. Bone's? Her face was long and pale, with a hectic pink in the cheeks. I smiled at her, but she did not smile back; and indeed though her gaze seemed fixed on me, I could not tell if she saw me at all. Spittle stood out at the corners of her mouth, and she rocked back and forth like some clockwork toy whilst one of her tiny hands plucked at a sleeve. Her toes were turned violently in.

Mazzoni crossed the room to kneel before her. "Felicity, *cara*, you must not be here. You know your mother does not like it."

Felicity showed no indication that she knew anything at all.

"Per favore," pled Mazzoni—but Cavitty suddenly stood over him, and the Italian rose and crept back to work. Cavitty knelt in Mazzoni's place, peering into the girl's strangely blank face, his features working with powerful emotion, his long-fingered hands twisting as if he would wash some stain from 'em. "No, Felicity, not in the painting room. The painting room does terrible things." He led the child out.

His words echoed in my brain as the morning wore on. Terrible things—what could he mean? But speculations did not prevent me from continuing to observe. Around ten the first sitter of the day arrived, Sir Malcolm Derby, a gap-toothed fellow, who was shown in by Mrs. Bone. She treated him in an obsequious manner whilst shooting a glance at her brother that seemed to say: *do not provoke him.* Two folding Chinese screens, which had leant against a wall, were pulled out to form a barrier across half the room, so painter and sitter might have privacy, whilst the rest of us went about our tasks. From behind the screen I heard 'em talk of what pose was desired, what garments should be depicted, Cavitty explaining to Sir Malcolm that he needed him only for his face. "It does not matter what you wear as you sit, for we shall dress you in the painting however you like."

Sir Malcolm did not quite understand—"Hem, ah," protested he—and Cavitty grew brusque as he explained for the second time that a hired model or a lay figure would be dressed in anything the gentleman cared to send round, so he need not be present for the rendering of it. "Ah!" cried Sir Malcolm, seeming to take no umbrage at the painter's irritability. But many another might have, and I began to see what an enemy Cavitty was to himself. Why indeed had Lord Shenstone chosen him?

Having been set the task of washing paint pots, I wished my labors were placed so I might peep round the open end of the screens. But as they were not, I listened for sounds: the arranging of the subject upon the dais, the faint whisper of brush on canvas. Cavitty frequently snapped at Sir Malcolm to sit still, and I recalled how Lady Shenstone had complained of him; he had a temper. Finishing my cleaning, I wondered: what next? Signore Mazzoni had gone to the engraving table to burnish copperplates. As for my nemesis, having done with paint mixing Cully Stringer had withdrawn to a corner where he sat on the floor with a sheet of paper pinned to a board, his tongue betwixt his teeth, his black eyes squinting whilst he struggled to depict a plaster cast of a head. Was this, then, the nature of lessons at James Cavitty's? Stringer had pulled his paper from a quire under the workbench. I took a sheet too, a board, two pins, and settled myself quietly against the wall farthest from him, by the portrait of Lady Shenstone. I decided to draw Stringer himself, proceeding to render him in all his beetle-browed churlishness. There! and there! He became in my picture all I hated of bullies like Buck Duffin and Mr. Bumpp, who had near broke my head on a snowbound street before Peter felled him. I smiled as I drew, for no one watched, no one judged. Stringer grew under my pencil into a noxious, sneaky-eyed lump of misspent youth, and though I was constrained from dealing him any actual blow, it gave me warm satisfaction to have at him thus.

But no happiness was unalloyed, and after a time I discovered his eyes on me, glowering over the top of his board. Whereas he seemed to hate to draw (he had fussed and grumbled over his effort, I plainly enjoyed my work, and his beetling stare demanded how I dared enjoy anything. All my pleasure gone, I looked away. Not half a day in the studio and I had provoked a rival.

After an hour Sir Malcolm emerged and departed, at which the master called to Stringer and me. "Show what you have done." He fixed his gaze upon Stringer's effort first. The apprentice proved not wholly without perception, for he had got the nose betwixt the eyes, the mouth beneath the nose, and there were two protrusions on each side o' the head that might be ears rather than pumphandles. But how wretched the whole, smudged and labored, no 'line of beauty' anywhere. Cavitty sighed impatiently. "Damn it, boy, do you not learn?" Snatching Stringer's instrument, he attempted to rescue the drawing but with little success, for 'twas like trying to revivify a dead man.

He turned to my work. Had I gone too far? "Good enough," conceded the artist, and I thought he smiled, his large teeth wolfish behind the thin, stretched lips. I wondered how he, who looked to paint truth and cursed when he must paint a lie, could have wronged Lady Shenstone. Uneasily I glanced about, at Mazzoni, the workbenches, paints, easels, screen; at the rear door, which led I knew not where. I thought on Annie, the blank-eyed child, Mrs. Bone, and was suddenly chilled to the heart. Fear set its teeth in me, and I recalled that Mr. Franklin had said I might withdraw if I chose. But how could I? He himself would not.

I made myself look at Cully Stringer. My drawing had

mocked him (he was not such a fool to miss that); too, the master seemed to approve my work, another blow, and his gaze promised vengeance. I sent him a defiant stare and had the satisfaction of carving a moment's doubt on his sullen features, but it did not last. His fingers curled to fists.

❦ 9 ❦

IN WHICH I tell of anger and fear . . .

A nd now, Nick," said Mr. Franklin, settling into his comfortable chair that eve whilst I perched on the edge of his bed, "the soldier must give his report. What have you seen and heard today?" It was seven, dusk beginning to mantle London, though sufficient light fell through the bow window to lend a soft glow to the gentleman's bald crown. His fringe of brown hair hung to his shoulders, and his crinkled eyes behind the small, squarish spectacles were alight.

I related all whilst he made small hums or plucked at his breeches, the sound of Mrs. Stevenson preparing supper drifting up the stairs. I told of Sir Malcolm Derby. "There arrived a second sitter," continued I, "a thin, nervous woman. Cavitty painted her for an hour, the allotment for each sitting, it seems; then came time for luncheon. There are two sets of stairs in the house. Servants—even Signore Mazzoni—do not use the main ones but go up or down by the back way. Cavitty departed by the front door. Mazzoni beckoned me through the rear. A storeroom lies beyond, about ten by twelve feet, where I saw a second lay figure hung on a hook, racks of paintings too. Most were by Cavitty but some were plainly not—a landscape, a Madonna—but I had no time to study 'em, for Cully Stringer trod on my heels. A second door in the storeroom gave onto the back stairs, and we went down to a corridor where I was led past a pantry and scullery to an eating room where a long trestle table was set with wooden plates. Three small, high windows let in light.

"A simple meal was laid: bread and some thick soup not near as good as Mrs. Stevenson's. Annie was already seated. Biggs too, with his sticking-up hair and his look to see that Stringer did not cuff him; he ate like some animal, noisy at his soup. Again I felt a sadness about Annie. She sent me a smile from her pale blue eyes, but Stringer soon extinguished that. She must like him no better than I, for she looked down and shuddered when he pushed past. How he leered at her! I longed to strike him.

"Signore Mazzoni sat across from them, I next to him. Cook arrived pretty soon, a tall woman built like an oak plank: Mrs. Cockle. She flung down more bread and some pippin apples on a pewter plate. 'Who's this?' asked she, staring. Mazzoni told her. 'Another mouth!' She sank down and began to eat too. She has streaky hair and a face greatly disfigured by the pox, and she complained that Annie must wear her cap straighter. She poked at Biggs too, as if he were a species of vermin, but she treated Stringer with great favor: 'More soup, more bread? A young man must eat.' "

"Was there talk at table?" inquired Mr. Franklin.

"Some. Mrs. Cockle asked how Master was and Stringer winked and said, 'How should he be?' 'Oho, the same, eh?' says Mrs. Cockle, squinting back. 'Sumping on his mind? He's been jumpy as a cat these days.' 'He's still jumpy,' answers Stringer. '*Why*, is what I wonders,' says Mrs. Cockle. 'Ain't there more money in the house? I hear there's more money.' 'I am very glad of that,' says Annie. 'And just why?' snaps Mrs.

Cockle, as if Annie has no right to speak. 'Because then Mrs. Bone will not be so angry,' whispers Annie. 'Hmp, true enough,' says Mrs. Cockle. 'But where's it come from, eh?' 'The master is painting gentry of a better class,' Signore Mazzoni told her as if to put an end to gossip, but Mrs. Cockle only looked sly. 'He's got a friend, *I* know. A lord who sends him custom. But can't he act nicer to his sitters? Many's the time I've seen 'em through the area window, amuttering. Can't he smile? Lord knows I must do!'

"The old gentleman who showed Mr. Ralph and me into the house on Saturday came in next," went on I. "He had been serving Master at table upstairs. He has a gray face, but his expression is kind. His name is Peasgood and he greeted me pleasantly and sat with a cracking of knees and ate his soup. Mrs. Cockle barked that Annie must be off to clear Master's table, so she hurried out. Her apronstrings were still atangle, and Stringer watched her in a way I still did not like. Biggs begged for more soup, but Mrs. Cockle only cuffed him and sent him to the kitchen to scrub pots. As for me, I ate hardly anything. And that is the household, sir."

"You describe 'em well. But who might be this 'lord' who recommends Cavitty to his friends? Inquire, Nicolas—discreetly."

"I shall. As for the rest of my day, it was spent in the studio. Cavitty painted two more sitters behind his screen. Sometimes Mrs. Bone poked in her nose, and I saw the child once more, though plainly she is not wished in that part of the house. As for Stringer and I, we prepared canvases and colors, whilst Mazzoni touched up what needed finishing: costumes and backgrounds, and I helped him dress a lay figure in a fine blue velvet suit, so you might've taken it for a lord. Stringer tried to copy one of the master's paintings but he huffed and grumbled so that I stayed out of his way and scratched in my book. See?"

Pulling the small volume from my coat pocket, I held it out. "Here is Signore Mazzoni. Cavitty. This is Annie. Peasgood. Mrs. Cockle. Biggs. Here is Mrs. Bone. Felicity too."

Mr. Franklin examined 'em, especially the child. "What a strange, empty stare, poor thing. Excellent work. And this—" (I had turned a page) "—your plan of the house?"

"It is." I had sketched the arrangement of rooms and stairs. "Cavitty carries in his pocket a book similar to mine, in which he makes notes or sketches. He allowed me to watch him paint."

"Did he? In hopes you will learn what Stringer cannot, no doubt. Tell of it."

" 'Twas his fourth sitter, around three, a vain young gentleman in a full-bottomed wig. 'Come round here, Handy,' said he, and I found him before a small blank canvas on the easel behind the screen, a 'kit-kat' they call it, a head-and-shoulders. 'As this is your first day, you must see all.' He bade me stand near. The sitter was perched absurdly regally, with drooping lids and a foppish air. He had asked to be portrayed as Alexander the Great—which meant, I learnt, that symbols of the conquerer would be dabbed in and the painting titled *Viscount Budwell as Alexander.*"

"So even a fop may be transmuted to a hero."

"Paint is an alchemist, sir."

"Bravo!"

"There were only blue and black on the palette. Mixing 'em, Cavitty began. He is very good. General shapes came first—the oval of the head, the shoulders, the torso; the details with a sable. The result was comical, like one of the satirical prints we saw in Carrington Bowles. Cavitty had exaggerated his sitter's vainness (I could not blame him), but when the man was allowed to come look, he seemed not to see the burlesque. He strutted back to his pose, and Cavitty laid in shadows and added a gleaming helmet on the hero's head. 'This must dry,' said he. 'At the next sitting I shall paint the flesh tones. Thursday, same time?' Budwell bobbed his head and left. The master turned to me. 'What do you think, Handy?'

" 'I think I should like to paint as well as you, sir,' said I.

" 'Ha, do not expect to climb too fast. Yet, though you draw like a cretin, if you learn to flatter you will rise quick.' The portrait of Lady Shenstone was visible round the edge of the screen, the gem at its center, and Cavitty gazed at it. 'I have found *my* way . . .' said he, greed and fear seeming to fight a war in him, as if he saw riches within his grasp but must cross a field of battle to get 'em."

Mr. Franklin pursed his lips. "There shall prove more to this than a stolen gem." Dusk deepened around us. "Go on."

"Mr. Banks arrived shortly after, a house agent. Peasgood came to say he would show him to the display parlor, but Cavitty said no, he must speak to him in the painting room. When he was brought in, they withdrew behind the screen. The conversation was in lowered voices, but I overheard enough to learn that Cavitty looks to let a house in Leicester Square, far finer than his present one. He hopes to move his establishment there."

"Does he? Hum, Leicester Square is costly, but a painter might by an address there ask more for a picture; he might get it too. He might make his name in Leicester Square."

"Not if Mrs. Bone can help it. She waylaid her brother in the entryway just after Mr. Banks left. The painting room door was ajar, and I heard her press him to tell who the visitor was and why he had come. When she had wrung his plans from him, she began to rant: 'What? Where's the money to come from when I have had to scrimp to make ends meet?' 'You have not had to pinch pennies lately,' Cavitty said. '*I* am master of this house and will have my way. My circumstances are improved.

We must move if I am to prosper.' 'If you wish to prosper, begin by treating your sitters better,' she replied, but he slammed the painting-room door on her and shot us such a look as would've set fire to ice.''

"Money provokes strong feelings," said Mr. Franklin. "So Mrs. Bone draws the pursestrings tight? There is some virtue in counting your farthings—and yet . . ." He pulled at his lip. "Plainly her brother is ambitious, and ambition may be a powerful incentive to crime." He turned his gaze to the bow window. Beyond it lay London, dark with night, where a thousand crimes took place hourly in the name of money. I reflected: poverty was the root of much evil—but not all, for there was in the hearts of many well-off men a need for more, which a mere sufficiency could never assuage.

Mr. Franklin's gaze came back. "What more, Nick?"

"Some sneaking business. Stringer and I were sometimes alone, for there is ever a coming-and-going. Near four, Signore Mazzoni was sent off to the framer's; Cavitty went out too. This left Stringer free to work mischief on me—but he did not. He grew furtive and, after assuring himself that both doors were closed, he began to search about the room, peering in cabinets and drawers, pawing amongst the oddments there. I heard him in the storeroom, scraping and cursing, and when he came back, he looked through ev'ry drawer of the mahogany artist's cabinet which Cavitty had also searched; but he did not seem to find what he sought, and pretty soon he stomped to me and snatched my sleeve: ' 'Ave you seen my drawing? Th' one I did this mornin'?' He had been looking for no drawing— it was in a leather folder that leant against a wall in easy view— but I said no, I had not seen it. 'If you see it you must say so, hear? And stop toadyin' to Master.' He let me go without harm. I was surprised he had not treated me worse, but he seemed to brood on something. I think he is frightened, sir.''

The gentleman's chair creaked as he struck flint to the candle on the table, its soft glow springing up. "I trust your intuition, Nick." He shook his head. "What currents run through that house? You do an excellent job of testing the waters, but I begin to misgive making you swim in 'em. The apprentice does no real harm?"

"All bluff, sir."

"Do not be overbrave."

"There is more. Cavitty returned about five, and shortly after another visitor arrived, Mr. Cope, a printseller. They stood in plain view by the engraving table, no secrecy. Cope has little black-currant eyes; he came regarding a series of prints Cavitty had just completed, *The Follies of a Lord*, which, I gathered, lampoon the vogue of something called 'connoisseurship.'"

"Having expert knowledge of art. Go on."

"Cavitty railed against it: 'The gentry who sneer they know a good painting from a bad or can tell a true Roman head from a copy?—pah!' Mr. Cope stood this awhile, but at last he broke in to ask why Cavitty wished to withdraw the series before even one was delivered. The subscription was excellent—'twas the best Cavitty had achieved, Cope said; many a subscriber waited. Further, three had already been printed; 'twould be costly to destroy 'em. 'Why must you have 'em returned?' 'I wish to alter 'em,' says Cavitty. 'But, why?' says Cope. 'That is my business. You will get your prints—but I must receive the plates back from duVerre tomorrow. I will make changes, and he will reprint 'em as I wish, and that is that. Do not fret. 'Twill be not a penny out of your pocket.' Cope protested that it was not only a matter of money but of the goodwill of his customers, but Cavitty was adamant; so the printseller bowed his head and withdrew, though he muttered that he did not like having to tell subscribers they must wait for prints already overdue. 'I do not care what you like,' Cavitty shot after him."

Mr. Franklin frowned. "How peculiar. Did you see any of these prints?"

"No."

"Did Cavitty say how he wished to change 'em?"

"Mr. Cope asked, but Cavitty only told him to mind his business."

"Let us make it our business, eh? Look at the copperplates when they are brought in tomorrow, if you can. I am interested in this duVerre too."

I told the rest of my day: "Just past five-thirty Mrs. Bone called us into the display room: Stringer, Peasgood, Cook, Annie, Biggs, me. Signore Mazzoni was there too. We stood in a line, and I thought Mrs. Bone and Mazzoni exchanged another look, though I could not say what sort. Cavitty was not present. Mrs. Bone stood straight as a stick, whilst Felicity peeped from behind her skirts. 'I cannot find my thimble,' says Mrs. Bone, 'silver with mother-of-pearl. My best thimble. It belonged to my grandmother. I know where I place things, and I cannot find it. A saltcellar is missing too. Three ivory buttons. Who is thieving in this house? Is someone thieving? If so, it will go hard with him, for they cut off the fingers of thieves, they cut off their hands.' She glared. 'We shall find this thief. *I* shall find him. I shall see him before the magistrate. I shall see him tried. I shall see a part of him cut *off*!' Taking a breath, she smoothed her bosom. 'Now, I shall expect to find these things returned. I shall expect this soon or there will be *dire consequences*. Do you understand?'

" 'Yes, ma'am,' we replied as one, shaking.

"At this her brother walked in. 'What the devil?' says he. 'I am catching a thief,' replies his sister. Cavitty blanched. 'Thief? What is missing?' 'My best thimble, for one,' says Mrs.

Bone, at which her brother forced a laugh. 'That is all? Good luck, then. But I need my helpers. At once.' He stalked out, and Mrs. Bone dismissed us with a warning glance that said the villain had best confess."

"Which seems to say," mused Mr. Franklin, "that Cavitty has not told his sister the diamond is missing. I wonder: did she ever know it came into the house? And this petty thievery—what to make of it?"

I had no answer. At that moment Polly rapped to say that supper awaited, and we rose and went down. William joined us upon the stairs. At table his father quizzed him about the progress of his studies at the Middle Temple, and William told of lengthy lectures and weighty tomes. "Yet you go much about London," observed the father.

"Why . . . some," replied the son.

"O, a very great deal. You could not love the law so much loved you not London more, eh?"

"I do not catch your meaning."

"I mean that I hope you board your books before you board the ladies of the town."

"O, Mr. Franklin!" protested Mrs. Stevenson, reddening.

He merely smiled. "I speak metaphorically, dear lady. What splendid pudding!"

There was pleasanter talk, the gossip of the house, and I listened, content. Though I had been in Craven Street but seven months, I began to think of it as home. Here was kindness, which I had rarely found at Inch, Printer; and after my trying day at Cavitty's, I was pleased to keep company with convivial talk and excellent food. Yet two things which I had not told Mr. Franklin troubled me. One had occurred just before I departed. Cavitty was already gone, Signore Mazzoni occupied placing works in the storeroom, leaving Cully Stringer and me alone. Annie came in. She gave me a friendly glance, but seeing Stringer she made to go, as if to escape—yet he was near enough to catch her. He pulled her to him. "I'll have you, I will," said he, and fondled her breasts and tried to kiss her. She struggled but there came into her eye a look that said she knew he would trap her one day and have his way. This filled me with such fury that if I had not been at the other end of the room I should have struck him, and damn the consequence. But Annie got free; she fled. Wiping his mouth, Stringer shot a glance from under his thick black hair that seemed to taunt me, and I felt more rivalry flare betwixt us.

Must I be Annie's protector? Did I wish to be more?

The other event occurred on my way home. It had been agreed that no coach should meet me at Cavitty's; each six P.M. I was to walk to the Strand, where Peter would collect me. With relief to be free, but also pride that I had acquitted myself decently, I nodded to Peasgood as I went down the three stone steps of the house. In St. Martin's Lane I strolled south. I had much to think on: Cavitty's volatile temperament, the denizens of number 23. But when I came to the spot by the Devil's Foot where Mr. Franklin had near been run down, the hair at the nape of my neck prickled. I peered at the cobbles where the gentleman had fallen. Had it truly been his old enemy Quimp who had sent his coach after him? Apprehension stabbed me. Was I watched? I cast a look behind—and, yes!—a furtive figure darted betwixt two buildings. I tried to dismiss it: foolish Nick, all you saw were boot heels, no proof they belonged to a spy; you must not report phantoms to Mr. Franklin.

Nonetheless I peered behind me the rest of the way.

❦ 10 ❧

IN WHICH I learn of poison and spy
upon a lord . . .

James Cavitty called me to him next morn at a quarter past
eight. He pointed to a picture he had just brought from the
storage room. "This needs a tree to balance its design. 'Tis
a conversation piece, meant for a tradesman's mantel, of no
great matter, so I shall give it you to see what you can do. A
yew tree, I think." His bulging eyes measured me. "You know
what a yew tree is?"

"I believe so, sir."

"Then paint one. Thin your color with spirits." Taking up
brush and palette, he showed me how. "Use the brush as you
would your pencil. Take it, 'twill not bite. Sir Bartleby's sister
wants to know how art likes you? Well, I need to discover if *I*
like you. The proof is in the pudding. Have at it, then, and call
me promptly when you are through."

"Yes, sir." Dry-mouthed I took the brush, whilst Cully
Stringer glowered from the engraving table, where he rough-
ened a mezzotint plate. That yew tree ought to be *mine*, he
chid.

One more mark in his book of vengeance.

I turned to the canvas. It stood on an easel next the west

wall. To my left, grayish light seeped through the large front window, beyond which I could glimpse Cranbourne Street. Faint noises sounded about number 23, and nearby Signore Mazzoni added a small white dog to a full-length; to my right Cavitty opened out the two Chinese screens to prepare for the morning's sitters.

Gripping brush and palette, I addressed my task. It was a small picture, two feet by three, of a sort by which many a rising merchant gained respectability. Because of its size it was cheap, and one got much for his twelve guineas, for the entire family was depicted, with a grand house in the background instead of the modest abode near Lincoln's Inn where they most likely resided. A middle-aged man, his dour wife, three lumpish children and a draggled hound. Plainly Cavitty had given little care to 'em—this was a bread-and-butter piece—but its design must be balanced by a yew. How simple. Yet I had not held a brush in my life, and though I had seen yews in the churchyard in Finsbury, where my dear mother was buried, to paint one was another matter, and I stood frozen whilst noises behind the screens said Cavitty set up his dais and would soon wish to see how I did. I glanced once more at Stringer's sneer before I lifted the brush, but the paint ran and I cursed in misery. How had Cavitty fashioned with the recalcitrant instrument such eloquent satire of Viscount Budwell?

Succor arrived in a surprising form: Signore Amadeo Mazzoni, who stood suddenly beside me, his curling hair as wild as ever about his dusky face. Placing a finger to his lips, he took the brush and with it began to sketch on a sheet of foolscap. His arm was like a length of oak, but it knew its job, and with a few swift strokes a yew emerged. When he was done his deepset eyes met mine. "See?"

My heart flooded with gratitude. "I do, sir. Thank you."

Stringer stared—"Here, now!"—but Mazzoni never looked

at him, only returning silently to his work. The brush once more in my hand, I made my own attempt. It was but a copy of the Italian's, but he had set me on the right path. Not that my tree expressed anything but a novice's struggle with inexperience—it was a sort of feathered cone from which Nature would turn her face—yet it was a yew, and if Cavitty did not in glazing and touching up the work utterly paint it out, someone at some far distant day might pronounce it a decent tree.

Cavitty emerged. He glanced at my work. " 'Twill do." With no more ado he snatched the picture away to the storage room.

Humbled, I considered myself fortunate the rest of the day to be allowed to attempt even the smallest task.

I learnt that Cavitty was more than a painter, for, after his nine A.M. sitter, a different sort of man arrived: a collector, seeking something to decorate the walls of his country house. "It is newly rebuilt in the Palladian style," said he. He was portly and wore fine velvet and black shiny shoes and carried a snuff box and a quizzing glass and spoke in high-flown terms of "artistic quality," though he was plainly more interested in the signature on the painting than in the style of the work. He would not look at a landscape by Cavitty. "No, I must have me a French one, an Italian or a Dutch." His nose wrinked in distaste. "Nothing English. Never." He sniffed him some snuff. "Have you a Rembrandt?"

Cavitty barely mastered his contempt. "My man on the continent finds those difficult to obtain. A Crivelli, perhaps?—I have that."

The gentleman reflected. "I would entertain a Crivelli."

"I hope it entertains *you*," muttered Cavitty as he went to the storage room, returning with the *Madonna* I had glimpsed yesterday. He placed it upon an easel. The prospective buyer used his quizzing glass to search out the signature before he stood back with an affected air. He tilted his head. "Genuine?" said he with a drooping eye.

"I assure you."

"There are many forgeries about."

"Your superior taste must tell you this is not one."

"O, no question!" The gentleman squinted. "And now you say it, the line is—"

Cavitty leered. "Ineffable?"

"The very word I sought! A *Madonna*? Hum, I suppose 'twould not be considered too popish, and I have a small room for such things, out o' the way. Further, it *is* Italian. You have not at present some mythological subject? No? Then I shall take this."

A price was named and acceded to, and Cavitty said he would have the picture framed and sent round. As the man strode out, Cavitty made a mock bow at his back. "A Rembrandt, eh? I shall try to see he paints one before *you* come again." This was likely the sort of "connoisseur" he lampooned in his *Follies*, and I saw why he thought him a fool, but something else was on my mind, for I had heard the name Shenstone pass betwixt 'em. I glanced at the portrait of Lady Shenstone, so graceful, so grave. The woman's troubled almond-shaped eyes seemed to look back. Had those eyes witnessed the fate of her husband's precious gem?

Mrs. Bone poked her nose in often during the course of the morning when sitters came and went, as if to assure herself that her brother treated 'em with deference; and once, near eleven, I heard further argument flare up: money again. Mrs. Bone conceded that there was more of it of late. "But I do not see where it comes from," complained she.

Cavitty's jaw tightened. "I get more for my work now. Is that not proof my reputation grows? And good reason why we

96

must move to Leicester Square?" I wondered that this altercation took place so publicly, but Mazzoni's and Stringer's expressions said they had heard such talk often.

In the midst of it Felicity wandered in, gazing about with her strange eyes in her long little face.

Mrs. Bone grasped the child. "More money, eh? Will all the money in England give me back my daughter? Damned orpiment!" She bore the girl from the room.

Orpiment. Cavitty paled at the word. Mazzoni and Cully Stringer knew to avoid his eyes, but he caught mine before I could avert 'em. "What do you stare at, boy?"

I turned quickly away.

Just past eleven I was sent to Cavitty's colorman, in St. Martin's Lane. The day remained chill under a hide-and-seek sun, so I was glad to nip into the warm shop after ten minutes' walk. I gazed at the pigments, dry and oil-ground, labeled on shelves: the reds, the blues, the yellows. Orpiment. It sat amongst the yellows, and as I called for the package which had been ordered I asked about it. A good color?

"There are better," the shopman replied.

"Pray, why?"

"Because you cannot trust your orpiment. Best use yellow ochre, young sir."

"But why cannot you trust it?"

" 'Twill not mix well with other colors. It darkens, 'specially if put with white lead. It may turn your picture black."

"Dear me."

" 'Tis poisonous too, sulphide of arsenic." He tapped his nose. "Very wise that your master no longer uses it, though he once did, and many still do because it goes on so well. But it always turns bad with time. Be off with you now."

I thought on this as I walked back to Cranbourne Street.

*   *   *

Mrs. Bone had called me aside as I set out. As I was neither a member of the family nor a friend or caller on business, she had made sure I understood that I might enter the front door at seven and go out it at six, but at all other times I must use the back way. This meant traversing a narrow alley to the rear yard, from thence entering the door that gave onto the small landing from which the servants' stairs went up and down. Accordingly I walked up this alley; finding the back door unlatched, I entered. No one was in sight. Passing through the storage room, I paused to peer at the dozen or so paintings. The Crivelli was prominent. I wished to look closer at it but, hearing voices just beyond, I thought it best not to dawdle. The door was ajar, and my fingers had pushed it perhaps a quarter open when I stopped dead.

Lord Shenstone, his countenance plain as day.

He stood not ten feet away, talking with Cavitty, who had his back to me. If his lordship turned his head only a little he would see me. My heart pounded, for if he recalled me he would tell Cavitty of meeting me at Augustus Broome's, which might lead to the end of well-laid plans. The storage room was dim, lit only by a small window at its rear. As silently as possible I crept backward 'til I felt the shadow of the nearest painting fall across my face. There I thought myself reasonably well concealed, though I would far rather have fled, but I feared if I moved I might be discovered. My fingers bit my palms. Why was Lord Shenstone back in town again? Why was he here?

I listened.

Through the open slot of door I could see Cavitty in an angry slouch. He said, ". . . you *assured* me, sir, that you would send Lord Pevsney to me. You promised that a word from you would suffice to recommend me. But he has not come, and now I hear he has got Imry to paint him and his wife and children. Imry! All London thinks Pevsney an arbiter of taste, never mind that he does not know a Carracci from a cockroach. If he had chosen me, 'twould have made my career. But he has slipped through my fingers. Why?"

Lord Shenstone appeared wearied. "I have sent many a man to you," answered he.

"No one so important as Pevsney."

"You are ungrateful for what you have got?"

"I want more! I want what was promised."

"You have much that was promised. Paintings from the continent. I have obtained 'em, and you have repaired 'em. You have acted as agent to sell 'em too, and I thank you for it—but you have profited well."

"Have not some of these pictures been your own, which you took from your walls, in your need of money?"

"What if they were?"

"I tell you, I do not prosper as I wish!"

"You wish to be the toast of London, but London will not toast a man who spits on her."

"She toasts Hogarth."

"Have you heard such a toast of late? At least Hogarth knows how to make a friend. Whereas you—"

Cavitty trembled. "Do not insult me in my own house!"

Shenstone looked wearier than ever. "I do not come to insult you. But I offer advice. You are an able painter, better than some who are better known. But you must—"

"Flatter?"

"—not go out of your way to offend."

"It comes to this: you advised my lord Pevsney not to be painted by me. Can you deny it?"

"He is my friend, I wish to keep that friendship. Others I have sent you, not so great as Pevsney, have chid me for doing so."

"They cannot complain of my abilities."

"Good God, man, they complain of how you depict 'em. Must you paint ev'ry blemish? Must you show only folly?"

Cavitty drew himself up. "I paint truth."

Shenstone started at the word, as if it were a blow. He recovered: "You must then find approbation in yourself, for you will not win it of the gentry. Sir Francis Dormand says you make him look like a cutpurse. I cannot recommend you more, and that is that. Come, sir, we must make an end. I have needed money, and you have acted as my agent when I could not, for such work is unseemly in a lord. Again I thank you, but I look to other means. Yet, however you depict others, you have painted my wife well. And my gem. I want the portrait. What more remains to complete it?"

"Touching up. Glazing. Framing," replied Cavitty betwixt his teeth.

"When may I have it?"

"In a week."

My lord slapped his gloves against his palm. "That is all then, except . . . 'tis unlikely you will meet my wife again, but if you should chance to do so, do not tell her I met you in town today."

"Why?"

Shenstone's heretofore mild expression flashed warning. Plainly Cavitty knew not to brook him, for he contented himself with a bitter flourish. "As my lord wishes."

"Then I bid you good day." With a crisp nod Shenstone vanished round the screen.

"You will see . . . I shall . . ." muttered Cavitty. I heard rapid footsteps, the opening and closing of a door, and Shenstone was gone. There followed the angry crash of a paint pot against a wall. "Damn you," cried James Cavitty, "may you never see your precious diamond again!"

100

*   *   *

I thought on what I had overheard. My lord had said he turned to "other means." That meant he still needed money. What new means, then? And why should he keep this second return to town from his wife?

I questioned old Peasgood.

Our domains were separate, yet we came together for luncheon belowstairs. After a repast much the same as yesterday's—stew and bread and Cully Stringer pressing himself upon Annie whilst I silently vowed to thrash him one day—the stooped old fellow beckoned me into the areaway. Leaning his sticklike frame against the grimy bricks, he proceeded to suck with little popping sounds at a long clay pipe. I was puzzled at his seeking my company, but he seemed only to want an ear.

"I know how 'tis to be a lad in service," mused his wheezing voice, "for fifty year ago I was such a one." I listened to tales of Lord This and Sir That, musty with age, whilst his rheumy eyes lit with past events, but when I saw my chance, I asked about matters nearer to hand. "Where, if I may ask, is Mr. Bone, sir?"

"O, dead. Of a pleurisy. Three years ago. Left no money. That is why Mrs. Bone came here to live with her brother."

"What is wrong with her daughter?"

Peasgood tapped his cranium. "Mad."

"Truly?"

" 'Tis a sad tale. She was once a bright-eyed babe. 'Tis Master's fault what happened, though Master hates it talked on. The girl is five years old now. At two, just after her and her mother settled here, she got into the painting room and ate of some paint that made her sick."

"Orpiment," said I.

"You know of it, then? Aye. The poor thing near died. When she could walk again she was as you see, with little brain to speak on, a lovely child but likely never able to take care of herself on God's green earth."

Peasgood's smoke curled up toward the sky; coach wheels chattered near our heads, whilst street vendors' cries drifted down from a world where chance might blight a life. Poor Felicity. I could not blame James Cavitty for the accident, but I understood Mrs. Bone's bitterness and felt deep pity for the child. Here was one source of the anger in the house.

"How long have you served Mr. Cavitty, sir?" asked I.

"Six years, since he let Cranbourne Street."

"How did he become an artist?"

"Started as apprentice to Mr. Megivvey, who painted many a fine gent. Married Megivvey's daughter after Megivvey died. Took over his studio and custom. 'Twas not enough for him, though, for he must go abroad, to see for himself how Hannibal Scratchi, and Paul Varnish and Raphael Angelo laid down paint. He itched for the Grand Tour, I mean, but had no money for't. But Master gets what he wants, so he looked about and attached himself to a young lord and went as his guide, asketching what he was bid and teaching his man about pictures and such. Was gone near a year, but came back to sorrow, for his wife'd been carried off by a fever. But he had her father's house. He sold it and set up here, in the spring of '52, when I was taken on. He brought some custom with him, but it has fallen off. 'Tis a pity they do not commend him to their friends."

"Yet I have heard that there are more sitters of late. A better class."

"O? It does not seem so to me. James Cavitty has his tempers, but he is not a bad sort; he will not beat you. He copies old masters for the dealers sometimes, to make ends meet. He would like to paint his own grand subjects, as the Italians do, but I have heard him complain he cannot, for them that buys pictures think English painters are good only for portraits."

"I like Master's picture of Lady Shenstone. Her diamond must be worth much."

" 'Tis famous, I hear."

"She brought it round?"

"How else could Master paint it?"

"She left it for a time, I mean?"

"I b'lieve so."

"What became of it then?"

"He painted it and returned it, did he not?"

I peered at the sky. "Who is stealing things in the house, sir? Do you know?"

Peasgood looked sad. "No. But I do not like it! 'Tis bad when a household comes to stealing." The old man peeled himself from the bricks. "We must go in."

I turned. At the narrow window Cook beckoned. Peasgood tapped out his pipe, and I followed him.

That afternoon I dissolved resin to make copal varnish, polished a three-quarters with beeswax, and Signore Mazzoni showed me how make drying medium, by boiling linseed oil over sugar of lead. Since he had helped me paint the yew, I had thought on him. Beneath his head of curling hair, his eyes took in much. He was dogged and uncomplaining, moving from task to task with steady dependability, yet I guessed that there was fire within. Ambition? He had not Cavitty's flair with the brush, but he was a good draftsman and knew how to lay in color. Sitters took to him too, for he knew how to give 'em the deferential "Sir" or "Madame," as Cavitty did not. I wondered: if Cranbourne Street were his, would he make more of a success of it? Cavitty must see how sitters liked him;

surely he would never dismiss Mazzoni. Yet as to what the Italian thought, he kept it to himself.

Would he be content to stay an assistant the rest of his life?

I began to learn that the man who put his name to a picture rarely painted the whole of it. The design might be his, the underpainting, the face or faces—but the rest was left to others. There were experts in landscape, drapery, hands, even animals, so that a portrait of my lady might have a face by A, hands by B, garments by C, shrubbery by D, a lapdog by E, whilst F did the sky. No wonder one saw workboys and apprentices hurrying pictures about St. Martin's Lane; they were delivering 'em to the next man in line.

Cavitty employed a drapery-painter; I saw him for the first time that afternoon: Mr. Noyce, a prinking fellow carrying (with assistance from Biggs) a six-foot portrait. Puffing, he unwrapped the cloth to show scarlet breeches and a scarlet braided coat. I thought 'em excellent, but Cavitty hardly looked at the work. Impatiently he drew Noyce aside. "Well? Have you found it?"

Noyce's eyes narrowed. "You know very well, sir, that I returned it to you."

Cavitty cursed under his breath. "I pray you do not lie. Be gone."

I was taken aback. Could "it" be the Shenstone Diamond? Had Cavitty sent the gem elsewhere to be painted?

Near four o'clock Monsieur Phillippe duVerre arrived. Again Cavitty wasted no time on pleasantries. "The plates, man? You brought 'em?"

"As you requested, monsieur. But I do not see—"

"Damn it, let me have 'em."

DuVerre merely inclined his head. They were in a paper-wrapped package, heavy by the manner in which he handed 'em over. I was at the workbench dissolving copal, and whilst

Cavitty unwrapped the copperplates at the engraving table I examined duVerre. He was thin to gauntness, perhaps forty, with a knife-edge jaw, a beaky nose, a small, almost feminine mouth. He wore fine green velvet and a tight-fitting wig, his eyes deep-set and heavy-lidded. He must have been here many times, for he nodded familiarly to Mazzoni, smiled too at Cully Stringer as if he had long ago taken the measure of the sullen boy's worth. Discovering me, he pursed his lips as if at a new species of insect, and I ducked my head.

A small ironic smile seemed a fixture of his face. He turned back to Cavitty, who had unwrapped the plates. They were large, about sixteen inches by twenty. I wished to satisfy Mr. Franklin as to their details but could make little of 'em. All I could see was that they seemed crowded with figures. Cavitty fixed his bulging eyes upon each before he carefully re-wrapped it and slid it into a slot of the cabinet next the engraving table.

He turned to duVerre. "As I told you, they must be re-worked. You shall get 'em to print again as soon as I am able."

"But are they not excellent as they are?"

"I shall be the judge of that."

"I have done sixty impressions of the first, which cost me many hours. What is to become of those?"

"You brought 'em, as I asked?"

DuVerre proffered a bundle of papers.

Coals remained in the morning fire. With a clang of the stove door Cavitty thrust the prints into it, and in less than a minute they were smoke. Mazzoni and Cully Stringer gaped at this, as did I, but Cavitty might've burnt straw for all the alteration in duVerre's wry gaze.

Nonetheless his fingers flicked at his sides. "I must be paid for those," he said.

"Ha, you will get your money."

"Pray, why do you do this?"

"To discommode a lord."

"You seem to discommode yourself, *mon ami.*"

Cavitty reddened. "I shall have satisfaction!"

DuVerre merely nodded. "As you will." His voice was soft as silk. "I shall await the altered plates—and shall print 'em as I have printed others to our profit in the past."

Cavitty thrust a poker at the charred paper in the grate, then hurried duVerre out. Through the front window I saw 'em upon the street. The Frenchman seemed to attempt to reason a moment more with the artist, but Cavitty only grew red of face, and with a shrug duVerre strolled off.

"And that is my second day in Cranbourne Street, Mr. Franklin," concluded I that evening at nine, in the gentleman's chamber. As before, I perched on his bed whilst he took his ease in his chair.

"You do well, Nick. What a picture you draw! I must warn you, though: I visit Cranbourne Street tomorrow, to study matters for myself, so do not be surprised when I arrive."

"There is one last thing, sir."

"Tell it."

"Signore Mazzoni and Mrs. Bone—"

"Oho, we must certainly hear more of them!"

" 'Twas half past five, near time for me to come home. I had gone into the display room to fetch a portrait Cavitty had called for. I saw no reason to knock. They were there, sir, in a corner, kissing."

"Did they see you?"

"I do not believe so, for I jumped back quick as I could and shut the door. I made some stir before opening it again. There is a further door, and when I came in again they were gone."

"Pray, what sort of kiss?"

"He held her close."

"Was she agreeable?"

"She held him too."

Mr. Franklin drummed his fingertips. "So, romance blossoms in Cranbourne Street. What else grows in that soil, Nick? And what is planted in Shenstone's garden that brings him secretly to town? How I long to dig it up!"

Shortly I went to bed, leaving the gentleman to delve alone. Again there was something I had not told, and I tossed beneath my coverlet remembering it. Annie had seen me out at six. We had stood in the entryway, I glad to be alone with her, for I longed to tell her something. "Cully Stringer—" I had said. "—if he harms you . . . if he attempts to get at you in any way . . ."

She came close. I had never been so near a girl. She smelt of cream and honey, and her breath touched my face. "You are a kind boy, a pretty boy," said she, taking my hand and pressing it against her breast so that I felt a softness I had never felt before. Her heartbeat seemed to blend with mine, and I trembled. How long did we stand thus? Whatever the time, the spell was broken by Felicity's face peering through the stair rail.

Pulling free, I stammered farewell. All the way along St. Martin's Lane I could hardly feel the cobbles beneath my feet.

🕸 11 🕸

IN WHICH Benjamin Franklin comes to call and I am near caught for a spy . . .

In the coach next morn I thought on what I had glimpsed betwixt Signore Mazzoni and Mrs. Bone. Her fingers had clung to his shoulders; he had clasped her near. Cavitty had got his toehold in his craft by marrying his master's daughter, but there was no eligible daughter for Amadeo Mazzoni to marry.

Yet there was a sister . . .

This speculation was extinguished by memories of Annie: her soft breasts, her shy, questing eyes. Last night I had dreamt of holding her as Signore Mazzoni had held Mrs. Bone. I had all but promised to protect her from Cully Stringer, but could I, barely thirteen, keep that promise? I was filled with apprehension wondering how.

I was surprised to discover James Cavitty already at work in the painting room when I arrived. The past two days he had not put his nose in before eight, but I saw him on his stool at the engraving table as I hung up my coat at seven, laboring on one of the copperplates which Monsieur duVerre had brought.

He barely looked round. "Put the boy to work, Mazzoni," muttered he.

Had the Italian seen who had stumbled upon his lovemaking yesterday? If so his deep-set eyes gave no sign as he set me varnishing a portrait. Nearby Cully Stringer added color to my yew tree. I hated seeing he was given the job, for he did it ill—but I could hardly protest. Again I felt the uncertainty of my position: neither apprentice nor permanent workboy, a sort of spy. I watched Cavitty. By means of scraper and burnisher, he effaced the parts of his design which he wished to alter, muttering softly, "Deny me, will you? . . . this will make you sorry . . ." I longed to get a close look at his work—but he was secretive about it, covering it if anyone came near and tucking the plate away when his sister put in her head, as she did around nine, wearing her customary frown. I now knew the meaning of the glance she exchanged with Mazzoni, but did her brother have any idea they made love?

Her look fell on me. Did she know that I had seen her with Mazzoni? What would she do should she learn that her brother had burnt sixty prints he must pay for?

She left without comment, and we all worked in greater ease. A sitter was announced at eleven, Cavitty grumbling that Peasgood must tell her he was ill and could not paint. The old fellow trudged dutifully to obey, but Mazzoni looked up. Unfolding himself from his task (how strong-built he was, like a wrestler), he scowled at Cavitty's back. *We—all of us—depend upon your whim!* his smoldering eyes seemed to say; *how dare you drive custom away?*

His hands opened and closed at his sides, but he turned back to work; like me he had no power. Yet he was right, I thought: the entire household would fall if Cavitty fell, and I wondered: the Italian might not say what he thought to Cavitty—but did he to Mrs. Bone? Would he report of the sixty prints?

At half past eleven Annie came in, curtsied, said, "Begging

your pardon, sir, but a gentleman wishes to see you about being painted."

Cavitty barked, "I cannot be bothered now."

But Mrs. Bone was on the maid's heels. "Go to your dusting, girl." She faced her brother. "You must see the man, James. He brings us custom. You have turned away a sitter this morning. This cannot go on. You must speak to him."

Cavitty threw down his burin. "Very well!" He stalked from the room.

The caller was Benjamin Franklin. Here, from my shorthand, writ that very eve in Craven Street, is his account of the meeting:

. . . I hired a hackney coach to Cranbourne Street, Nick. ('Twould never do if they saw Peter, who delivers you, deliver me.) Upon knocking, I was let in by Annie, who is as pretty as your drawing made her. I caught sight of Felicity as well—her little face startled me through the stair rail—but I had no time to contemplate it, for in less time than it takes to sneeze, Mrs. Fanny Bone was there in her high-collared dress to see why I came.

"Good day, ma'am. I am here to talk of being painted by James Cavitty," says I.

"How very nice," says she, a smile on her lips but none in her eyes.

"O, yes," says I, "Lord Shenstone recommended him," but all she answered was, "My brother has done an excellent painting of his lady. Fetch the master, Annie." The maid scurried off whilst Mrs. Bone fixed her smile on me as if to measure my purse, but after a moment she said, "I must make sure . . ." and hurried off. Felicity remained on the stair, and I tried to engage her by a trick with string and coins, but her odd little gaze never altered.

James Cavitty charged from the painting room. "Sir?"

I bowed. "Benjamin Franklin. You have been engraving, I see."

"What?"

I pointed to the tiny curls of copper on his apron. "The burr from your plate."

He glanced at 'em. His fingers twitched. "You know of engraving, then."

"I am one of your *dilettanti*, that is all."

His look expressed no fondness for *dilettanti*.

"I wish to be painted," said I.

"He would be pleased to talk of that," put in his sister.

He turned upon her. "I can do that best without *you*. See to the household, if you please."

With a treacly smile she mounted the stair, Felicity in tow.

Cavitty took me in, as I did him. He is as you described, not tall yet with a sinewy, knotted frame, his brown hair pulled straight back, which emphasized his outstarting eyes that seemed to damn my soul. All in all a remarkable presence, without an ounce of amiability. A genius? A thief? I knew not what to make of him.

"I have heard good report of you," said I, "but I must first see your work. May I?"

"I must get back to my engraving—" (What is so urgent about this engraving, Nick?) "—but if it will not take long . . . here . . . in the viewing room." He waved me through the door on the left, watching impatiently whilst I looked about within, at the marble hand on the table, the pictures on the walls. You are right, Nick: he is skilled, though he paints his subjects with a satirical wit which cannot always please.

I faced him squarely. "I have played false with you, sir. I do not wish my picture painted. I am come to retrieve the Shenstone Diamond."

His brown eyes roiled at these words. "What?"

"I come from America, on business for the colony of Pennsylvania. But I do other work. I dissembled because I did not wish your sister to hear what I desire. Yet now we are alone, I speak plain." I held out my hand. "Give me the diamond, and I shall trouble you no more."

He gaped at my palm. He stared into my face. "But I do not have the diamond."

"You must."

"I say I do not."

"Lady Shenstone did not give it you?"

"She did."

"Return it, then."

The man licked his lips. "See here, by what warrant—?"

"Lady Shenstone, herself."

"She asked you—?"

"She required my aid."

He barked a laugh. "Ha, she should have better asked her husband."

I tutted. "You know very well why she did not, for she was persuaded by you to do a foolish thing: to deliver into your hands a gem worth a ransom. Or were you the fool in promising you could keep it safe? In either case her husband must not learn she has made this error."

"What do I care what her husband learns?"

"Come, sir, have you done painting the diamond?"

"I have."

"Then give it me so I may return it to the lady. You have no right to trouble her."

His harelike eyes calculated. "Tell Shenstone, then, and be damned," he flung out.

I was ready for this. "John Fielding, sir. Principal Magistrate

112

for Westminster. You have heard of him? The Blind Beak, they call him. Hard as flint. Cruel as fire. Despises thieves."

"Here, I am no thief!"

"You will be called one and hauled up before this same Fielding if we cannot resolve the matter betwixt ourselves. They cut off a man's hands for taking a loaf of bread, and you appear to have made off with much more. Your hands will surely go, sir, if not your head. Can you paint without either? Come, act in your best interest. Where is the gem?"

He was shaken by this. "I tell you, I do not know."

"You persuaded my lady to bring it to you."

"Her husband's idea. He must have it in his wife's picture."

"You could have painted it in his home. Or from sketches."

" 'Twas inconvenient."

" 'Twas arrogant. When did she deliver it?"

"Monday last, in a rosewood case."

"What time o' day?"

"Morning."

"Hour?"

"Ten."

His tale accorded with Lady Shenstone's. "What did you do with it?"

"Placed it in an artist's cabinet, in my painting room."

"Does this cabinet lock?"

"Yes."

"You locked it?"

"Until I sent the gem to Noyce."

I stared. "What? You let it out of your house?"

Cavitty swallowed. "Noyce is my drapery man, but he can paint a diamond too. Lady Shenstone must have the gem back next day, she said. I had no time to do the thing myself. Noyce was set to do her clothes, so I sent the gem round with 'em."

"Sent it with whom?"

"Signore Mazzoni, my assistant. I trust him. He has worked for me many years."

"Noyce painted it, then?"

"And the clothes. They were already sketched in monochrome. All he must do is drape a lay figure and apply the glazes. Three hours' work at best."

"Did he return the clothes and gem himself?"

"Next morn, just past nine. The painting came two days later, after it dried in his workshop."

"So you are certain the diamond was returned." A faltering look in his eyes made my heart sink. "You *are* certain?"

He had turned gray as ash. "He brought back the clothes. He brought back the little box too, and I placed it once more in my cabinet. I locked the cabinet, but . . . but"—he opened his hands—"I do not know if the gem was truly there, for when Noyce returned it I did not look into the box."

The ticking of a clock sounded loud from the entry. I shook my head. "You have been careless, sir." Could I credit such folly?

He drew himself up. "Damn it, I was engaged with a sitter. Noyce arrived. He said, 'Here is the gem,' and held up the box, and I said, 'Put it there,' meaning in the cabinet, and he did so and I locked the drawer and dropped the key in my apron pocket and went back to my sitter."

"So the gem might not have been in the box?"

"It *must* have been. Noyce would not try to trick me."

"No? We shall see. Besides your sitter, who saw him bring in the box?"

"Mazzoni. My apprentice. A boy-of-work named Biggs."

"Who else in the house knew it was there?"

"My sister."

"Have you told her it is missing?"

He blanched. "She must never know!"

"She may have to learn. We must presume that if some persons in your employ knew the gem was here, all of 'em knew. You say you are certain you locked the cabinet the second time?"

"Yes, for I later found it broke into."

The clock sent more loud measures of time through the walls. "This grows worse," said I.

To give him credit he hung his head. "Do you think I do not know?"

"So the gem has been stolen? Someone took it from your cabinet?"

"What else can I conclude? I was busy that day, I did not look into the drawer until just before Lady Shenstone came to retrieve the gem. When I made to take it out, I was thunderstruck to discover the lock sprung, the rosewood box open, the diamond gone."

"Why not tell the truth to her ladyship?"

"I did not lie. I told her the gem was misplaced."

"Come, sir, half-truth at best."

"I hoped to retrieve it, can you not understand? I had not paid heed when Noyce returned it. In desperation I hoped he might still have it. I even hoped it might be found about the painting room. Or in the house."

"So you bought time at her expense. What of the rest of the day before she came to retrieve her property—were you always in the painting room?"

"I was out often."

"Whilst others came and went?"

"I presume so."

"What visitors did you have?"

115

"My printer, to pick up some copperplates. A gentleman, to talk of buying a *Diana and Actaeon* of Rosso Fiorentino, which had come into my possession. Sitters."

"So there was much opportunity for mischief."

"More—for the back door is customarily left unlatched from seven o' the morn 'til six in the eve."

Could there have been worse news? Silently I cursed Cavitty's heedlessness, for all London might have crept in to steal the gem. Had it even been in the rosewood box? "Do you suspect any particular person?" asked I.

"No one and ev'ryone."

"But have you questioned any?"

"Only Noyce. I wished to keep from my sister—"

"There are worse consequences than your sister. Further measures must be taken. 'Tis is your fault the Shenstone Diamond is lost. Who knows but you are in complicity with the thief." He made to protest, but I held up a hand. "That would be the view of the law. How would you answer it? You need not hold out your wrists for the irons; I shall not take the matter to the magistrate just yet. But you must help me all you can. I may need to question your household, perhaps even your sister."

"But—"

I was stern. " 'Tis Fielding or I, sir. Make your choice."

He made mouths, flung up his hands, yielded.

"Good. Now. I must see your painting room. I prefer your household not know my real aims at present. Tell 'em I am come to have my portrait done. I may even have you paint me, if it comes to that."

"Very well. You do not know how this spoils my plans," muttered he as he led me out. . . .

* * *

Thus Mr. Franklin told me. I had longed to know what passed between him and James Cavitty during the half hour of their absence, but I bent close over my work when they walked in, for fear some accidental look might give us away. Mr. Franklin paid me no mind; he was amiable as he was shown about. For his part Cavitty looked glum—plainly the anger which customarily animated him was gone. Mr. Franklin made particular examination of the engraving table, but there was little to discover, for all the copperplates were snug in their slots. He was introduced to Signore Mazzoni. Cully Stringer hunkered by a wall with another of his wretched scribbles, but he watched. This was a dangerous moment, for he might recognize Mr. Franklin and recall that I was the boy who had stood next him in the street, yet his look showed no suspicion.

Mr. Franklin halted before the portrait of Lady Shenstone. "Remarkable, sir. So that is the famous diamond."

"Cursed thing," was Cavitty's bitter response, at which Stringer ducked his head. Why? With a twitch of his shoulders he returned to his labors, but he had been shaken. By what? What did Cully Stringer have to do with our mystery?

Mr. Franklin departed soon after, and James Cavitty returned to his engraving gloomily; plainly his visitor had prodded him to face some dire thing.

At lunch belowstairs Annie touched my shoulder as she walked past, which Biggs saw and leered. After the meal old Peasgood treated me to another quarter hour's reminiscence in the areaway. I heard more of Lord This and Sir That. He told me that Master sometimes worked late. "Likes to be alone, he does." I had little time to reflect on this however, for Mrs. Cockle's sharp rap on the windowpane warned that I ought to be back in the painting room.

I went, to find no others yet returned.

Time to investigate, Nick.

My heart beat fast, but I must take my chance. Watched only by painted eyes, I went to the artist's cabinet. It was made of mahogany, desklike: two sets of drawers on either side a knee hole, these partitioned to hold dry pigments, and a wide central drawer, all with white porcelain knobs. The top could be lifted to form an easel but was at present closed. I tried the main drawer. At first it seemed secured, but a jiggle and a sharp pull made it yield. So weak a lock? Had the gem been taken so easily?

I opened the drawer.

It was about two feet wide and the same deep, four inches in height. There were pens and chalks on the left side, sheafs of sketches on the right. I glanced through 'em. A few were studies for portraits, but most were designs for mythological and biblical scenes. Would Cavitty ever get to paint 'em? There were in addition three small octavo volumes bound in soft kid, similar to the sketchbook I carried. I had noted that Cavitty kept one like it in his apron or coat pocket. I thumbed through 'em. They proved of varied use. Some pages revealed small, quick drawings—I recognized Peasgood, Annie, Felicity, Mrs. Bone, scenes of St. Martin's Lane—but there were also records of painting methods: ". . . half-length of Bardwell, underpainting, umber and flake white; hunting coat, *terre verte* and Prussian blue; face, carmine, gamboge . . ." etc. There were also dates and names of sitters and visitors. I found Noyce's name frequently, duVerre's, Cope's. I came across Lord Shenstone's once or twice—no surprise, and on one page a comic sketch of my lord peering at a painting through a quizzing glass, his intelligent face transformed into a booby's. Putting ev'rything back, I felt deep inside the drawer. Nothing. What had I expected? Had Cavitty searched the drawer in desperate hope that the Shenstone Diamond had somehow escaped to the back? Had Cully Stringer sought the same?

Suddenly there came footsteps, and I started like a hare, but they proved only clatter from the street.

Hurry, Nick.

The copperplates Cavitty had labored to change. Quelling fears—my mouth felt dry as dust—I went to the worktable to pull from its vertical slot the first of the eight. Cavitty had completed the engraving part of the job, but he meant to refine his alterations by aquatint, for he had dusted the surface with asphaltum. The brownish tint made it hard to read. The grand hall of some fine house? Many paintings seemed to hang on walls there, and a man, well-dressed, seemed to lead others about. As I struggled to make out details, the sharp smell of aquafortis filled my nostrils from an ill-sealed jar, and I was reminded how I had burnt my finger in the etching bath at Ravenet's.

A hand on the latch, unmistakable. Pushing the plate back into its slot, I snatched up a burin.

I turned to see James Cavitty in the doorway.

He snapped, "What are you about, boy?"

"I w-wished only to get the feel of the tool, sir," stammered I. "I should very much like to try my hand at a plate."

Striding to me, he snatched the burin from my hand. "You will in future ask before you disturb my work. I may train you to the plate sometime, but not today. Get back to your varnishing."

"Yes, sir." Creeping to the easel, I did as I was told. Cavitty remained at his worktable the rest of the afternoon scratching at his plates. I had hoped Annie might bid me good-bye at six, but she was nowhere in sight, and I slipped out and walked off alone. Did secret eyes trace my steps? If so I could not discover 'em.

119

❧ 12 ❧

IN WHICH I hide in a housemaid's
bed . . .

Outside Mr. Franklin's bow window London's rooftops were a dusky silhouette as, at nine P.M., I finished my third day's news.

"Brave, Nick," said the gentleman. "Resourceful too." His grave eyes warned. "But do not take unwonted chances. Passions are roused, secrets are hid; some deep game is being played. It cannot be mere chance that both James Cavitty and Lord Shenstone suddenly find themselves with sufficient funds for one to let a house in Leicester Square whilst the other pays all his creditors. I have inquired into Shenstone's debts. Though large, they are discharged. Entirely with funds obtained by selling paintings through Cavitty? In any case, I have unearthed more. Shenstone's wife told us he was gone to his estate in Oxfordshire. He came back once with her knowledge and once without, we know—yet on the second occasion he did not return to his estate. Learning of a club he frequents in Wardour Street (I delve, Nick, I delve), I set Peter to watch disguised as a St. Giles man. My lord departed with hearty laments to his fellow clubmen that he must to Oxfordshire—but Oxfordshire is west, Nick, and his lordship set out east."

"How?"

"By the Dover coach. Does this not add interest? Packets from Calais dock at Dover. Some bring antiquities from Rome—what passes for 'em, at any rate; paintings too, from France, Italy, Holland, to satisfy the art-mad mob. Is that Shenstone's business?" Mr. Franklin looked speculatively at me. "Are you up to more prying?"

"To help you, sir."

"To help Lady Shenstone—and only if you take great care. I wish you to look into Cavitty's storeroom, at the Crivelli and any other continental master you may find. At the Rosso Fiorentino in the viewing room too. Shenstone said you have an eye; let us test it: are these pictures truly by the artists whose names are writ on 'em?"

This gave me pause. I had small experience of art save what little I had seen about London. Should I know a true Crivelli from a false one? But, "I shall do my best, sir," replied I. "They are forgeries, you think?"

"I do not know what to think." He shook his head. "What a strange matter, in which the more we bring to light the more we discover darkness."

Next morn: to Cavitty's again. Many houses were agitated by strong feeling—even Mrs. Stevenson's had its spits and spats—but number 23 seemed especially fraught. There was Annie's fear of Stringer, Mrs. Bone's watchfulness, Signore Mazzoni's suppressed rebellion, Cully Stringer's meanness, Cavitty's haughty desperation. And of course the passion of Mazzoni and Mrs. Bone and my own confused desires regarding Annie.

As I set to work I was further troubled that on this, my fourth day at the painter's, we appeared no nearer the diamond. What had seemed an easy journey had run aground.

How to chart a clear course? Not that Mr. Franklin did not delve, as he said—manfully too. After his interview with Cavitty he had gone straight to the drapery man, Noyce, pressing him hard, but Noyce had insisted the diamond had been in its rosewood box when he returned it, and he took great umbrage at being questioned. "I believe he spoke true," Mr. Franklin had said. He had also inquired into Lord Shenstone's character: "Nothing but good reports," he had told me. My lord was upright, a patron of the arts, a connoisseur who had learnt much from the Grand Tour. Yes, he had had money troubles (he *would* game), but he seemed to have overcome 'em. Last, Mr. Franklin had driven round to Lady Shenstone, to tell her he did his best.

"Seen your husband?" asked he.

"Not since the day he surprised me," she had replied.

He did not tell her he had been observed in town twice.

I had offered a thought: "Mrs. Bone says things go missing in the house. Might the person who took 'em have taken the gem?"

Mr. Franklin considered. "A thimble is one thing, a diamond another. I shall think on your idea."

I bent my attention to the task Mr. Franklin had set me. I must find time alone in the storeroom; time, too, to slip into the viewing room on the other side of the entryway—yet it seemed I never would, for there were always people about. Viscount Budwell returned, to have his countenance glazed. Cavitty seemed to have forgot he would come and grumbled at this further interruption to his engraving. For all his desire to make a success, he treated his sitters haughtily, as if they ought to be grateful he found time for 'em. Would a shop merchant who snubbed his custom retain much trade?

But Cavitty made quick work of Budwell, turning him into a

comically weak-chinned Alexander in less than three-quarters of an hour. 'Twas a measure of the Viscount's wit that when he peered at the result he only preened. What a glass in which to view himself!

Monsieur duVerre arrived around eleven, to see if any of the returned plates might be ready for printing.

"Do not hurry me," Cavitty snapped. "I am only now ready to etch the first three. The day after tomorrow shall be soon enough." Reluctantly he let duVerre examine the three he had named.

When he had looked at 'em the Frenchman said, "I see your aim." His eyes lifted. "But is it wise?"

Cavitty reacted as if his honor had been impugned. "I shall show how wise I am. Stringer!" The apprentice scrambled to him. "Take this round to the *Gazeteer*, the *Public Advertiser*, the *Morning Post*." He pushed a paper into Stringer's hand. "Advertisements," he crowed to duVerre, "for my revised *Follies of a Lord*."

You are a fool, monsieur, the Frenchman's answering look seemed to say. But he only bowed. *"Si vous voulez.* I shall come back in two days. *Au revoir."* He walked out.

Cully Stringer left on his errand, and shortly Signore Mazzoni departed to pick up some lengths of linen. Cavitty hunched over his engraving table; he and I were alone.

"Beg pardon, sir," said I, "but I have some few moments before luncheon. May I draw from the paintings in the parlor across the way?"

He did not even look up. "As you please." He seemed happy to be let be, and I slipped out.

I hoped to run into Annie in the entryway, but she was not in sight. Entering the viewing room, I shut the door. Silence reigned, and I stood a while, alone. There, by the farther door, Signore Mazzoni had clasped Mrs. Bone, and for a moment their tangled passion seemed to fill the air of the chamber, like some musky perfume. On the small round table lay the marble hand which I had drawn. My gaze turned to Cavitty's paintings. What acid in his brush! He was a virtuoso at satire, but his virtuosity might be his curse.

There were four continental paintings: a little Watteau, a pair of wrestlers by Signorelli, a Mantegna head of a man, his brow swathed in a vermilion cloth, and the Rosso Fiorentino, in which Actaeon, just turning into a stag, was brought down by his hounds whilst Diana gazed on. It was about two by three feet and dashing in execution, a study for a larger work, I guessed. I took out my sketching book and drew as I had told Cavitty I would, in case he came in, all the while studying the *Actaeon*. Were there false notes? The picture seemed well done, with none of the awkwardness of the *Europa* at Augustus Broome's, no cupids with two left feet. Genuine, then? Yet Cavitty was skilled; he might have painted it. But if so, what did that have to do with the theft of the Shenstone Diamond?

I had no better luck with the Watteau, the Signorelli, the Mantegna; they seemed excellent. What a glasslike surface had the Mantegna! How pretty were Watteau's little pink flowers in that trembling wood!

A prickling of hairs at the back of my neck made me turn.

Felicity Bone stood not six feet away.

I had not heard the rear door open, the child enter. She wore a white ruffled collar and rose-colored velvet smock, her toes pointed awkwardly. Her thin dark hair hung straight about her face, which tilted as if she listened to distant voices. She gently swayed, whilst a jewel of spittle hung at the corner of her mouth.

"Hello, Felicity." I found my voice.

She gave no sign she had heard.

I stepped closer. "I am drawing pictures. Should you like to look?"

Her chin seemed to lift a little.

Taking this as encouragement, I knelt to show her my book. "See? Here is your mama. Here is Cook. Signore Mazzoni."

She had a sour smell. Her fingers fluttered, lifted. She touched the sketch of the Italian.

"What do you do!" came a stern voice, and I leapt up.

Mrs. Bone stood like an avenging angel in the rear door.

"I . . . I was drawing from the paintings, ma'am," gulped I. "Master gave me leave. Felicity came in. I . . . I was only showing her my book."

The woman's eyes flashed. "You spend a good deal too much time in this room; I do not like it. My brother gave you leave to come here? I give you leave to go. Do so at once."

"Yes, ma'am."

She wrapped an arm round her daughter as I crept out.

I spent the afternoon wishing I had discovered more of use in the viewing room. I thought on strange, voiceless Felicity. I thought on Annie too. I wished to speak to her—I longed to touch her as I had before—but there was no chance, for she came into the painting room but once, and Stringer's black eyes fixed so sharply upon her that she dared not give me a glance. I saw her at lunch too, but she was sent up almost at once to clear Master's table. She chanced one quick look at me, a wavering smile that seemed to say, *See how I obey, how I accept?* and I felt a wave of pity. (I had not yet learnt that pity is not love.) Stringer pawed at her as she passed, and I longed to bloody his nose.

Yet something ate at Stringer; it had ever since I came to Cranbourne Street. What? He was not in favor with Cavitty—

he must know that—but it was more than knowing he displeased his master day after day. He jumped at sounds and peered out the windows, front and back, as if he thought someone might watch.

What agitated the apprentice?

At four Cavitty poured acid into an enamel tray, and the stink of niter filled the room. Diluting it, he began to dip his plates. This was aquatint: printed, the etched copper would yield rich shades of gray. He tilted the copper into the liquid, tiny bubbles fizzing as acid ate metal, and I felt a tingling in the fingertip which I had burnt. Stopping out some of the copper, he dipped again. When he was through he handled the plates like a miser's hoard, wrapping 'em in paper and sliding 'em back in their slots as if they were gold. Why the secrecy? Surely all London would see 'em soon, at Cope's.

Done by five-thirty, he hung up his apron and went out, Signore Mazzoni departing shortly after.

Stringer looked here, there, then stomped to the bench where I worked. He gave me a great shove. "Go home, Handy."

Surprised, I stumbled but righted myself to face him. " 'Tis not yet six."

His lips curled. "Who cares? I'll not tell."

"I must stay."

"Damned mole!" Grabbing my collar, he snarled, "Go, or I'll give you a drubbing."

I longed to strike him—but I did not, for I saw in his caprice my chance. "I will leave," said I.

"Ha!" He flung me from him.

Going to the peg by the door, I exchanged apron for coat, and slipped into the entryway. No Annie, though bent old Peasgood bobbed his head as he passed.

"Good day, sir." I left the house.

In Cranbourne Street, I walked by the painting-room window, in case Stringer watched. Then, with a quick glance round, I nipped into the narrow passage beside number 23 and darted along it. My plan was to re-enter by the back door and slip into the storage room so I might look at the little Crivelli as Mr. Franklin had asked. Pausing at the end of the alley, I peered into the rear yard. Nothing save bedsheets blowing on a line. Did the back door make a movement? But when I came to it I found the little anteroom by the servants' stairs deserted. Creeping softly, I heard faint sounds from the kitchen below as I slipped into the dim-lit storage room to the left.

Once more I stood amongst the dozen or so paintings in their racks: Viscount Budwell smirked at me, and there just beside him was the Crivelli. I did not like to discover that the door opposite was half-open, for if Cully Stringer were still in the painting room he might hear me. Could I softly close it? I reached, gripped the iron latch.

My hand froze, for voices came from beyond: Stringer's—and another which I recognized, and my skin crawled, for I was certain it was Bertie Hexham's.

Mean, foppish Hexham, who had skulked about St. Martin's Lane—what did he here? He was no friend to Mr. Franklin—or to me, and I was filled with terrified bewilderment. His father had worked for Quimp. Did the son now too?

I stood listening as I had listened to Cavitty and Lord Shenstone but with far more fear. I could not see Stringer and Hexham; they were on the other side of the screens. I longed to run but stayed rooted, for I must hear what passed.

"You are mad to come in the house," came Stringer's voice.

"Your back door was open"—Hexham's insolent drawl. "You told me it was often open."

"Yet we were to meet in the alley."

"I do not care for the alley."

127

"But—"

There was the sound of a blow. Hexham striking Stringer? "And *we* do not care for *you*. You have not produced what we seek. We promise reward to those who serve us, we punish those who do not. You know this, yet you do not keep your word."

Stringer made a moan. This became a cry: "Ah, sir, no . . . !" and I stood in agonies. Plainly Hexham did something to Stringer. A twisting of arms? Worse? Stringer emitted a wail and, recalling Bertie Hexham's cruel nature, his black, polished boots and whip-like stick with which he was used to strike servants who provoked him, I near cried out myself in the shadows.

Stringer's cry ended in a whimper. "Now, see here," came Hexham's voice again. "I have made promises of my own. They depend upon you." (Was he, too, afraid?) "And therefore I shall—what was that sound?"

In my hiding place I turned to ice, for I knew why he asked: I had gripped the shelf on which the Crivelli rested, the painting had slid, and though I tried to save it, it had dropped with a thump. A wave of silence rushed toward me from the painting room. "I told you you should not come here," hissed Stringer.

"Who is that?" demanded Hexham, and I heard the crack of a stick against a boot.

I could not have replied even if I wished, for my voice was locked in my throat.

Rapid footfalls moved toward the screens. In a second Bertie Hexham would round 'em, marching with his stick into the storage room to discover Nick Handy. He would know my face. He would know I was Benjamin Franklin's boy. And then—? But I dared not think further. I heard Cully Stringer following. My body tensed to flee, but I felt helpless. Indeed they were so near they must catch me. Sucking a great breath, I steeled myself to be discovered.

And then a hand gripped mine, pulled, and like a marionette I let myself be drawn back into the small rear entryway. This same hand relinquished mine, slammed the door, twisted a key rapidly in the lock.

Annie. She peered up at me with her light blue eyes, a finger upon her lips.

We turned toward the locked door. "What?" came a disgruntled cry on the other side as rushing footfalls stopped. There was an angry debate. If they pursued and ran into Cavitty, they should be asked to explain their business—yet they must learn who might have listened, and there came a pounding on the wood and Cully Stringer's angry demand: "Open this door!"

Annie made frantic motions that I must go up the servants' stairs. "My chamber. Second door on the right," whispered she.

"But you—"

"I shall see to 'em. Go."

I stared into her eyes. I went.

At the top I found myself in a narrow corridor under the rafters, but, unable to bring myself to hide, I hovered just out of sight in case Annie needed aid.

I heard the key in the latch, a rush, then Stringer's gruff: "Damn it, girl, why did you close the door upon us?"

Annie's voice, innocent as you please: "I did not know, sir, that you were there. Pray, who is this other man?"

This slowed Stringer. "Why . . . a fellow of the painting trade. None of your business. Hear, did you spy upon us?"

"Was there something to spy upon? I came to lock the door, as is always done near six. How should I know you were still in

Master's painting room? Why were you, sir? And with this gentleman? Shall I tell Master that you were?"

Stringer faltered. "No need of that. I shall tell him myself, seeing as it's his business I'm about."

"Is it his business? And look, you have knocked down one of Master's paintings. He would not like to hear you had done that." There followed more silence, in which Stringer and Hexham must have exchanged glances.

"Get to work, then, girl," Stringer snapped. "Come, sir, you may go out this way."

A scrape of boots, and the back door shut.

I sank against the newel post like a wilted stalk. Annie's footsteps mounted. On the landing she took my hand. "He will come back. He will look for me. He twists my arm sometimes."

I gazed into her upturned eyes. "You were brave, Annie. Truly."

"I have saved myself from worse." She searched my face. "He talked of spying. Did you spy, Nicolas?"

"Why . . . no. I was in the storage room . . . they seemed to think—"

She stopped my lips. "Say no more. Cully will be back. If you do not wish him to know you were there, you must hide in my room."

Should I? Peter would worry when I did not meet him in the Strand, but Stringer must not catch my scent. I let myself be led a dozen paces to a mean, low-ceilinged chamber on the north side of the house, all that Annie owned of privacy. In it were a narrow bed, a rickety table with a basin and ewer, a small, cracked glass on the wall, one bleak cupboard. A foot-wide window let in dusk's dying light. Shutting the door, Annie went to the window to peer out, and I imagined her there often, dreaming of realms she would never visit. She turned. "And so you are here, young sir. I have thought how I should like you to be."

"Annie—"

"You must have far better quarters at Sir Bartleby Bart's."

"Only one room, hardly larger."

"But you have fine clothes."

"Some."

"I have one dress besides my maid's poor shift, and I have had no reason to wear it since I came to this house. How old are you, Nicolas?"

"Thirteen."

"I am fifteen. You are taller than I, but that is the way with boys. Yet I am almost as tall as you." She stood very near, her eyes meeting mine. "I should like to please you, Nicolas. Thirteen is old enough to be pleased?"

I swallowed but had no chance to answer, for an angry thumping rattled the door, followed by Cully Stringer's snarled demand. "Are you in there, girl? I know that you are."

"Go away," cried Annie, though she trembled.

"You will let me in!"

She drew herself up. "No! I shall call Mrs. Bone! I shall tell Master of the man you spoke to in his painting room!"

A muttering. "Damn you. Very well, then." Stringer stomped off.

Annie met my eyes. *You see how it is*, they said, and I read in 'em the history of thousands of serving girls. What fortitude she must muster, for it was likely only a matter of time before the apprentice found a way to have her. If she fought, would he beat her? If she complained, would she be credited? In any case, her virtue mattered little; housemaids were meant to serve.

Her breath touched my face, her voice a murmur. "May I please you, Nicolas? I should like to. You are not like Cully

131

Stringer. You are kind." She raised her chin, she placed her lips against mine, and I felt heat rush through my bones and my arms lifted to return her embrace. How soft felt Annie, how pliant. Her mouth taught me. Her hands were shy but grew bolder, and mine grew bold too. "I should like to please you, Nicolas," whispered she. "Will you lie with me, for my little room is so dreadfully lonely and cold."

❧ 13 ❧

IN WHICH murder is discovered in
Cranbourne Street . . .

I was an hour in Annie's chamber, a schoolboy in a new sort of school. Annie taught me of her, of myself too. She guided my lips and hands, and such of the rest of me which must bring us to our end. She was both tender and ardent, and when we lay quietly side by side she whispered that she hoped I had liked it well.

I could but nod in languorous amazement.

Standing, she washed herself with vinegar and water, and in the dying light I looked at her pale curves, her breasts, the mysterious woman's part of her. I had heard it called "knowing" a woman, but I felt I knew little. I was lost in wonder.

Returning to the narrow bed, she lay beside me and gazed into my eyes. I felt uneasy under her scrutiny, for I saw that she might hope more from me than I could give. I believed I should rise in life (I hoped I would), whilst Annie might remain mired in floors to dust and plate to polish. I could not take her from her fate—I had no means. I met her searching look. I could not be certain she harbored the hopes I seemed to read, but the possibility made me restive. Plainly this was not her first time; she knew the old dance well. Fifteen. Who had debauched her?

Her struggle to escape Cully Stringer—was it a struggle to escape him *again*?

She stirred. Rising, she put on her petticoat and simple housemaid's shift, and I dressed too, turning my back as if, our intimacy over, I must hide my nakedness.

We faced one another in the shallow space betwixt wall and bed.

"I must be down soon," came her soft voice. "I shall tell Mrs. Bone I was busy tidying the upper floors. I am glad you came to my chamber, Nicolas."

"I am glad too. But I know so little of you. How did you come to Cavitty's?"

"From a fine house. A lord's."

"Lord Shenstone's?" I did not know how this idea sprang to my lips, but she replied, "Why . . . yes. How did you know? You must have seen him calling upon Master. He does, now and then. Is he not handsome? Gentle too—he always speaks well to me. He gave me this." Reaching deep under her mattress, she drew forth a man's ring set with a blood red stone.

I stared at it, no gewgaw. "Why did he give it you?"

"As a remembrance. When I left his employ." She hid the ring once more. "Do not tell Mrs. Bone. She would not think it right for me to have such a thing."

I felt that I did not know Annie at all. "My lord must have liked you a great deal."

"O, yes."

"Because you served him well."

"In ev'ry way."

I had no idea what to make of her story. "Do you know why he continues to come here?"

"Some business to do with paintings."

"O? The man with Cully Stringer—have you seen him here before too?"

"Not in the house, but he hangs about the street."

I felt a shiver of alarm. "How long has he done that?"

"P'rhaps a week. I saw him and Cully just yesterday, at the corner of St. Martin's. They talked with another man."

"Who?"

"I do not know. He sat in a black coach. He drove off." Her brow furrowed. "Why are you truly here, Nicolas?"

My face felt like a hot, tight mask. "To learn."

She gave me a wan smile. "I have taught you something, then. I must go down." She pecked my cheek. "Go out the back. 'Twill be safe. The household will be readying for supper." Cap askew, she slipped like some quicksilver sprite through the door.

I stared after her feeling a great emptiness in my hands, a longing about my heart, a weight on my soul. Shortly I crept out as she advised, meeting nothing more untoward in the yard than bedsheets fluttering like ghosts. I prayed no one spied me.

In the Strand Peter exclaimed in joy when he saw I was come at last.

"Lord, child, you are late," chid Mrs. Stevenson when I returned to the warmth of Craven Street just before eight.

"The painter kept me, ma'am. I shall tell Mr. Franklin." I hurried upstairs.

I found the gentleman pacing by his window, beyond which London huddled under the first black of night. Relief flooded his face as I slipped in. "Thank God you are come!—I was about to speed to Cranbourne Street." He peered at me. "No trouble, lad?"

I shrugged out of my coat. How to answer? If I said yes, he might withdraw me from Cavitty's, and I did not wish that; I must see Annie again. Too, I longed to help recover the Shenstone Diamond. And I had become attached to Signore Maz-zoni, Felicity, Peasgood, even to Cavitty; and to the hours of labor in the painting room. Persuading myself that omission was no perjury, I told him of overhearing Cully Stringer and Bertie Hexham, but not that they had pursued me. I was late, I said, because of some "unfinished task." I said I had spoke to Annie but not when, and I told what she had said about the man in the black coach. "She came to Cavitty's from Lord Shenstone's," added I. "She showed me a ring he gave her when she left his employ."

"But how did you come to be shown it?"

"It was under her mattress."

Mr. Franklin's eyes narrowed. "You were in her chamber, then?"

I saw that I had trapped myself. "Why . . . yes, sir. Did I not say?"

He stood very still. "That, then, rather than some 'unfin-ished task,' is why you were late?"

I nodded.

"What took you to the maid's chamber?"

Red-faced, I confessed how Stringer and Hexham had near caught me. Polly's cheery hum drifted past the closed door, and William's brisk footfalls told he returned from the Inns of Court, but I felt no cheer, and the city bells tolling the hour sounded like death knells. Mr. Franklin plainly saw what had happened betwixt me and Annie, and I sank further into mis-ery. What was more wrong, lying with Annie or lying to Mr. Franklin? *Thirteen has made you more a man than I bargained for today*, his look seemed to say as he dropped into his chair. "When a boy becomes a man, it gives him no right to lie to his father."

"Never again, sir!" pled I. "Never!"

But I was surprised when a sigh rather than a thunderclap escaped him. "Yet sons do lie. And to their fathers." His right hand equivocated. "I did to mine; and, truly, a boy must learn some dissembling, to make his way in the world." His eyes flashed. "Nonetheless, though I encourage you to play a role at Cavitty's, you must not do so with me. I require truth of you, Nick Handy."

"Yes, sir, truth, sir, always. I promise."

"Well, 'twas only a small deceit, a little thing." He linked his fingers across his belly. "And so you have learnt what 'tis to be with a woman, eh?"

I flushed. "Begun to learn."

"Learn more then, how not to father a child out of wedlock." He described sev'ral means. "Will you remember?"

"Yes, sir," said I.

"Very well, no more on the subject. Tell the rest of your day—and make ev'ry word true."

Scruplous to detail, I told him what Stringer and Hexham had said. "As for the continental paintings, they were excellently done and might well have been from the hands of the masters whose names are upon 'em—though as to that, Cavitty has great skill; I cannot say he did not do 'em."

"Or that he did not alter some lesser works which Shenstone delivered him from Paris or Rome, to both their profits? Bertie Hexham called on Cully Stringer, did he? And tried his petty tyranny? Damn it, who employs the fop? What the devil is he after? Excellent work, Nick—but there may be more peril than I imagined. I am sorely inclined to remove you from Cavitty's."

"O, no, sir. Please. Let me stay a while longer."

He chewed his lip. "Only upon condition that you take no chances."

My fifth day at Cavitty's, Friday, the mid-April sky a cloudless China blue over Cranbourne Street. Arriving, I found Biggs lazily scouring the front steps, his carrot-red hair sticking up. As I stepped from the coach he smirked at me but I ignored him. I peered about. Was Bertie Hexham awatch? Feeling I must make the most of my reprieve from Mr. Franklin, I slipped along the side passage by which I had yesterday fled. In the rear yard the bedsheets had been taken down. On the landing inside the back door, I glanced up the narrow servants' stairs, where just twelve hours ago Annie and I had lain.

As I passed through the storage room a faint, unpleasant odor seemed mingled with the customary pungency of drying spirits.

I walked into the studio.

Mr. Franklin had been busy yesterday, calling upon Cavitty's colorman, he had told me. There he had learnt that though Cavitty had for some time been tardy with his bills, he paid promptly now. Pray, how long had he done so? A good two months, the colorman had said. "Would that I had known Bertie Hexham hangs about St. Martin's Lane," Mr. Franklin had added. "I should have asked the colorman if he knew aught of him."

Signore Mazzoni and Cully Stringer were already at work when I put on my apron. Mazzoni set me to cleaning brushes. As I did so, I fretted that half the days 'til Lord Shenstone's official return were past. Why had my lord gone to Dover? Was he still there? Would we discover where his precious gem had vanished? "I do not see how it can still be in Cavitty's household," Mr. Franklin had said. Ev'ry five minutes Cully Stringer shot me one of his sour looks. Did he suspect me of overhearing him and Bertie Hexham? I was alarmed that Hexham lurked near number 23, for he might easily spy me arriving or leaving. Had he already? Was it he who had seemed to dog my steps? His bullying of Stringer seemed to have been driven by fear for his own skin. Who turned the screws on him, then? Quimp?

Eight o'clock passed, eight-thirty, and Cavitty did not come in. No longer in a fever to complete *The Follies of a Lord*? I glanced at the slots above the engraving table where the eight copperplates customarily rested. I counted only seven. Had he delivered one to Monsieur duVerre after all? The large pan of acid sat out ready to etch, its vitriol smell wrinkling my nose. I was certain Cavitty had emptied the pan when he was done yesterday. Had he come back to work in the night?

Near nine a boy delivered a set of clothes for a portrait of a merchant which needed finishing, and Signore Mazzoni sent me to the storage room to bring the lay figure so we might dress it. The screens were still up. Passing the dais with its oddments of properties, I felt some apprehension entering the storage room, seeing that I had near been caught in it twice, but I told myself no harm could come. The Crivelli sat on its shelf, undamaged, and Viscount Budwell's portrait gazed out with the blunt, mock-heroic stare which Cavitty had painted upon it. The light from the small, high window fell upon a foot of the lay figure, sticking out from behind a full-length at the back of the small chamber. I moved toward it, stopped.

The figure wore a boot. It should not wear a boot.

The hairs at the nape of my neck prickled, but I made myself take three more steps. Small steps can make long journeys, and this was one, for, peering round the full-length, I felt a great, dismal sinking in my heart. James Cavitty sprawled on his back, sightless eyes staring. Blood daubed his chest, and a graver was buried in his throat.

*　*　*

My hand leapt to my own throat. My first thought was of Mr. Franklin: he must see this before others do! before they trample upon clues!

Could I manage it?

But first I must manage myself, and that was hard. Stumbling back, I fought the bile that threatened to surge from my belly. I closed my eyes, I clenched my fists, but the stink of death, blood and a giving-way of bladder and bowels, compounded my nausea. It did not help that when I forced myself to look once more, I saw flies about the dead man's eyes, battening upon calamity.

Who could have done this?

I turned away, shaking. I must have a plan. Biggs? Was he possible? Desperation made me hope, and I felt in my breeches pocket. I always carried two shillings; there they were. I had never found use for 'em, but I had one now.

"What keeps you, Handy?" came Signore Mazzoni's voice.

"Coming!" Cavitty's body was almost on top of the lay figure. Forcing myself to bend over the dead man, I tugged the flopping, awkward mannequin into my arms. It was cloth upon wood, and I struggled it out and closed the door. Panting, still feeling ill, I brought it round the screen.

Cully Stringer's lips twisted at sight of me. "You look sickly, Handy. Too much work? P'rhaps you'd best run home to Bartleby Bart."

"*Basta,*" chid Signore Mazzoni, but he too stared. "It is a standing pose. Hang it up." He gestured at the armature by one wall, on which the hinged figure would be pinned.

I felt sweat on my brow, and my knees wobbled, but I contrived to raise the dummy on its hooks.

When I turned the Italian was by my side, examining me out of his deep-set eyes. "You are unwell?"

"F-feel faint," murmured I.

"Faint as a girl, eh? Wot'd I tell you?" jeered Stringer.

Mazzoni gestured toward the street. "Get some air, then. *Presto.* You must dress the dummy."

Stumbling through the entryway, I near fell down upon the stoop, but my mind began to clear. Looking about, I was surprised to find the world unchanged: a bill-poster slapping up his broadside, a coach rattling by, the sky at nine-fifteen a pure sweet blue that belied murder. I steadied myself by these signs.

Biggs was still sanding the steps in his squinch-eyed way. "Hear, don't dirty me work!"

Descending the steps, I went to a corner of the house where we could not be seen. I hooked an arm at him. "Biggs."

"Wot?"

"Come here!"

Sauntering over, he screwed his smudged, ugly face up at me.

I rubbed the two shillings together under his nose. "One for you now, if you go where I tell you, and one when you return with a reply."

His little eyes narrowed. "Wot? Go off from Master's without leave?"

"This coin gives you leave. No more than half an hour there, half back." With my stub of pencil I scribbled a note, tore the page from my little book, wrapped the shilling in it and thrust it into the urchin's paw. "Number 7 Craven Street, the Strand. Ask for Benjamin Franklin."

"Franklin, eh?" Biggs eyed me, the paper, pushed it in a ragged pocket, ambled off.

Faster, damn you! cried I in my heart. The traffic of Cranbourne Street was a soundless parade.

Creeping back into the cursed house, I waited hoping no one went into the storage room. At least I had a task to occupy my hands; it gave me reason to avert my face.

Let Mr. Franklin be home.

Yet I suffered doubts. Was I wrong not to tell Mrs. Bone of my discovery? Ought I to have called a constable right away? But I had made my choice, and time ticked molasses-slow whilst my fingers tugged breeches, shirt, and waistcoat upon the limbs of the lay figure, so the folds of the garments might be properly painted. To my right the life-sized portrait of Lady Shenstone looked down as always, the diamond at its center. What would she say when she learnt James Cavitty was dead?

Signore Mazzoni came to help me pull on the velvet coat. I slipped a boot on each hinged foot, and together we arranged torso and limbs in a brave armorial pose. Mazzoni had already set the wine merchant's painting on an easel, so he had no need to obtain it from the storage room. *"Dove e il maestro?"* asked he as he took up the brush. "Did Signore Cavitty go out?"

"I haven't seen him," came Stringer's reply. Creeping to the workbench, I mixed paints, stealing glances at Mazzoni and Stringer. A terrible thought only then crept upon me: one of *them* might have murdered Cavitty! I peered for signs of guilt. Did Mazzoni's hands tremble? Did Stringer look secretly pleased to've done the deed? Would not such an act be the slaying of the golden goose?

The clock on the wall crept toward ten. All the while James Cavitty lay in the storage room, and though he could feel nothing this side of eternity, I hated to think of him sprawled there, and I fought hot tears.

Abruptly the front door of the room burst open. "Mr. Cavitty is not at present to be found?" I whirled round. The man who owned this voice strode in, Peasgood hovering behind him. The man waved a hand. "Nay, Mr. Peasgood, I shall wait for him in his painting room, for I was to sit for him this very hour, were you not told? Good morning, all." A brisk bow. "Benjamin Franklin."

Black buckled shoes, a familiar sturdy body, a wise dome of head with a fringe of brown hair—it was truly he. *I am here, Nick, do not fear,* his brief glance assured me, and I sent back a wavering smile, whilst beside him Biggs rubbed thumb and finger at me with unmistakable meaning: *I have earned my second shilling, see?*

❧ 14 ❧

IN WHICH Mr. Franklin picks the
pocket of a corpse . . .

I prayed Biggs could not read, for I should not like him to be privy to what I had writ Mr. Franklin, who looked about expectantly as if James Cavitty must arrive in the studio any instant. Sitters did not customarily burst in, and for half a moment no one seemed to know how to deal with the man. Peasgood gazed helplessly. Stringer cleared his throat. 'Twas Mazzoni who came forward. He bent his head of wildly curling hair. *"Perdonne me,* signore, I did not know the master was to paint anyone this morning."

"He was to paint me," said Mr. Franklin firmly. "Where is he, pray?"

Mazzoni turned to Peasgood. *"Per favore,* inquire of Mrs. Bone where her brother might be, for there is a gentleman who says he is to have his picture done."

Peasgood went out on wobbling old legs.

"He shall be found," assured Mazzoni.

"I am glad to hear it," replied Mr. Franklin. "Meanwhile I shall look about." As if nothing were more natural than to make one's self at home he began to stride here and there, peering at the merchant's unfinished portrait, the lay figure on

144

its hooks, the engraving table, where he frowned a moment into the etching tray. Glancing at the conversation piece Cully Stringer labored over, he patted the young man's shoulder, "Good, excellent!" as if he meant it, though Stringer replied with little more than a grunt. He came to the boy who cleaned brushes at the workbench. Bending near for the seeming purpose of examining my task, he whispered, "Damnable business! You have done well, Nick." Then he wandered behind the screens, and I heard his footsteps moving toward the storage room. "Perhaps your master is behind this door?" came his voice.

Mazzoni looked up. "It is only where we keep unfinished paintings."

I heard the opening of the door. "Dear God," sounded Mr. Franklin's cry.

The Italian frowned, met our eyes, set down brush and palette and vanished behind the screen. There followed a silence, in which I was aware of my heart pounding, until Mazzoni's own bark of dismay cut the air, followed by some words in Italian whose meaning I did not know but whose import was plain—he had come upon the horror.

Stringer scrambled up to rush round the screens. Thumping steps. A gasp. With a glance at me Biggs scurried too, I following, 'til we were, all five, crammed into the storage room with scarce space for another elbow, staring down at James Cavitty's fly-specked corpse.

I had seen Mr. Franklin in such circumstances before, by the bodies of Ebenezer Inch and Roderick Fairbrass and Abel Drumm, all murdered, and I fixed my gaze on him now, to steady me. First came a grave taking-in, very still, his large gray-brown eyes proclaiming what a pity it was that men treated men thus in this world. But his right hand tightened upon his bamboo stick. *Justice must be done; the madness of the*

145

world must be tamed if we are to govern our fates! his grip seemed to proclaim, and I felt stronger to know he would do his best.

Mr. Franklin turned. "He has been murdered." His manner was far different from the airy mien he had affected a moment ago. "Do any of you know aught of this?"

Blanchings and mouthings answered him in varying degrees of consternation. "Why, nothing . . . I know nothing," protested all three, whilst Biggs wiped his nose and Cully Stringer stood as white as flour. (Did he see in the corpse a portrait of what Bertie Hexham might do to *him*?) Only Mazzoni seemed to show genuine regret. His deep-set eyes brimmed, and he wiped his hands over and over on his painter's apron as if he might wipe out the deed itself. Had he been truly fond of his master?

Mazzoni mastered himself. *"Dio,* we must move him from this place . . . it is not right . . . Help me to take him into the painting room." He knelt.

"No." Mr. Franklin bade him stand. "First we must have the law. And we must inform the poor man's sister. You," he spoke to Stringer, "fetch the nearest constable. And you— Mazzoni is your name, if I recall aright—ask Mrs. Bone to come to the painting room. Do not alarm her. I shall tell her what has occurred."

Mazzoni's dark eyes did not like this. *"Il signore* must not take this matter upon himself. It is true that you were first to come upon the body, but you are not of this household. We cannot ask—"

Mr. Franklin shook his head. "I have had much experience in such affairs. Believe me 'twill be best if you leave 'em in my charge."

Mazzoni frowned. Yet he was but a painter's assistant, whilst Mr. Franklin was a gentleman, and he gave way with a brooding nod, jerking his head at Stringer to tell him to do as had been ordered. Stringer backed out.

"I shall bring Mrs. Bone," Mazzoni ground betwixt his teeth and left.

Mr. Franklin turned to Biggs.

The little creature squinted from him to me. *Wot's up?* his eyes demanded.

"You. Wait in the painting room. And no word to anyone that you came to Craven Street."

Biggs sauntered out.

Mr. Franklin clasped my shoulders. "Are you well, Nick?"

His touch told me how tight-wound I had been, for my knees nearly gave way under it. But I stiffened my spine and mustered a smile. "Well enough. I am heartily glad you were to be found at home, sir!"

He smiled back. "No gladder than I. Clever of you to send Biggs. And in the state you must have been! You kept your wits—good lad." His expression sobered. "But is this not a black turn of events? If only I had guessed the affair might lead to murder!—could I not have known? But since it has, we must redouble our efforts." He knelt, knees cracking. "Look." I dropped close beside him. "See how the graver has entered the throat? Thrust from behind. What is this black smudge upon it?" He sniffed. "Ink, no surprise, for an engraver's tool spends much time in proximity to ink. Damn me, what does this mean for Lady Shenstone? Has it to do with the diamond?" Crawling backward, he peered at the floorboards. "Look you, these marks," he pointed, "the track of Cavitty's heels. He was murdered elsewhere in the house, then dragged to this place."

"Does this mean a woman could not have done it?"

"He was small. A determined woman may do a great deal.

We must trace these heel marks, but first—" Returning to the body, he began to go through its pockets. As he did so I noted that Cavitty was not wearing his leathern apron. Not at work, then, when he was struck down? How limp lay his long-fingered hands. A lump rose in my throat. He had had his fits of anger, and he might prove to have known more of the Shenstone Diamond than he claimed, but that did not prevent me from mourning him. He had exposed folly by his art but folly cried out to be exposed and the world might've learnt much from James Cavitty.

"See?" murmured Mr. Franklin, drawing from the right-hand coat pocket one of Cavitty's small octavo notebooks. He waggled it. "One day the law may be so well trained that the likes of Ben Franklin are not needed; but, as experience teaches me that most London constables have little more brains than newts, I take matters into my hands." He dropped the notebook into his own pocket. Rising, he gazed down. "What an indignity is death." He peered about. "This is the little Crivelli, eh?" He tapped the painting. "Would I knew its true provenance—and much else besides." He glanced out the second door, onto the back landing, up and down the servant's stairs. Returning, he began to trace the faint drag of Cavitty's heel marks, round the screen and into the painting room, bending now and then to squint through the quizzing glass that hung from its black velvet cord at his neck.

I followed. We ended by the engraving table. The painting room was deserted save for us, and Mr. Franklin gazed fiercely round, pulling at his lip, as if he might recreate by force of will what had occurred. Angry words? A struggle? Had the victim been struck without warning? The graver was gleaming sharp, a steel shaft; 'twould have taken no very great effort to plunge it deep. "Murdered here, it seems," said Mr. Franklin. "See you, upon the floor?"

With queasy distaste I discovered red-brown smears. Blood.

"Unnoticed in the morning's activities, no doubt. Indeed, the blood might well have been taken for paint. The weapon appears to be what was at hand. Meaning the deed was not planned? An act of fear, then, anger, desperation? I do not like it, for, lacking the logic of forethought, such deeds may be hard to trace." He scrutinized the portrait of Lady Shenstone. "What did you witness, ma'am? Was the gem upon your breast its cause? Have you noted nothing unusual about the engraving table, Nick?"

I looked at it. "That of the eight copperplates of *The Follies of a Lord* only seven are in their slots?" said I.

"Nay, the eighth is here."

"Where?"

He gestured. "In the etching bath."

I peered into the long, shallow enameled tray with its stinging smell of aquafortis—and indeed a plate lay there, but ruined, for the niter had eaten away all save a ghost of an image.

I frowned. "It is the size of the other seven. Indeed, it must be the missing one. But why has it been spoilt?"

"If we knew that, we should know a great deal more, I believe." Tearing a corner from a sheet of foolscap, he dropped it in the bath. It turned rapidly yellow, then brown, wrinkled and began to dissolve. "See, the niter is undiluted." His eyes met mine. "Someone meant to destroy the plate."

"Cavitty?"

"More likely his murderer." Taking up wooden tongs, he lifted out the plate. In a basin he poured water on it from a jug, to stop the bite.

"But, sir," said I, "another plate is in the bath; 'twas concealed by the first."

He looked. "You are right. Quickly, pull it out!"

149

Using the tongs, I lifted it and placed it in the basin so he might pour water on it, too. 'Twas a smaller rectangle of copper, less than a fourth the size of the first. Plainly something had been engraved upon it, but its image, too, had dissolved, to pitted, blurred unreadability.

Mr. Franklin shook his head. "What can this mean?"

Hearing the front door open we turned.

Old Peasgood stood there. "Phillippe duVerre to see Mr. Cavitty." The manservant peered about in puzzlement. "What, Master is not yet here? I have been unable to find him elsewhere."

"He is here," replied Mr. Franklin. "Show in Monsieur duVerre."

Peasgood went out, and in a moment the Frenchman stood before us. He was as lean and elegantly dressed as during the other two occasions I had seen him, and equally self-possessed. His glass, gray gaze flicked about the room, puzzled to find no familiar face save mine. He made a little nod to Mr. Franklin. "*Bonjour*, monsieur. I expected to meet Monsieur Cavitty. Where is he, if you please?"

Mr. Franklin nodded back. "Meet him for what purpose, may I ask?"

DuVerre wore a tight-fitting white wig. His glittering eyes narrowed. "Before I reply, may I know who asks me? You are perhaps new in Monsieur Cavitty's employ?"

A small smile. "I am not in his employ." Mr. Franklin offered a bow. "Benjamin Franklin, sir. From America."

DuVerre started. "Not *the* Benjamin Franklin?—who writes of the electrical fluid?"

"I have writ somewhat of it."

"*Mon dieu*, you are too modest. You are famous in the most enlightened circles in France." DuVerre returned the bow, quite low. "Phillippe duVerre, from Paris, at your service, monsieur. I am honored to know you. But"—he gestured at the otherwise untenanted chamber—"what do you here?"

"What else but to have my picture painted? You?"

"I am James Cavitty's printer, come to obtain copperplates of him. He sent word they were ready to be printed."

"The Follies of a Lord?"

"You know of them? You are a subscriber, perhaps?"

"Pray, when did he send word?"

"Why . . . yesterday."

"But you could not come 'til today?"

"He sent word very late."

"And the subject of these engravings—?" But Mr. Franklin's inquiry was cut short, for Signore Mazzoni at that moment came in.

"I have been unable to find Mrs. Bone," said he. "She has gone on some errand into the Strand."

"A pity," said Mr. Franklin.

DuVerre glanced from one man to the other. He frowned. *"S'il vous plait,* what is this about?"

Mr. Franklin faced him. "No very good thing. I fear I must inform you that James Cavitty is dead."

DuVerre stood very still. "Can it be? But . . . how? Some accident?"

"His own graver, buried in his throat."

The Frenchman's hand lifted to the neck cloth above his ruffled shirt. "Murder, you say? B-but I was to print his plates . . . his printseller chafes that they are overdue . . . he owes me . . . the subscribers to the series have waited many weeks . . ."

"They must now wait forever, it seems."

"Who did this thing?"

"That is what I wish to learn. The body has just been found. It lies in his storage room, dragged there from this spot." Mr. Franklin indicated the bloodstained floor. Looking where he

151

pointed, duVerre achieved a deathly pallor, whilst Mazzoni paled too. Biggs had wriggled in, and he also stared at the red-brown smears—whilst Mr. Franklin stood with his head half-bowed, a hand stroking the end of his bamboo stick.

There came sounds from the front door of the house, and Mrs. Fanny Bone strode in, looking about as if she expected to find disorder and foolishness. She was dressed for town in a trim dark dress and dark blue coat and a small felt hat that for all its ribbons seemed severe above her narrow face. Her eyes bulged slightly, like her brother's. They flicked from face to face whilst her frown deepened. Her gaze sought Mazzoni. *What can this mean?* it asked, and she looked suddenly vulnerable, a woman who had held a household together by force of will but whose will had limited power. Mazzoni made a move toward her—would he actually have held her, to console her?—but Mr. Franklin stepped betwixt 'em.

He made a little bow. "Benjamin Franklin, ma'am. Perhaps you recall me—I came to inquire of a portrait. I am returned to have it done, but I find a dreadful thing has happened. Would you wish to sit down before hearing of it?"

All color drained from her face. "Not . . . not Felicity?"

"No. Your brother. I am very sorry to tell you that he is dead."

A hand slowly rose to her mouth as if to stifle a cry. "I find I must sit after all." Her voice was as hollow as if it were come from the grave, and it was Biggs who whisked a stool from the wall to place behind her. She sank upon it.

After a moment she lifted her face. "How?" came the single, searching word.

"Murdered. Stabbed with his graver. He lies in the storage room."

"Who did this?"

"I do not know."

Her eyes examined me, duVerre, Biggs, Mazzoni. Could any of *you* have done it? they seemed to ask. She struggled to master herself. "If he is dead, he is dead. Poor James. Who could hate him so?" She rose. "I must think on this, I must decide what to do." She was ashen, but she shed no tears. "Has a constable been called? I must see my brother. You need not accompany me." Skirts rustling, she walked behind the screen whilst we shifted our feet in awkward waiting.

When she returned it was solemnly. Though plainly shaken, she held her chin high as she went to the front door. She turned. "Someone must tell the servants. Will you do so, Signore Mazzoni? Inform 'em I shall take charge; this household will not be dissolved. Now, I must be alone. Will you wait for the constable, Mr. Franklin? I am sorry you are discommoded." She walked out.

DuVerre's fingers flicked at his sides. "I must go. But the plates—" Glancing at the seven remaining in their slots, he emitted a shaken laugh. "But why should I take them, when it is all over with Cavitty? What a terrible thing." He stared into Mr. Franklin's face. "Who, indeed, could hate him so much?"

"Perhaps it was not a *crime passionel*, monsieur."

DuVerre blinked. *"Hélas."* With one last grim glance about the room, he hurried out.

Stripping off his paint-smeared apron, Mazzoni shrugged into the plain brown coat which hung on a peg next to mine. "I must ask Peasgood to call the servants. I must tell them, as Mrs. Bone asks."

"Do so," said Mr. Franklin. "I shall await the constable."

In a moment Mazzoni was gone.

Biggs still leant against the wall by the door.

Mr. Franklin regarded him. "What do you know of this?"

The urchin ran a sly hand through his brush of reddish hair. "Nothink—savin' that you lied about comin' to 'ave yer picture done."

"Have you never lied?"

"I does it best when I'm paid."

Mr. Franklin took this in. "I cannot fault you for seeking remuneration for your talents." He opened his purse. "Here is the second shilling which was promised."

Biggs bit the coin. He slid out of the room.

Mr. Franklin shook his head. "What a waste of talent—the boy might stand for Parliament."

"Or hang at Tyburn, sir?"

A thin smile. "Many a promising lad strangles on a string."

Clumping boots proclaimed that Cully Stringer returned with the constable. This proved to be Mr. Gampers, a large looming man with a brow like a knotted fist and no great intelligence in his eyes. Mr. Franklin led him to the storage room, I following, where he stood a moment over the body. "Hm," grunted he before beckoning us back round the screen to glower at the painting room as if he dreaded the news it might bring. From his bottle-green watch coat he pulled a notebook and a bitten stub of pencil and took Mr. Franklin's name and mine and Stringer's and demanded why we were here and what we knew of the murder. I could not give up the pretense of being here by grace of Sir Bartleby Bart, but I lied as little as possible. For his part, Mr. Franklin told who he truly was. Stringer came last, answering in such a gulping manner as to make him seem guilty of all the crimes in London. Mr. Gampers fixed a hard gaze upon him. "Yer master was unmarried, ye say? I must speak to his sister."

"She is sorely distrait," interposed Mr. Franklin. "May she be left alone awhile?"

Gampers gloomily agreed. "Very well. Assemble the rest, though."

Stringer darted to do so as if sprung from a trap.

A moment later we were all in the viewing room across the way. Plainly Signore Mazzoni had had time to spread the news, for there was a bleak pallor on ev'ry face, and varying degrees and sorts of feeling: Mrs. Cockle moaning and sniffling dramatically, Peasgood's head wobbling as if he had had a great blow, Annie sending me a brave but tremulous look from under her askew little cap.

Positioning himself by the marble hand on the table, Constable Gampers proceeded to put more questions, scribbling the replies in his book. It proved a dreary quarter hour, for nothing helpful emerged that I could see. Mr. Cavitty was a good master. No one knew why or when the deed had been done. The issue of motive was broached and dispatched by ringing silence, and I had the sense, when Constable Gampers at last closed his book and prepared to depart, that he was satisfied he had done his duty by filling three pages, no matter that his jottings shed no light. "Save me from officious men," muttered Mr. Franklin when Gampers had gone to make his report.

Yet he had never spoke to Mrs. Bone. "*I* shall speak to her, Nick," murmured Mr. Franklin quietly to me. "Let us see if we can lure her down."

❧ 15 ❧

*IN WHICH Mr. Franklin asks
questions of a sister and prevents the
letting of a house . . .*

W hat now?" moaned Mrs. Cockle when Constable
Gampers was gone.

Peasgood emitted a sigh. "To our places, that is
what. Mrs. Bone is now mistress of the house. We must await
her orders." He beckoned, and Cook, Annie, and Biggs shuffled out after him.

Signore Mazzoni and Cully Stringer remained. Mr. Franklin
cleared his throat, his spectacles glinting in the windowlight.
"I must speak to Mrs. Bone, to inquire what disposition is to
be made of her brother's body." Mazzoni looked like protest-
ing, but Mr. Franklin held up a hand. "A gentleman's obliga-
tion. Go up, if you please. Tell the lady that Benjamin Franklin
wishes to see her." He added, "I hope the lady can provide,
now her brother is dead." Mazzoni trudged off, but as I
watched his strong back push through the door I wondered
what private conversation he and Mrs. Bone would hold
before—and if—she deigned to descend.

Mr. Franklin turned to me. "What is your name, boy?"

I saw I must still pretend to have met him only today. "Nick
Handy, sir."

"Can you write?"

"Yes, sir."

"Then remain with me, for I may wish some notes taken, and I do not care to scribble 'em myself. You—" to Cully Stringer, who shifted his feet by the door, "return to your work."

"Here now, wot work is there now Master is dead?"

"Had he set you a task?"

"Sev'ral. I was useful to him, I was."

"Respect his memory, then, by completing those tasks."

Stringer lurched out.

"A troubled young man," said Mr. Franklin when he was gone. He fixed his eyes on me. "Well, Nick, which one of 'em did it?"

"Perhaps none, sir. You do not forget Quimp?"

"O, I never forget Quimp. Nor the Shenstones. Bertie Hexham too, damn him. You will indeed have many notes to take." Waiting, he paced silently whilst I reflected on other times when we had come across murder. It was always upsetting, but its ragged rents must be sewn up, for if not, what was to keep bloody disorder from spreading to all the world? Beyond the heavily draped window, London stirred, horsebells jingled, and a vegetable-seller cried the finest potatoes in Christendom.

The door swung open, and Mrs. Fanny Bone walked in.

Signore Mazzoni stood in the entryway behind her, looking as if he would come in too, but Mr. Franklin gently but firmly closed the door. He turned to James Cavitty's sister, I beside him.

Her narrow face below the severely pulled-back hair was difficult to read. It showed great strain. Sorrow? I thought I detected the tracks of tears upon her cheeks, but one may cry for many reasons. She had put on a black dress—prompt, I thought, for many a woman would have been too distrait to think of mourning colors so soon. She clasped her hands before her, a handkerchief in 'em, her mouth rigid as she peered at Mr. Franklin out of those outstarting eyes so like her brother's. Her soul was flinty, but I could not condemn its hardness. Her brother had longed to make a success of his art; she had wished only to secure a home for herself and her daughter.

Her throat worked. She formed hoarse words. "You wish to speak to me, Mr. Franklin?"

"I do."

"To help, I am told. I cannot allow it. You have done enough. You owe no more."

"Yet I do."

"How?"

"The truth is, I am not a gentleman come to have his picture done."

She blinked. "Whatever can you mean?"

"Shall we sit?"

Alarm and suspicion spread across her features, but she nodded. "I believe we must." Lowering herself onto the sofa, her eyes found me. "Why do you hang about? Return to the painting room at once."

Mr. Franklin raised a finger. "I should like him to remain. If you will allow." He settled into the chair opposite her. "He is my boy."

"No. He is the son of Sir Bartleby Bart's sister."

A pained look. "I fear not. He is in my employ. I placed him in your house." Mr. Franklin spread his hands. "There is no Sir Bartleby Bart."

Several heartbeats passed, during which the skin on Mrs. Bone's face seemed to creep tighter over her skull. "What do you say?"

"A friend of mine played Sir Bartleby. An actor in my impolite little game."

The woman flared. "It is more than merely impolite!"

"Forgive me."

"What, sir, are you about?"

"Your notebook, Nick?"

I took it out.

He bent toward Fanny Bone. "Dear lady, you know of the Shenstone Diamond?"

"Of course I know of it. My brother painted it only a week ago."

"And do you know that the diamond is gone?"

"What do you mean?"

"Missing. Stolen perhaps. I see you did not know." Whilst she stared in dismay, he told of Lady Shenstone's coming to him, of my being placed in Cranbourne Street, of his interview with her brother. "It seemed a matter only of theft," concluded he. "I never thought it should come to murder. If I had, I should have acted to prevent it. What you must know now is that when I spoke to your brother he agreed to allow me to help in the recovery of the gem. You see why I wish to go on with the task?"

"The law must do that."

"It has been here and gone. To what effect? London is rife with crime. Do you think your brother's death will be taken much note of? Yet I can help. I am a friend to Sir John Fielding, the Westminster magistrate; I can obtain his sanction, his aid, if need be. Yield to me, ma'am. Let me search out who did this crime."

Mrs. Bone's chest rose and fell, anger crumbling to confusion in her eyes. I examined her. She might have done the murder herself; desperation might paint that anguish upon her face, and if so, she would wish to dismiss Benjamin Franklin. Yet to refuse him might say she feared the truth. I turned my gaze to the gentleman, waiting. In the tale he had told, he had left out a great deal: Bertie Hexham, Quimp; he did not show all his hand. The house clock ticked.

"I must know who murdered my brother," breathed Mrs. Bone at last, but looking as if she had grave doubts. "How will you discover it?"

"By questions—of yourself, to begin. May I?" At her nod, he leant forward. "Who hated your brother?"

"You do not mince words."

"His murderer went to the point. So must we."

She struggled to answer. "James was not beloved—he was temperamental, impatient."

"There might be sev'ral who wished him dead?"

She paled. "May not one dislike a person without wishing him dead?"

"As you say. I mean . . . had he enemies?"

"No one I would give that name. I am sorry, but—"

"I seek only what is true. No one with a reason to murder him, then?"

"No one I can think of."

"Did your brother behave out of the ordinary, of late?"

"He was never easy. Yet in past days, yes, he was more fretful than usual—no wonder if he knew the Shenstone Diamond had been stolen. He also had some idea of removing to Leicester Square; that may have made him excitable."

"Did you approve of this move?"

"I did not."

"Pray, why?"

"My brother's temperament lost him custom sometimes, but he had come to make a decent living here—due mainly to

160

my management of this house. Why move when we were well off as we were?"

"Yet I have heard you had more money of late."

"That is true."

"How did he earn it?"

"By sev'ral means. In addition to painting portraits, he was a dealer, obtaining works for wealthy men. He sometimes copied paintings too, though he hated to do so. And his engravings—he planned a new series, which he had much hope for."

"Yet why should he have *more* money than usual, a great deal more?"

She stared at her hands. "I do not know. Did he have some enterprise he did not tell me of?"

"I cannot answer that," said Mr. Franklin. "He was more excitable of late, you say. Was he at all fearful?"

She stared unflinchingly. "My brother was a fearless man."

"Would stick at little?"

"He went after what he desired, if that is what you mean."

Mr. Franklin stroked the head of his bamboo. "I am sure, ma'am, that you love your daughter very much."

"More than my life!"

"Her father, Mr. Bone—where is he?"

"Ran off to India, good riddance to the fool."

"So he could have no part in this crime? Now, I should like to learn where ev'ryone is disposed about the house. You yourself sleep—?"

"On the second floor. Felicity's bed is in my chamber. She sometimes wanders in the night, so I always lock the door."

Whilst I jotted, Mr. Franklin satisfied himself as to the rest of the household. James Cavitty's bedchamber was to the right of his sister's. The servants slept above, in attic rooms—Peasgood, Annie, Signore Mazzoni, Cully Stringer. Only Mrs.

Cockle had a room belowstairs, and Biggs's bed was a pallet in the kitchen, by the coals. "When was the last time you saw your brother alive?" asked Mr. Franklin.

"Just before eight last night, when he went out."

"Where, pray, did he go?"

"He did not take kindly to questions, and so I did not ask him. 'Twas before supper. Cook left a bit of cold joint for him, but 'twas untouched in the morning, she said."

"Did you hear him come in?"

"I thought so, round about ten."

"But cannot say for sure?"

"I had retired by then."

"Did you see or hear anything after that time which might bear upon his death?"

"No. I read my devotions, then blew out the lamp. I was asleep before eleven."

"And Felicity did not 'wander,' as you describe it?"

"Only to climb into my bed at cock's crow, for the half hour before I must rise."

Mr. Franklin's brow furrowed. "But in the morning no one remarked at your brother's seeming absence?"

"*I* did not remark it. He was used to rising in his own time. We did not always breakfast together; indeed he frequently went directly to the painting room, so that I might not see him 'til one or two."

"So each part of the house assumed he was elsewhere—convenient for murder. To another matter: I am told you leave the back door unlatched by day. But the front remains well-locked? And both were locked last night?"

"No. That is, yes, they are customarily locked—but," Mrs. Bone licked her thin lips, "Peasgood informed me that this morning he found the front door off the latch."

"Ah! Do you know any reason why that should be?"

"None."

"So the murderer might've entered freely?—I do not like to hear it. To another matter. I am told there have been small thefts about your house."

"Over the past few months."

"Who did 'em, do you know?"

"If I did, the thief would pay dearly!"

"You do not suspect anyone?"

"Many had opportunity. I have wondered if the little ragamuffin Biggs . . . but . . . I do not know."

"I ask only in passing. Is there anything more you may tell me which might bear upon your brother's murder?"

"Nothing." Her stays creaked. "Mr. Franklin, the Shenstone Diamond—is *it* the reason for the crime?"

"It is worth a small fortune."

"You think my brother may have had it all along? And was done in to obtain it?"

"I do not know. When I spoke to him he seemed truly to have no idea where it was. By the by, the engravings your brother worked on, *The Follies of a Lord*—did you know he had taken 'em back from duVerre?"

Her eyes widened. "What? But they were well completed."

"He did not seem to think so. He had decided to alter 'em in some way."

"How?"

"I hoped that you might say."

The woman's shoulders heaved. "O, James, James! What were you about?"

Mr. Franklin was solicitous. "Something secret, ma'am, which we must bring to light. To which end: further steps. Will you inform your household that I have befriended you? That you have given me leave to come and go, and freedom to inquire? Do so, and I shall do my all to bring your brother's murderer to justice."

Silence pressed about us, whilst she examined the kind face watching her. *Can I trust you?* she seemed to inquire. Yet in what Mr. Franklin had not asked, about her fights with her brother, her relations with Mazzoni, I saw that he did not entirely trust her.

She yielded. "I shall place myself in your hands."

"But do not reveal that the boy works for me."

"I shall not."

"To your poor brother's body. Shall you have someone in to prepare it?"

"Dear God, I must." For a moment I thought her facade might crumble, but she mastered herself with that iron will with which she ruled the house. "Will you see to it, sir?"

"Gladly."

Mrs. Bone gazed toward the window. "Lady Shenstone." She turned back. "I met her twice. When she came to sit." Her voice asked plaintively, "She too suffers?"

A nod. "She blames herself for the loss of her husband's diamond."

"How I curse the thing! Recover it for her, sir."

The door opened and Felicity walked in. Wordlessly she lay her head in her mother's lap.

Mrs. Bone stroked Felicity's hair. "I must go up."

Before mounting, she spoke to Peasgood as Mr. Franklin had asked: "This gentleman has the run of the house. Inform the others. Help him in any way you can. Answer all questions. He will see to my brother's body." Then she was gone.

As Peasgood went to obey, I wondered how the others would take to a stranger's questions. Mr. Franklin and I were left alone in the entryway. "Now," said he, "Shall you return to the painting room, to play your part some more?"

"I should like to. I may learn something of note. I promise to take care."

He regarded me. "Well, you are no object of murder. Why was Cavitty?" He thumped his bamboo. "To know so much, yet to see so little!"

A rapping sounded upon the door.

Mr. Franklin turned and opened.

A round-faced fellow with a very black moustache and very eager eyes stood on the stoop: Mr. Banks, the agent to whom Cavitty had talked of letting the house in Leicester Square. He peered in in some surprise. "I am here to see James Cavitty." He entered. "Where is his manservant, sir? Who are you?"

"A friend. Benjamin Franklin."

"Noah Banks, sir."

"Your servant. Mr. Cavitty was to meet you?"

"At this very hour."

"To settle Leicester Square?"

"You know of that? He is to let it—on very good terms, I may add." More officious peering. "But I must see him in person, to sign papers and receive monies. Will you tell him I am here?"

"I am afraid that is impossible. I must deliver bad news." Mr. Franklin told it.

Mr. Banks made gaping mouths. "Murdered? But this is dreadful! What am I to tell Lord Pye, who owns the house? He very much counted on me. On this arrangement. A very great surety is due. And a half-year's rent."

"Generous terms to Lord Pye. Mr. Cavitty made no objection?"

"It is a very desirable house."

"Then you will easily find someone else to take it. But I am sorry, a dead man cannot move to Leicester Square. Come, this is a sad day for this household and an unfortunate one for you, but you will find another client. You had best go."

Mr. Banks departed muttering.

Mr. Franklin turned to me. "A half-year's rent? A significant sum. And Cavitty murdered the day before he was to pay it. More." He pulled a folded newspaper from his coat pocket. *"The London Advertiser,* fresh this morn." He tapped a small square of print. "Read this."

I did so:

> "James Cavitty, artist, proposes to publish by subscription eight prints by his hand, newly altered, entitled *The Follies of a Lord,* in which the foibles of a London connoisseur are satirized. Printed by Philippe duVerre. Apply to the artist at 23 Cranbourne Street, or Cope, Printseller, the Strand."

"Note, Nick, *a* connoisseur. Cavitty, then, aimed at a particular person? Damn the murder, it has prevented more than one thing, *viz.*: the letting of a house, the selling of prints, the answering of questions. How still is a dead man's tongue!"

166

16

*IN WHICH Mr. Franklin seeks truth
upstairs and down . . .*

It was by then past noon, the odor of one of Mrs. Cockle's stews beginning to fill the house; life went on despite murder. "I wish to see more," said Mr. Franklin. "Belowstairs, Nick. Lead the way." Though I had heretofore used only the narrow back stairs, I took him down the front, past the still room and scullery, to the servants' eating room with its long trestle table and three high windows through which light spilt in dingy rays.

He looked about. " 'Twill do. Fetch Peasgood, if you please."

I found the old man in the areaway, wreathed in pipesmoke. He tapped out his pipe and came.

We walked in to find Mr. Franklin paddling his fingers on the mantelpiece.

The old manservant bowed. "What do you require, sir?" asked his croaking voice.

"But a few moments of your time. A lamentable business, is this not? Tell me, did you see or hear anything last eve which might bear upon your master's murder?"

"Nothing, sir. I made my rounds as customary and latched

167

the doors and snuffed the candles and was abed by ten, sound asleep. These old bones rest well."

"And when did you rise?"

"At six."

"To find the front door off the latch?"

"Yes."

"Surely that was not customary."

"O, no, indeed. Never happened afore, to my knowing."

"What did you do when you discovered it?"

"Told Mrs. Bone, for I could not find Mr. Cavitty. Yet I was not deeply concerned, for I discovered no disturbance nor nothing missing. I thought Master himself may have left it unlatched when he went out."

"He was used to going out early?"

"No."

"But you sought a harmless explanation when no harm appeared? Quite right. Now tell me: who might've done this terrible deed?"

"Dear me, I am sure I do not know."

"No idea at all?"

A helpless sigh. "None, sir, I fear."

"I am sorry to hear it, for I counted upon your wisdom. Nonetheless something may come to mind; it often does with reflection. Save it for Ben Franklin, eh? Thank you. Send Biggs, if you will."

Peasgood doddered out, and in a moment the boy-of-work replaced him, sauntering in with his wry leer that proclaimed he saw through all pretenses.

His manner said he knew he held one good card in the game.

Shutting the door, Mr. Franklin peered at him as he might at a troublesome smudge on his sleeve. Then, wearing a smile that more than matched Biggs's for irony, he took out a shilling and tossed it up and down whilst he questioned him in much the same way he had Peasgood. Eyes on the coin, Biggs squirted out answers, but they amounted to little. He had not done in Master, he asserted, and he had no idea who had—though he hoped it was Cully Stringer so he might have the pleasure of watching his heels kick at Tyburn. "I want 'is tongue to turn black!" He did not always sleep by the kitchen fire, he told us, but sometimes slipped out the area window, "on bizness about London, that bizness bein' none o' your bizness, and aplucking out my toenails one by one shall not wring it from me." I thought he might be one of those boys who were employed by thieves for slipping silently through small chinks in great houses—but Mr. Franklin did not press him on the matter, at which Biggs's face fell.

"And were you out last night?" asked the gentleman.

Biggs thrust out his chin. "I were, so I seen nor heard nothink in this house. Wot're you and yer spyin' boy about?"

"Seeking truth," replied Mr. Franklin. "And willing to pay for it too. But—" Giving the shilling one last toss, he caught it in his purse. "—as we have heard nothing to our purpose from you, there will be no payment today."

Biggs's eyes narrowed. "Here, now—!"

"O, there will be payment—if you can keep our secret."

"You think I can't?"

"I hope you can do a great deal more. Who in the neighborhood sees to the washing and dressing of bodies?"

"Mrs. Cray."

"Fetch her. And if you should like to have that shilling you will keep your eyes peeled for Benjamin Franklin."

When Biggs was gone the gentleman called in Mrs. Cockle, who made a moaning show of sorrow. Her slatlike body swayed as she whimpered through her apron, which she tugged up over her mouth. "I do my job and mind my business and that is all I know!" Last came Annie, who looked more disheveled than usual, ribbons untied, apron crooked, wisps of hair flying about her face. At sight of her I flushed, whilst for her part she looked abashed to discover me scribbling in my book, and I felt a stab of guilt that I had not been honest with her.

Mr. Franklin attempted to put her at ease. "Pay no mind to the boy. He writes notes at my request."

Plainly she still was affrighted.

He took her hand. "Dear child, I mean only to help. I should like to hear anything which might bear upon the mystery of your master's murder."

Gazing into his face, she stammered that she did not know how or why such a terrible thing should come about. To closer questioning, she said that she had been abed by ten. No, she had not known Master had gone out, and she had not heard him return. As for the morn, she had been up and about by seven but had noted nothing amiss. "I . . . I liked Master . . . he was always fair . . . I shall miss him," quavered she, tears spilling.

"There, there. From whose employ did you come to this house?"

She glanced at me. "Why . . . from Lord Shenstone."

"Was he fair to you too?"

"Yes. Always fair."

He patted her hand. "It is a terrible thing to lose a good master, whether you must leave his house or he is taken from you in this terrible way. Now. I am here to make things right. If you recall or discover anything which may help me to that end, send to number 7 Craven Street. Or you may speak to this boy," he nodded at me, "for he has consented to be my messenger. That is all for now, child. You may go."

Annie fled.

When the door was closed, Mr. Franklin puffed a breath. "Nothing seen nor heard by ev'ry one of 'em? Impossible. Who lies? Upstairs, Nick, for I must visit James Cavitty once more."

I led him by the back way, and shortly we were in the narrow storage room. The flies were thicker, the smell of death stronger. I did not like to look again on the dead man—his crumpled, useless form—but if Mr. Franklin did not shirk, though the wrinkling of his nose said he should like to, then neither would I. He knelt with a creak of bones to squeeze the arms and legs and fingers of the corpse. "Fothergill," murmured he (John Fothergill, his old physician friend), "has taught me to judge of the time of death by the looseness or rigidity of the limbs. When I felt 'em earlier they were quite immovable, but now they begin to ease. 'Tis an inexact science, but I surmise the man was struck down last night, somewhere betwixt ten and one; that is why I inquired so particularly as to what the household noted before it slept."

With a handkerchief he began to draw the thin steel graver from the dead man's throat. Slowly it came, gore-smeared, and I had to fight a terrible nausea. The body shifted under the pulling, as if to protest this last indignity, and I wondered where the artist's soul was now. Where it could observe our mortal folly? Did it laugh? I longed for it to cry to us the name of him—or her—who had done the awful deed.

Mr. Franklin slipped the weapon, kerchief-wrapped, into a pocket. Deeply shaken, I followed him from the chamber.

We found Signore Mazzoni and Cully Stringer in the painting room, working as on the day I first came, as if the master might at any moment burst in to examine whether or not they did well. Near the front window, the Italian dabbed at the portrait for which he and I had dressed the lay figure, whilst

Stringer varnished Viscount Budwell nearby. Both looked round with slitted eyes. Who is this man? asked their gazes. Why does he require the boy to scribble?

Mr. Franklin gave me a nudge. Reminded that I must keep up pretenses, I pushed my small book in the pocket under my apron and went to the workbench to grind red earth. I kept my eye on Mazzoni. How large were his hands, knots of sinew. His expression burned with resentment.

Mr. Franklin went to him. "Peasgood has told you of Mrs. Bone's intentions?"

"We are to answer your questions, *si*."

"Why should we?" burst out Stringer.

"Because the mistress wishes it, *ragazzo*," snapped the Italian, "and if you displease her you will answer to me."

Stringer ducked his head.

"Leave us," said Mr. Franklin to the apprentice, "but do not go far; I shall want you presently."

With a louring glance at me Stringer scuffed out.

Mr. Franklin turned back to the Italian. The one P.M. light had brightened, sending golden shafts across the floor. Out upon Cranbourne Street coach wheels clattered. He asked the man's history, learning that Amadeo Mazzoni had been born in Cremona, was apprenticed to Vicellino Stamati in Rome, and had come to London at the age of thirty.

"Why leave your native land?"

"I was told Italian craftsmen were respected by your English gentry."

"They are, but surely you sought more than respect."

"To make my way, then."

"To gain an establishment of your own? To be your own master?"

"Why should I not seek these things?"

172

"You should. I wish you luck. How did you come to work for James Cavitty?"

"I met him in *Roma*, when he acted as guide to a lord."

"You knew him well there?"

"We had . . . dealings. I helped him to obtain some works for his patron: a little Bellini, a Tintoretto."

"And you called upon him when you arrived in London? He remembered you?"

"*E fortunato*. He looked for an assistant, and so—"

"So you are here. Fortunate indeed. How long did you serve him?"

"Four years."

"And has that brought you any nearer an establishment of your own?"

The Italian's lips compressed. "Not very near."

"Not to despair, sir. It took me many years to found my own, and I started with nothing. Now, to last night—" But the Italian's replies shed as little light upon the murder as any others. He too had eaten supper, gone to bed. Cranbourne Street was a house of habits, it seemed, and those habits had been universally followed. He could say nothing helpful about the early morn either, being fast asleep, he said, 'til he rose at six-thirty and came down to find Peasgood fretting about the unlatched door.

"Who should wish to kill your master?" asked Mr. Franklin.

"I do not know."

"Had *you* reason to wish him dead?"

Mazzoni had restrained himself, but Mr. Franklin's question was like a bellows to coals. The Italian took a step forward, and for a moment I thought he might strike Mr. Franklin. I stiffened. Yet though the Italian was younger and stronger, Mr. Franklin knew many tricks of fighting (I had seen him lay more than one man low), and I had no idea what might follow. But a shudder checked Mazzoni, a bleak look spread over his face and he said, quite pale, *"Il signore* Cavitty was a good master to me! I tell you, he was good!"

Mr. Franklin nodded. "I believe he may have been."

At this moment the front door opened, Cully Stringer poking in his head. "The lady for the body." Mr. Franklin nodded, and a small, plump woman, no more than five feet tall, with very pink cheeks, bustled in and was directed to the storage room, from which she emerged a moment later to inform us in a shrill voice that someone must help her move the dead gentleman out upon the dais. "I shall work upon him there."

"Ecco, I shall help." Mazzoni trudged after Mrs. Cray. Mr. Franklin gave me a nod, and I followed him to the entryway, where Cully Stringer kicked sullenly at the wainscoting.

Mr. Franklin gestured at me. "Write all he says."

I took out my book and pencil.

He proceeded to wring Stringer's history from him. He was the son of a Kentish cooper, it fell out, whose wife had been persuaded by her son's idle doodles that he was meant to be an artist; she had wheedled her husband into finding a London apprenticeship for him. He had been with Cavitty since the age of twelve. He was now sixteen.

Mr. Franklin regarded him. "Now, boy, did you do in your master?"

The apprentice's Adam's apple leapt in his throat. "What? I never!" Yet his manner seemed to betray some guilt. Because of Bertie Hexham? Quimp? Did he believe—or know—that one of 'em had stabbed James Cavitty?

He was a damned accessory to the deed if he had unlatched the door.

"You protest your innocence," said Mr. Franklin, "yet you play some game."

"I . . . I do not know what you talk on. I play no game."

Mr. Franklin touched the young man's arm. "You are afraid," cajoled he. "I see that you are. For your life? What have you fallen into? Come, I mean no harm. Unburden your heart. Tell all to Benjamin Franklin."

Stringer stared at the hand upon his sleeve, then into the sober brown eyes scrutinizing him; and I thought for a moment that he might yield. But something powerful had locked his lips—terror, I thought—and he set his jaw and swung his head from side to side.

Mr. Franklin released him. "A pity. Murder has come into this house. Think on that. Might it visit again? Back to work, boy."

Stringer left, and Mr. Franklin shook his head. "I do not love a bully, but one may pity one. Do you know, I almost pity Cully Stringer?"

At his nod we returned to the painting room, where I crept back to my mortar and pestle, and Mr. Franklin went to the engraving table to frown at the destroyed plate upon the pitted wood. Mazzoni and Stringer bent to their tasks, but they watched him. With the quizzing glass that always hung round his neck, he made a great show of peering at the plate.

"Destroyed, do you note?" said he.

Mazzoni came to look. He seemed surprised. "The first of the *Follies*. But, why?"

"You do not know?"

A shake of head.

Mr. Ralph had told us that engravings were sometimes copies of scenes the artist had previously painted. "Is there a painting of this?" asked Mr. Franklin.

Mazzoni nodded. "I did the draperies myself."

"What did it depict?"

"A lord. Showing guests about his country home."

175

"And where is this painting now?"

"Sold."

"To whom?"

"A gentleman. I do not recall his name."

Mr. Franklin turned away. "Mrs. Bone will know; I shall apply to her." He glanced toward the screen, behind which Mrs. Cray worked on James Cavitty's corpse singing a merry tune, as if the washing and dressing of dead limbs were all the world's delight. He strode to the door. "That is all for now— though it is not the end. Look to truth. Farewell." He walked out without a word more.

❧ 17 ❧

*IN WHICH Mr. Franklin reflects
on murder and pursues truth
out of town . . .*

We scraped through the afternoon in tasks left by the dead master. Mazzoni painted, Stringer varnished, and I ground color in oil and tucked odds and ends in cupboards and, when I could make no more work, huddled on a stool and drew a plaster torso. Walking by, Stringer struck me. "Mr. High and Mighty, awritin' things for the gentleman!" His blow reminded me that my book was still in my pocket; I wished I had given it to Mr. Franklin.

We all seemed to have forgot luncheon, and when Annie came to announce it long past one, we trooped down dejectedly. Two themes ran in murmurs round the servants' table: *Who could have done the awful deed?* and *What would become of us now?* The answer to the second lay with Mrs. Bone, and we gazed up speculatively, I picturing her thin, rigid form clasping Felicity to her breast. What would she do? What could she, if she awaited the doom of creditor's bills?

James Cavitty's body was to be laid out in the viewing room. A table being prepared, Mrs. Cray oversaw the last journey of the artist before his final one to the grave. I watched him carried by, waxen, his eyes mercifully closed, his long-fingered

177

hands crossed upon his chest, all the anger in him stilled. Secrets went with him. Could Mr. Franklin resurrect 'em?

At five, Signore Mazzoni was called upstairs. He came down a quarter of an hour later with a new light in his eye, striding straight to me: "*Attenzione,* take this letter to Sir Bartleby Bart explaining what has happened." Handing me an envelope, he said so no one else could hear, "Do not fear, I spoke for you." I had no idea what he meant, and he continued more loudly, "You are not needed at Cranbourne Street the next two days but are to return Monday morn, if Sir Bartleby will allow." Meaningly he eyed Stringer and Biggs. "*La padrona* will then have something to say to us all."

Stringer glowered at me as I went to put on my coat by the door, and I darted out quickly and hurried to the Strand, watching all the time for spying eyes. As I was early, I strode breathlessly on to Craven Street, arriving just in time to prevent Peter setting out to retrieve me.

In the front parlor Mrs. Stevenson was stitching up a Jacob's ladder. She sat in her clean dress by warm coals in the grate. I paused by the door. How dependable she looked in her white housewife's cap, how kindly, and I near rushed to kiss her round cheeks. "Thank you for a house in which murder is not done!" I longed to say.

She looked up. "Back so soon, Nicolas? Goodness, what high color you show. I hope you do not get the fever."

"O, no, ma'am. Thank you, ma'am. I shall go up." On the landing Polly hummed "Under the Greenwood Tree," as I mounted to Mr. Franklin's chamber.

I found him by the bow window. Beyond its casement a rose-colored dusk lit a sea of chimneypots spewing coalsmoke in gray, slanting plumes. London. He turned with a book in his hands. "You are early, Nick." He tutted. "What a day! But see

178

what I have been perusing: *An Essay on the Theory of Painting,* by Jonathan Richardson." Turning a page, he read, " 'The artist must avoid all low and sordid actions, all base and criminal passions. The way to be an Excellent Painter is to be an Excellent Man, to be placed amongst those whom all the world allow to be Gentlemen.' Ha! The way to be an excellent painter is to *appear* to be an excellent man—is that not nearer the mark? James Cavitty had no talent for appearances. Is that what did him in?" He shut the book. "Tell of Cranbourne Street."

I described the afternoon.

"Mrs. Bone did not come down?"

"No."

"But sent Signore Mazzoni with a note for Sir Bartleby Bart. Well, as I am the inventor of that redoubtable gentleman, I shall receive it." I gave it, and he broke the seal. "Hum, though she told Mazzoni 'twas for Sir Bartleby, she knew you would deliver it here, for it is writ to me. (I wonder how much she confides in the Italian.) In any case, she says little more than what he told you: that you are not to return 'til Monday. What does she intend? And what to make of Mazzoni's 'speaking in your favor'?" He tossed the note amongst other papers. "We must wait to find out. Now, as you have reported your afternoon to me, I shall tell you mine." Leaning upon his desk, he said, "Naturally I went first to Lady Shenstone, to tell her of the murder. Poor woman. There were no telling starts of guilt, though she displayed more agitation for herself than sorrow over Cavitty. Plainly she regards him as the one person who might have led us to her husband's diamond. All this for a polished stone. Never live for *things,* Nick; seek truth—speaking of which, the date of Lord Shenstone's official return is three days hence. Will that bring truth nearer our sight? In any case I spoke to John Fielding. Having been just apprised by his constable of the murder, he complained bitterly how his plate was heaped with crime; thus he was glad to let me look into matters for him—if he promised to pass on any significant gossip and to let me know if a valuable gem turned up in some receiver's hands. But a summation is due. Sit upon the bed." He sank into his armchair. "Be my judge. Say when I go astray."

Having in times past sat thus whilst he picked over the strands of some knotty matter, I took my place willingly.

Shadows deepened about the room as he spoke. "Lord and Lady Shenstone. A happy marriage, it seems, my lady assuring us she loves her husband despite his precious diamond, which he adores too much. He determines that a picture of her must be done; the gem shall be prominent in it. Having settled upon a painter, he leaves town—yet he does not truly leave; or, rather, he returns to town for purposes we do not know, taking coach for Dover, which is the opposite direction from his country estate. None of this he tells his wife. Meanwhile she is left to say if the artist is to have the gem overnight. The artist persuades her, she delivers it to him—and it disappears.

"The painting and the gem are all that link Shenstone with Cavitty, it seems—and yet we learn that the pair have for some time carried on a private business involving paintings from the continent. This business is at an end—there is a falling-out, bitter words—but more connects the two, for Cavitty's maid came from Lord Shenstone. This maid possesses a valuable ring which Shenstone gave her. Does it bear upon our mystery? Furthermore, both my lord and Cavitty seem well-off when just months ago they stood on shaky ground.

"To the artist. He is ambitious, likely marrying his first wife more to advance himself than out of love. I do not suggest he had any part in this wife's death, but her demise was undeniably convenient, for it set him up in his own studio. His sister

180

arrived to live with him; she managed his money well, by her account; but he still did not prosper for, though he had talent, he had an ill temper and an inclination to satire, which did not endear him to patrons. Yet he longed to rise; he sought a name amongst the very men whom he despised. The sister had a daughter, poisoned by arsenic, for which the sister never forgave her brother. Meanwhile she is made love to by his assistant, an Italian whom he met in Rome. Did Cavitty suspect their liaison? In any case this assistant bears watching, for he burns with ambitions which go beyond Fanny Bone.

"The gem comes into this *ménage*. It vanishes. Where? Who took it? For what purpose? Cavitty vows that he does not know where it has gone. Do I leave out anything, Nick?"

"Cully Stringer, sir."

"Indeed we must not forget him. What a suspicious note he adds, squeezed by Bertie Hexham, who is in turn squeezed by another man. Quimp? Does Quimp seek to lay his hands on the famous gem? But if neither he nor Cavitty knows where it has gone, who does?

"Then: murder. Cavitty looks to let a house in Grosvenor Square on the same day his advertisement for a series of satirical prints appears. On the night before that day he is stabbed in the throat. Who did it, Nick?"

"Someone wishing to prevent the removal? His sister?"

"Would she kill the man who fed and clothed her? And put a roof over her loved child's head?"

"Someone wishing to prevent the printing of the satires, then?"

"Who should wish to prevent that?"

"The man satirized."

"Precisely why I wish to see the painting from which the first plate was made." On the little table beside Mr. Franklin rested two objects: the pocket notebook he had taken from

James Cavitty's coat, and the small copperplate we had discovered under the larger one in the acid bath. He picked up the plate. "Nothing but ghosts of lines. Something was here, but it is irrevocably effaced." His eyes met mine. "Mere chance that it came to be in the acid?"

"If not, who placed it there?"

"And why?" He exchanged it for the octavo notebook, about four by six inches, its soft kid cover spotted with paint, its edges worn. "I have perused this—not a great deal of interest, mostly jottings of sitters and business to attend to, buying pigments, linen. But there are appointments: the one he kept with Lord Shenstone, for example; today's with the house agent, which, alas, he could not keep; other names: Noyce, the drapery man, Cope, Cavitty's printseller. Philippe duVerre provides the most suggestive entry." Mr. Franklin's eyes met mine. "Cavitty was to meet him at his establishment last night."

I felt a prick of excitement. "So that is where he went."

"Where his notebook *says* he went. What do you make of the Frenchman, Nick?"

"He is cool, not easily unmanned. But Cavitty's death shook him."

"He surely did not like it—though he was moved less by sorrow than by the inconvenience it caused. Do you recall what Ravenet said of him?"

"That he had to leave France."

" 'Twas only rumor, and yet . . ." Night had come on, Mr. Franklin but a silhouette. He stirred in the dark. "There were two crimes, Cavitty's murder and the effacing of the copperplates. How do they relate? Damn me, where is the Shenstone Diamond?"

* * *

182

Mr. Franklin went out that eve, as he often did. William supping with fellow students of law at the Middle Temple, Mrs. Stevenson, Polly, and I ate without their company. I took great pleasure in the small dining room off the warm, flagged kitchen, candles flickering like talismans to ward off evil. It was very different from Cranbourne Street, with its angers and murder; yet though I ought to have been happy to stay away from Number 23 I longed to return, for I chaffed to unmask the unknown.

Apples and cheese concluded our repast. Eyes bright, Polly pressed me for details of my day: "Tell ev'rything, Nick!" How to answer? Mr. Franklin liked to keep his investigations to himself (Mrs. Stevenson fretted him if she thought there was any danger), and he had told 'em only that he had placed me for a week or two with a painter, to see if the craft liked me. I dared not speak of lost gems and murder, but Polly's question proceeded from a desire for news of a world she could not explore, so I tried to please her, inventing gossip, embroidering truth.

Escaping, I mounted to Mr. Franklin's chamber to gaze out his window. London was mist-wrapped, the Thames a river of pitch in a cave of night. A cur howled, wanton laughter pealed, and a drunken man stumbled in a spill of light from a tavern near the Strand. In spite of these stridencies Spring hung like the note of a wildly beautiful song in the air, and I was troubled twice over, because of Annie, whose memory made me ache with desire, but more because of James Cavitty. Murdered! His pocket notebook still lay on Mr. Franklin's chairside table. Picking it up, I idly turned its pages, peering at the sketches interspersed amongst the writing: Mazzoni, Cully Stringer, Nick Handy. I was surprised to discover myself, for I did not know he had limned me. There I sat over my sketchbook, drawing. The portrait did not have his usual sting—it showed a student struggling at his art, in contrast to his portrayal of Cully Stringer, who was made into a boorish lump. Had Cavitty seen some of himself in me? Tears started to my eyes, for I could not help recalling Ebenezer Inch, my former master, who had also treated me well before he was taken by violent death.

A rapping on my door. "Up, Nick, for country air." Peeping over my coverlet in gray dawn light, I made out Mr. Franklin in his maroon dressing gown. Beckoning, he shut the door, whilst I stumbled to my feet. He had remarkable energy. I had heard him return to the watchman's cry of "Three bells!" Now at six he stirred like an eager colt.

Rubbing sleep from my eyes, I dressed. By six-thirty we were headed out of London, on the Great North Road.

"Before I left Cranbourne Street," said he in his round beaver hat, "I sent Peasgood to inquire of Mrs. Bone who had bought the painting from which that engraving of *The Follies of a Lord* was took. 'Twas the third earl of Bolfing. We go there now." I gazed out at fleecy blue sky. Beneath our wheels the road was treacherous with spring mud, but Peter drove expertly, so no quagmires entrapped us. Swallows dove. Farmers readied their fields for planting. At Finsbury we stopped by my dear mother's grave for a moment of remembering before plunging on.

Mr. Franklin talked on forgery. "Cavitty and Shenstone were conjoined in some enterprise that suited their talents, their connections. Cavitty could paint, and Shenstone knew men aplenty with the desire for art and the money to buy it. Did Cavitty, then, turn out Titians and Watteaus whilst Shenstone helped him pass 'em on?" He smiled. "But enough of speculation. Shall you hear of building forts in America?"

I had heard the tale before but always like to hear it again—spying Indians, massacred settlers, and the feel of winter in a faraway wilderness I hoped to see one day. His tale of Pennsylvania militiamen, whom he had commanded in 1756, lasted long enough to deliver us to a large Tudor manse much torn apart, for work was in progress upon it, the third earl giving his country home a fashionable Palladian facade.

Even the gardens were dug up to be replanted *à la mode*.

The earl himself was not present—or at least not present to such as we, a servant haughtily informed us; but the picture gallery was open to curious travelers, so we were let into a long echoing room flanked by tall windows. Some famous names hung there; I was especially taken with a Rembrandt *Elijah*. A number of dull family portraits gazed out too, but there were sufficient comic works to lighten the tone; the earl had a taste for satire. Two Hogarth paintings poked fun at electioneering, and his *Harlot's Progress* was on view, under glass.

We found James Cavitty's painting halfway along. It was large, some five feet by six, depicting a monstrously vast picture gallery in a wing of some gentleman's estate, the walls crowded with pictures, some hung on top of others, some pushed askew, the floor littered like a dockside warehouse with wooden crates from which paintings and marbles burst in a mad profusion. The most prominent crate had writ upon it *Masterpieces of Europe*, whilst the one next it, in barely smaller letters, proclaimed: *Fakes, which may pass for Masterpieces.* The lord of this domain led about a mindlessly gaping coterie of London gentry, and he passed by the two crates blithely unheeding of their labels. The implication was plain: he would hang anything on his walls. He wore a look of rapacious avidity, but we did not know his face.

"Plainly aimed at the *faux connoisseur*," said Mr. Franklin when half an hour later we ate luncheon in an inn yard under a beech bursting with greenery. Crocuses pushed up through the hillocks nearby. "The third earl has a fine sense of irony to hang that which might be taken to satirize him. Cavitty's painting was excellent, was't not? Yet, having seen the original, we still do not know how the artist altered his engraving of't." He rose. "To London, for more seeking. Come, Nick. Come, good Peter."

During the jostling hours back to Craven Street, Mr. Franklin seemed to doze. For my part, hardly aware of the villages and little farm steadings that passed, I puzzled over who had done the murder. I longed to lay out the truth for Mr. Franklin when he woke, to see the approving light in his eye, but I could not find my way to it. I began to be distracted by something else. In addition to our own, four or five conveyances had dotted the inn yard, one set afar off by a copse—a black coach. Many such coaches were black, but this one jogged behind us now—or one that looked like it. It stayed well back. When Peter slowed, it slowed, and when he traveled fast it hurried to keep up but never drew near. I watched it as the road curved, its driver a cloaked shape, its occupant a mystery. Should I wake Mr. Franklin? But he need not be fretted by the imaginings of a boy, though I kept an eye peeled and vowed to alert him should the coach draw near. It never did, and as we entered Moorgate, upon the twisting, crowded ways of the City, it vanished, and I sank back. Had its business been with us?

I was startled to find Mr. Franklin awake. "You saw the coach too, eh? Followed us, did it?—but who should take so great an interest in plain Ben Franklin?" He stretched. " 'Tis near three. I shall leave you at Craven Street, where you are to practice your Latin, which has sorely suffered during your time at Cavitty's. Yet you are to sup with me this eve at Mrs. Goodbody's; the lady takes a very great interest in Cranbourne Street. For my part, I go to call upon Phillippe duVerre."

186

18

*IN WHICH we sup with a lady, hear of
a Frenchman, and Cranbourne Street is
shaken once more . . .*

I found genitives, datives and ablatives very hard to fix my
mind on when murder was so much more interesting a
subject, but I bent myself under Latin's yoke. In the manner of English skies, the morning's blue gave way to gray by
four, gusts at five, rain at six, devolving to dripping eaves and
running gutters at seven, when Mr. Franklin returned to take
me to supper. As usual Polly begged to go, whilst her mother
stood by the door, frowning. She was little fond of Mrs. Goodbody, who wooed her beloved lodger from Craven Street; thus
we ran a double gauntlet. But, braving it, we were driven by
Peter in clean-washed air. Swaying through the inky streets,
Mr. Franklin hummed. He was eager to reveal something—his
eyes shone bright—but I knew I must bide my time 'til he
chose the moment.

We were at Mrs. Goodbody's by eight: a tidy red brick
house, number 52 Wild Street, near where Mr. Franklin had
practiced printing when he first came to London, at age nineteen. Betsy, the maid, showed us to the parlor where our hostess stood by the hearth. Comfort Goodbody was a handsome,
plumpish woman, somewhat of Mr. Franklin's age, in a dark

187

green dress with a white satin underskirt, her reddish hair, little touched by gray, tucked neatly under a cap. Her eyes were blue, wise and kind, her smile welcoming. She smelt of apples.

She allowed Mr. Franklin to kiss her hand before examining me. "You are growing, Nicolas. An inch taller, to be sure." She pursed her lips at the gentleman. "He is becoming a man."

"Indeed, in many ways."

We sat round the fire and, Betsy delivering libations, Mr. Franklin began by inquiring of Drury Lane, where Mrs. Goodbody was wardrobe mistress under David Garrick. This led to a quarter hour's news of Mrs. Cibber and Mrs. Clive and the other actors and actresses amongst whom the gentleman had recently exorcised murder. "And are the designs for new lighting, which I made for Garrick, proceeding?" asked he.

"I assure you they are, and certain to make a great improvement."

Candlelight flickered, the fire crackled. I sat deep in a well-padded chair. As the man and woman conversed I thought how fortunate I was to be amongst 'em. Their cadences might turn grave or bantering, but they were always well-expressed, and I hoped one day I might talk so wittily. Yet I heard more, for underlying their words flowed a current of intimacy. Mr. Franklin was far distant from his wife; further, he was uncertain how much longer he must remain in London. I had often observed how the ladies liked him—he was not the handsomest of men, built like a sturdy keg, but 'twas words more than looks that conquered women, it seemed, and no man was better at words than Benjamin Franklin. In short he had the needs of a man, and from the moment he had encountered Mrs. Goodbody at Drury Lane he had taken special note of her and she of him. This had flowered, they had formed an understanding, and when he crept in at three bells o' the morn I knew 'twas likely from his dear friend's arms.

I had come in two short months to love her too. Much like Mrs. Stevenson, she was another mother to me.

Plainly Mr. Franklin had already confided much of our mystery to her, for 'twas she who had sent him Lady Shenstone. "To my visit to Phillippe duVerre," said he at last.

I slipped my small book from my pocket. Here from its pages is what the gentleman told us:

. . . After leaving you, Nick, Peter delivered me promptly, so that I arrived by four. I had already sent word I wished to speak to duVerre, so I was expected. He lives not far from Joshua Reynolds, near that same Leicester Square to which Cavitty wished to move his establishment. He has a fine shop in Princes Street: a display room and a workshop just behind, where his assistant, an ink-smudged fellow with huge arms for pulling the press, serves him. His living quarters are above. He has no wife.

He is handsome, of the ascetic type, with a head like one o' those marble Romans the gentry put about their houses these days. He met me with great punctilio in his short white wig and his tight-fitting suit of clothes. He was solicitous about Cavitty's murder, pressing his hands together and hoping I brought news about who had stabbed him.

"I am sorry to report that the villain is not yet discovered."

We stood in his workroom. "Damn him for discommoding me!" muttered the Frenchman.

I looked surprise. "Is not the dead man more discommoded?"

Small spots of red appeared in his cheeks. "Do not mistake my meaning, monsieur. I only meant that I counted upon printing the *Follies*, and now I cannot."

"Your fee has flown, you mean?"

"I am disappointed that I cannot collect it." His fingers flicked at his sides.

"Only natural." I had no desire to provoke him. "It is remarkable how many people murder disappoints—though it always pleases one."

"Hardly *this* one."

"Just so."

He rose and fell on his heels. "And why has monsieur come to me?"

"Mrs. Bone has given me leave to look into her brother's death."

"But why?"

"Because I have brought one or two murderers to ground. It is a hobby of mine."

He peered at me whilst his assistant grunted at the press handle. "How very peculiar. I pray you bring this one to ground as well."

"I am on the scent." I told him of the acid-eaten copper-plate.

"Incroyable!"

"I agree. But why should it be destroyed at the same time Cavitty was done in?"

"Might it not have been put in the acid long before he was murdered?"

"You are right. For that matter, it may have been dropped in hours afterward. And yet—" Pulling the other small plate from my pocket, I showed it him. "This too was in the bath."

He hardly looked at it. "O?"

"It is just as destroyed. Do you know what it might be? What picture may've been engraved upon it?"

"Mais, non. Cavitty never showed me such a thing. It is the size of a book illustration."

"Indeed, likely that is what it is—or was. You help me well. But what book? Cavitty sometime did such work?"

"I believe so."

"Any recent?"

"You must speak to his assistant about that. Or the booksellers."

"I shall surely seek 'em out. As for the *Follies,* they satirize collectors of art, that much I have learnt—but not how Cavitty wished to alter the plates."

"*Je regrette.* I cannot help you there either, for he would not give me leave to print even one 'til he had altered all, and that, alas, he never did."

"You did not see any of 'em?"

"I glimpsed one or two, but not enough to guess his intent."

This seemed to go against what you overheard, Nick, but I did not say so. "He discommoded more than you, then: his subscribers, his printseller."

"Monsieur Cavitty was a very willful man."

"He angered you by it?"

"At times."

"You disliked him?"

A smile, almost of contempt. "Anger is a waste, and I do not like waste. Anger would not have been to my profit. James Cavitty was not a successful painter—I mean, he did not find the patronage he sought. But he had begun to make a name in satire. He was no Hogarth, but he did well in prints. Who knows what he might have achieved? His latest series was subscribed well. The town began to look for his name at the bottom of an engraving. He sneered at this sort of fame—he wanted to paint prophets and angels, like Michelangelo or Raphael—but he could have made a reputation in the printshops, and thus I would have done handsomely too. *Enfin*, I am sorry he has slipped through my fingers. Do I speak too frankly?"

"You speak honestly. But, then . . . why did you not speak as honestly yesterday? Why not confess that Cavitty visited you the night before his murder?"

DuVerre appraised me. "I see why you are successful at your hobby. But you knock at the wrong door. I did not tell you he had visited me, because he did not."

"He was meant to."

"Why do you believe so?"

"You confess that he was?"

"Is it so very important?" He spread his hands. *"Voilà*, I confess, with neither shame nor guilt."

I took out the paint-smeared notebook. "He wrote the appointment in here."

"Ah." He glanced from it to me. "Mrs. Bone has chosen well."

"But the appointment was not kept, you say?"

"It was not."

"What was its purpose?"

"I do not know. Cavitty asked to see me. I merely acquiesced."

"When did he make this appointment?"

"Wednesday."

"One day before the murder. Were you in the habit of meeting at night?"

"Pas du tout. But he was capricious as well as willful. Thinking he wished to deliver some of the *Follies*—and planning in any case to be at home—I sent word he might stop round when he wished."

"Were you surprised when he did not arrive?"

"No. A note came at seven to say he had another engagement. It said he was going to Lord Shenstone's."

I frowned. "To see whom? My lord? Or his lady?"

"I presumed his lordship."

"His lordship was out of town."

"O?"

I felt jostled upon a new track, laid with snares. "Did you save the note?"

"I had no reason to do so."

"Do you know his lordship?"

"Shenstone? He has bought prints in my shop. I crossed his path at Cavitty's two or three times."

"Cavitty painted his wife. You have seen the portrait?"

"Indeed. *Une femme très belle.* Not the usual satire."

"He painted the Shenstone Diamond too."

"The famous gem. The question I ask, monsieur, is . . . why did Shenstone choose him to paint anything? They plainly did not care for one another."

"How do you know?"

"I have heard that they fought."

"Why?"

"I cannot guess Shenstone's reason. As for Cavitty, he could be provoked by a trifle."

I looked about duVerre's well-ordered workshop. All was scrubbed, neat, tidy, no wayward ink on wall or jamb.

Would that our mystery were so tidy.

The burly assistant continued to crank the press amidst prints hanging to dry. I turned back. "So Shenstone may've been the last man to see Cavitty alive. . . ."

DuVerre lifted a brow. "Surely, monsieur, you cannot think his lordship—?"

"I do not yet know what I think. Thank you for speaking with me." He bowed and we returned to the display room, where I examined the engravings hung on the walls. How skilled the Frenchman is. He had done the prints for sev'ral artists—half a dozen names were in evidence—and I praised his work, which drew from him a smile which seemed to know such praise was due. "England is fortunate to have you, sir,—but, why did you leave France?"

He answered easily, "There are fewer French engravers here; I do not compete against so many. I am appreciated by the English far more than ever I was in my native land."

"I see." Amadeo Mazzoni had replied similarly. How well did the two know one another? "Plainly you have improved your fortune," said I.

"By hard work."

"Hard work sweetens success. But I see that someone is here, to inquire about prints . . ." A fellow in a fine yellow coat had just walked in. "I shall take my leave." Yet I did not go, but, as the Frenchman went to greet the arrival, I wandered into the printing room, where I accosted the thick-set assistant who worked the press. "Excellent work. And a very fine shop. How long has your master occupied these premises?"

A coal-eyed face swiveled up. "Four months." His accent told that he was French too.

"And before that?"

"In Watling Street, near St. Paul's."

I patted him on the shoulder. "O, not near as good a street . . ."

Mrs. Goodbody smoothed her dress as Mr. Franklin ended his account. "Is Lord Shenstone the man who stabbed James Cavitty?" asked she.

"Shenstone was out of town."

"You seem to think he may not have been."

The chatter of a lamplighter's pole sounded from the street. "If he was not, it may be very bad for him! What did he at

Dover? And what was his business with Cavitty the night before the murder?—if it was he whom Cavitty visited."

Mrs. Goodbody tilted her head. "And if it was not? If it was Lady Shenstone he went to see?"

The gentleman puffed air. "Then she plays some very odd game." His fingers drummed. "But I have more news, from Joseph de Medina: The Shenstone Diamond is for sale."

Mrs. Goodbody set down her drink. "Can it be?"

"De Medina says so, and I believe him, for no one knows the world of gems better than he. He assures me that negotiations are now proceeding to sell it to a continental buyer, a Dutchman, he believes. 'Tis meant to be secret, but men whisper, especially about so famous a gem. Rumors float—but this is more than rumor."

"But who is selling it, sir?" asked I.

"On that head rumor appears silent. Only one thing is certain: the man will reap a fortune."

"Or woman," amended our hostess as flames sighed in the grate.

Mr. Franklin smiled. "You need not remind me that your sex is capable of wickedness, ma'am."

"La, sir." She rose with a rustle of skirts. "But here is Betsy. Let us sup."

Mrs. Goodbody's cook outdid herself, with a pigeon pie, roast veal, salmon with fennel, followed by a pudding made of apples and cream covered in brandy-soaked crumbs, and we rode home at eleven pleasantly stuffed by the repast, Mr. Franklin silent and thoughtful, rocking to the clip-clop of our mare echoing against brick and plaster and time-worn wood. In the light of passing streetlamps he wore a look of deep thought, his lips pursed, his brow knit.

What would bring an end to this?

* * *

Sunday I rose late, past nine, but when I hurried to Mr. Franklin's chamber I found him barely risen. Morning passed in desultory fashion. Around one he and William went to dine with the Quaker mercer, William Collinson, with whom Mr. Franklin had corresponded for years. Left at loose ends, I wandered by the Thames watching wherries and lighters under a ragged sky whilst I skipped stones in the dun brown current. Tall masts lifted from the westward docks, and Parliament stood like a bulwark against the southward curve of the river. I fought a desire to walk to Cranbourne Street just to gaze at the windows of Number 23. Did Annie have Sunday free? If she did, might I see her? But I did not go but trudged doggedly to help Mrs. Stevenson about the house and put my notes in order for Mr. Franklin.

Were the person who had murdered James Cavitty and he who sought to sell the Shenstone Diamond one and the same?

Monday morn drew round, the coach driven by Peter delivering me to Cranbourne Street by seven, all breathless, my coat pocket carrying my note, signed with Sir Bartleby Bart's name, giving me leave to hear out Mrs. Bone.

I entered by the back way.

I discovered disarray.

Pictures were tipped from their shelves in the storage room as if a great wind had blown through it, and when I hurried into the painting room, I spied more to appall me: the Chinese screens flattened upon the floor and all the properties which I had so carefully put away—draperies, plaster columns, the stuffed goose—strewn about as if by a madman. The drawers of the artist's cabinet were spilt, copperplates lay on the floor, brushes and paint pots were scattered.

Cully Stringer stood in the center of the room, trembling.

Eyes narrowed, he turned. "I don't s'pose *you* know anythin' about this, Handy?"

"W-what?" was all I could reply.

In a sudden fury he flung out an arm. "Can't you *see*? Someone broke in last night. Did a proper job, they did. Even tipped the master's body from his table."

"T-tipped him?" Though I was stunned, I noted that amidst the destruction Lady Shenstone had not been touched, as if she were inviolable. She stood in cool dignity on her easel, witness to yet another infamy she could not name.

I looked back at Stringer, pale beneath his black shock of hair. His words had lashed out at me but not his fists. Fear rimmed his eyes, he quaked as if with ague, and I shook too.

*IN WHICH Mr. Franklin prints some
pictures, I am closeted with a girl, and
two conspirators tell over their days . . .*

I became aware of commotion about the house, a confusion
of footsteps and voices. Stringer seemed rooted in place, so
it was easy to slip past him into the entryway. It too had
not escaped attack, for the carpet was flung aside, and the ar-
moire by the stairs had been emptied of drawers, which lay
scattered. No one was in sight, no one to gainsay me; so, with
fearful anticipation, I pressed on into the viewing parlor. Disorder met my eyes here too: cushions flung up from chairs,
more drawers spilled, the delicately pointing finger of the marble hand broke by the heel of some boot. Though appalled, I
tried to make my mind work calmly. Observe, Nick. Look
close. Plainly there had been a search for something—yet, in
spite of the appearance of haste, care had been taken; the
household had not been waked in the night.

The chamber smelled of rose petals, to cover the odor of
death. My gaze found James Cavitty. A trestle table had been
erected at the far end of the room where, in a velvet suit finer
than any I had seen him wear in life, he had been laid out so
people might pay their respects before the funeral this eve.

How many had come? He seemed to have few friends, but in any case I hoped none arrived now, for his body had been tumbled upon the floor, where it sprawled ignominiously, like one of his lay figures, jaw slack, wig askew, the neck cloth which had covered his wound pulled aside so the puncture showed like a bruised, puckered mouth.

At this moment Signore Mazzoni came in. His dusky eyes met mine. "So, you are here." A glance at the body. *"Dio mio.* You must help me put him on the table. *La signora* Bone must not see her brother like this."

We went to the man and, I at the feet, Mazzoni at the shoulders, succeeded in lifting him. How heavy he felt, a weight of spiritless matter! But we arranged him upon the table, the Italian replacing his wig whilst I refolded the cold, limp hands.

We stood back.

"Please, sir, what happened?" asked I.

"Someone came in the night. The front door was unlatched. Peasgood found things as you see them."

I could hardly believe it. "Unlatched a *second* time, sir?"

"It is what Peasgood says." Mazzoni waved a hand. *"Basta,* to the painting room. It must be put right; you and Stringer must do it." He gazed bleakly round the walls. Some paintings lay on the floor, others hung askew. Had something been hid behind one? Was that why they had been disturbed?

"Yet they took none. . . ." murmured the Italian. He frowned at me. "Hurry, boy." His voice rang with a tone of command I had never heard before.

By ten Cully Stringer and I had returned the painting room to near its former state. Objects had been scattered but nothing broke save a crockery pot in which brushes waited to be cleaned, so it was a matter only of picking things up and scrubbing spilt paint from the floor. As we worked I wondered: did the intruders find what they sought? I shuddered. Murder, then this: desperate acts. Did more wait in store?

At ten-thirty Mrs. Bone called the household to the painting room. Mid-morning light slanted wanly through the big front window as Mrs. Cockle shuffled in sniffing, followed by Annie, who sent a pale glance my way. Both wore black, as did Peasgood, who looked raddled by his morning's discovery and the setting aright which he must do, for even belowstairs had been searched. Biggs slipped in. He had been absent from the kitchen hearth again last night, I had learnt. Out about London? I peered at the cynical-eyed urchin, who met my look boldly. How far could he be trusted? Biggs, Stringer, Signore Mazzoni, and I had been given black armbands and, wearing 'em, we stood respectfully against the west wall with the rest as Mrs. Bone came in, in black too, her features chalk white. Felicity wore a severe ebon frock and clung to her mother's skirts. Did the poor waif understand what had occurred? Could she comprehend death, much less murder?

Mrs. Bone was plainly under great strain but proved mistress of herself, and after a moment, in which she sent Signore Mazzoni one of her quick, meaning glances, she cleared her throat:

"We have been broke in upon as you all well know. I shall speak of that later. First: you have been wondering what will become of you. Such thoughts are natural. I am here to answer 'em. I shall not mince words. My brother is passed on, but I am determined his death shall not scatter this household. My news to you is that Signore Amadeo Mazzoni will become master of the painting studio." There was a stir at this, followed by glances at the Italian, who stood a little apart. He refused to meet any gaze, but he was not expressionless, for there was an unmistakable air of triumph about him.

200

Mrs. Bone went on. "I have run this household well and shall continue to oversee it. This new arrangement is unusual—how often does a woman employ a painter in this fashion?—but necessity requires it, and I shall not give up to convention what my brother won hard. It will be difficult at first; Signore Mazzoni has not the reputation of my brother. But he is equally skilled—equally, I say!—and so I have directed him to complete all unfinished works. We shall present these to the ladies and gentlemen who commissioned 'em, we shall hope for the best. I count upon quality to persuade." Something near a smile trembled upon her lips. "We hope that one day the name Amadeo Mazzoni may count for something." She sobered. "As a practical matter this will redound to all who choose to remain. Peasgood has said he will stay, yet I am aware that some of you may feel the house is cursed. This is foolishness, but if any amongst you wishes to give notice, speak up now." Only silence met this. "Very well," said Mrs. Bone. "As for you," her eyes found me, "Signore Mazzoni will be as good a master to you as my brother, and you may remain under the terms of your uncle's agreement 'til such time as he removes or apprentices you. I have writ a letter expressing this." She held out a sealed paper. "I hope you may stay."

I took the note. "Thank you, ma'am." Her eyes conveyed by a brief, meaning widening that the note was for show; she well knew there was no Sir Bartleby Bart. Did Mazzoni? Did his "speaking for me" mean he had argued that I be allowed to remain? Truly, he needed more than the likes of Cully Stringer to make a success.

Mrs. Bone's expression darkened. "I must make one emendation. Unknown persons entered this house last night. Three days ago, someone murdered my brother. If any of you are found to have colluded in this—or, God forbid, to've done the deed—I shall prosecute you to the lengths of the law. I shall see you hanged. I shall show no quarter." Turning, like an icy wind she blew out of the room with her daughter.

A shudder ran amongst us. "I must," said Mrs. Cockle, "boil my beef," and she hurried from the chamber. Annie followed. Peasgood. Biggs.

Signore Mazzoni remained with Stringer and me. He turned his gaze upon us. "You have understood Mrs. Bone's words? I am master of painting now?"

"Yes, sir," said we.

"*Bene.* You shall do as I say. I shall make a success." He looked out the window, eyes alight. He seemed to peer into a hopeful future, yet there was no haughtiness to him; and, recalling his way with patrons, ingratiating but not obsequious, I believed he might make a success. Mazzoni would depict the *ton* however they wished; he would never paint their blemishes, and it would hardly prick his conscience that his brush lied.

Had he lied otherwise? Had he murdered?

There was, at once, a new atmosphere in the painting room, as if Mazzoni had long planned how to replace Cavitty's uneven hand with his more steady one. I took over painting the background of the conversation piece. This had been Stringer's job, and I braced myself for his cry of protest, but he was mute. Struggling with inner demons, he submitted meekly to his new master's command.

I had not known what time Mr. Franklin meant to return, so I was relieved when just past eleven he came into the painting room. Peasgood, who had shown him in, informed him of the housebreaking.

Mr. Franklin was grave. "The latch left open again? By whom?"

Peasgood's old head wobbled. "We do not know."

"And the body desecrated—what effrontery! A ransacking, you say. Was anything taken?"

"We are missing nothing yet, sir, but cannot tell for sure, as there is much still to put aright."

"How, pray, is Mrs. Bone?"

"Aggrieved. But she was capable of speaking to us. No one is to be let go."

"Very fine of her." Mr. Franklin rubbed his jaw a moment, but roused himself. Though the news was bad it would not deter him; he had come to print the second and third of the *Follies*, he said, and meant to do so. "They, at least, were not destroyed by acid." Plainly Mazzoni did not like his first hours as master challenged, but he made no protest. Doffing his coat and pulling on Cavitty's apron, Mr. Franklin went to the workbench. He had printed currency for Pennsylvania, so he knew what he was about. Inking a plate, he wiped it with a brisk slapping of his palm, fit dampened paper onto it. The blankets and tympan came next; then: into the press, and crank it through.

When the gentleman peeled off the paper he turned the image so I might see. The face of the satirized connoisseur had become Lord Shenstone's.

Handing me the first engraving to hang, Mr. Franklin printed the next, which proved Lord Shenstone too, even more damning than the other—my lord was a poseur and an opportunist, it said; he passed on forgeries. If these had been distributed, would London have distinguished betwixt truth and calumny? Remembering the leering faces of the mob outside Carrington Bowles, I felt sure they would have fed on the slander. Shenstone's reputation would have been besmirched, his name become a laughingstock.

Yet were they slander?

Mazzoni looked at the prints too. He appeared shaken, and his dusky eyes showed he saw all too well what the publishing of the prints would have meant.

Did they confirm that Lord Shenstone had murdered James Cavitty?

"I do not like it," muttered Mr. Franklin. Going to Cully Stringer, he drew him aside. "I have told you I am your friend." His voice was low, but I could hear each word, Stringer staring with gaping longing, as if he wished more than anything to unburden himself. "Come to me at any time." Mr. Franklin gave his arm a squeeze, and though Stringer said nothing his eyes yearned like a friendless pup's.

Mr. Franklin called Peasgood to him. "Did anyone inquire of the watch, to see what he saw in the night?"

"No . . ." came the quavering reply.

"Then I must do it." Though the prints were not yet dry Mr. Franklin took 'em down. He turned to Mazzoni. "By the by, did your master engrave book illustrations of late?"

"Not that I know."

"But he sometimes did such things?"

"*Sì.*"

"Thus he might've had old plates about. Depicting what?" This question seemed directed only to himself, and he strode out carefully carrying the prints.

Luncheon was a glum half hour. Signore Mazzoni was not amongst us. Did he now eat with Mrs. Bone?

Afterward I stole a moment with Annie, beckoning her into the still room where we could not be seen. Its confines smelt of herbs. We stood close. "How are you, Annie?" said I.

Her round face with its flyaway wisps of hair turned up. "I am glad not to lose my place."

I brushed a tail of hair from her brow. "Do you know anything of this? Of the murder? Or who came in last night? How the door came to be unlatched yet again?"

"O, Nicolas," cried she softly, biting her lip, "why do you ask?"

"Because the person who did this thing must be caught."

"If I told . . . O . . . O . . . I am a wicked girl!" Clasping my hand, she held it to her breast, so that once more I felt soft flesh beneath cloth, the beating heart. I was stirred but bewildered. What did she mean?

"Told what, Annie?"—but at that moment Cully Stringer loomed in the door. How long had he listened? I made ready to fight him if necessary, but to my great surprise his black-browed face was gone almost as soon as I saw it.

I turned back. Annie was rigid with some powerful emotion. "Has he harmed you . . . forced you . . . might he—?"

"I am a wicked girl!" sobbed she.

"Annie!" But she fled before I could catch her, leaving me alone in the little chamber, empty-handed. I was in no settled state as I mounted the back stairs, but more was to come: Cully Stringer caught my arm as I passed the storage room. He pulled me in amongst the paintings.

He held me near, hands gripping like iron, a fierce deliberation on his face. Was the fight to be now? Recalling all Mr. Franklin had taught me, I braced myself to give as good as I got—but no blow came. Sweat gleaming on his lip, he poured fear-soaked breath into my face. "Hear. This Benjamin Franklin. You writ for him. What of him, then?"

"What do you mean?"

He shook me. "Answer me, mole! D'you trust him?"

"Yes," chattered I.

"Where's he live?"

"Craven Street. Number seven. Near the Thames."

The apprentice wiped a hand across his mouth. "Number

seven." As if I were no longer significant, he thrust me away and pushed out of the room. "Is it really so?" I heard him mumble, bleakly hopeful. "Really, really so?" Clumping round the Chinese screens, he left me to rub my aching arms.

Mr. Franklin tipped back his cup of tea, which Mrs. Stevenson had just delivered. "And that is all your day, Nicolas?"

I sipped from my own cup. "All, sir." We sat in armchairs in the front parlor looking out upon Craven Street. It was just five; Signore Mazzoni had given me leave to depart two hours early, to tell Sir Bartleby of Mrs. Bone's offer.

Mr. Franklin gazed over his cup rim. "Sir Bartleby shall allow you to remain in Cranbourne Street only so long as you keep safe," said he. "Annie called herself 'wicked,' did she? You must try to discover why. And Mazzoni is painting master, eh? Does he bed Fanny Bone, do you think? More to the point, did he murder Cavitty to gain his foothold? Did the sister collude? Would she do in her brother to gain a living for her lover and a father for her daughter?" Sinking back, he shook his head. "Yet Shenstone remains to plague us." Beside him on the sofa lay the two prints, now dry. "Here my lord dispenses money for forgeries"—he tapped one—"and here"—he tapped the other—"having discovered 'em to be false, he passes 'em on to an even more gullible fool. London would've roared. Did Shenstone stab Cavitty to stop him?"

"How would he learn that Cavitty altered the plates in this way?"

"Just so. DuVerre knew they were altered. (He claims he did not know how, yet he may.) Did he tell Shenstone?"

"Why should he?"

Mr. Franklin fretted. "Why and why and why? Alas, I do not know. For that matter, Mazzoni might've told him. Or Cully

Stringer. Or anyone in the house. Better ask if there was some truth to the attack. Was Shenstone truly a purveyor of false pictures?"

"And murdered Cavitty to conceal it?"

"He recouped his fortune somehow, so two powerful motives may have incited him. But if Shenstone is our murderer, why did he not drop the second and third plates into the acid?"

"He believed only the first had been altered?"

"Possibly. To other matters. I went to the Hazard today. Take out your book, lad." He laced his fingers across his chest. "Write my tale."

The Hazard was London's most infamous gaming house. This what I set down:

. . . Lord Shenstone [said Mr. Franklin] told his lady the great turn in his fortunes came at the gaming tables. Thus I took myself round to Gideon Kite's iniquitous den, where Shenstone claimed to've made his killing. I did not like to go—as you will recall, it was at one of its card tables that I delivered Quimp himself a nasty defeat which near got my brains beat in—but I did, and the evil little dwarf, himself, consented to see me. Kite wore his macaroni wig and his red, painted smile, and cooed that I must play him a hand, "for old time's sake." I demurred, putting questions. Yes, Shenstone used to play there often, said Kite, faro, *vingt-une*, roly-poly. "He had a positive relish for it!"

"Was he lucky?"

"Luck is a will-o'-the-wisp. No, he was not."

"He won, then, no grand sum of money?"

"Tush, he lost heavily, poor man. But I hear he has replenished his fortune. Do you know him, Franklin? Persuade him to come round, and if there is fleece to be sheared we shall both have something from it." No, said I, and departed. Kite is a damned, conniving ferret, yet I believe he told true about Shenstone: my lord did not recoup his fortune by gaming.

But that was not all, for I went next to Cope, Cavitty's bookseller, who had heard of the murder and unburdened himself of many sanctimonious mutterings. I inquired if Cavitty had lately worked on engravings for a book, but Cope knew of none.

I went, too, to the Shenstone townhouse, where I learnt surprising news. But your pencil grows dull, Nick. Shave it so you may write more. . . .

❧ 20 ❧

*IN WHICH Mr. Franklin tells of a
lady and a lord . . .*

Mr. Franklin continued his tale:

. . . Lord and Lady Shenstone reside in a grand house in St. James's Street, not far from St. James's Palace. I was shown into its drawing room just past two, all gilt and white, with three tall windows.

I was in no easy state of mind. Might my lady's husband be a murderer? How far could I trust her?

I found her playing with her little son, Tobias, a lad of four; Toby, she called him, and urged him to greet me like a man, which he did, making an excellent bow. He rode for a while on a broomstick horse. Plainly his mother hated to part with him, but she called the governess to take him.

She wore a green lawn gown, her rich, brown hair covered by neither wig nor lace. Her umber eyes peered anxiously as she bade me sit in the chair opposite. "The diamond? Have you found it?"—this in one quick breath. At my regretful no she heaved a sigh. "Then all is lost."

"It may yet be recovered."

"At this date? With Cavitty dead?" Her fingers knotted. "I

must inform you, Mr. Franklin, that my husband is returned."

"He is here now?"

She nodded bleakly. "A full four days before I looked for him."

"When did he arrive?"

"Saturday, noon."

In time to stab an artist? "Did he say why he came back early?"

"His business was concluded sooner than expected."

"He is in the house this moment?"

"He is—though would he were not, Mr. Franklin! Would he were about town as of old, cheerful, for he has not gone out since he returned."

I was moved by her agitation. "Indoors ev'ry moment? Surely he has taken the air a little. Perhaps last night?"

"No." Her chagrin deepened. "That is . . . I cannot say for sure. We do not share the same chamber. He locks himself in his library. He broods dreadfully. I must tell you more: I have informed him about the diamond. I had to, for he wished me to wear it. When I told him why it was missing, he raged and cursed. He would fly to Cavitty, he shouted, he would wring out of him where his diamond had gone. 'You cannot,' said I. 'Cavitty is murdered.' At this he stared in such a manner that I blurted ev'ry detail, including all I have learnt from you—little enough, though you are not to blame. Since then he is sunk in despair." Tears spilt upon the woman's cheeks. "What irony. I feared his ire would be turned toward me, but he has turned it upon himself, it seems, and closets himself and mutters and eats little and will see no one save our precious Toby, whom he holds upon his lap whilst he mutters over and over, 'What have I done?' "

I tried to put the best face on it. "Surely this is a passing fit. He will recover. You can weather the storm."

"Can we? I hoped so, but finances have begun to trouble me. The housekeeper brought me several bills, long past due, which I did not know about. But when I knocked and told my lord of 'em, he cried through the door that the creditors must hang, for they never could be paid."

I did not know how to answer this. "You must not give up on the diamond. Ben Franklin is on the scent, and he is a persistent hound. May I ask more questions?"

She dabbed a handkerchief at her eyes. "If you think they may help."

"First: did James Cavitty come to see you the night before his murder?"

"Whyever should he do that?"

"That is what I wish to learn. Someone put it in my ear."

She was adamant. "If he came—and he did not—I would never let him past my door unless he brought the diamond and begged forgiveness!"

"I shall, then, pay the rumor no mind. But I am still curious about Cavitty. Why did your husband choose such a little-known man for your portrait? Others are more fashionable."

"I presume because they were on the Grand Tour together."

"Ah! I had heard Cavitty guided some young man about Italy; I did not guess it was your lord. So they have known one another some time."

"They were abroad near a year."

"And have kept up their acquaintance?"

"They have had dealings in paintings."

"What sort, pray?"

"I do not know."

"Your husband does not make you privy to such matters?"

She wiped the tearstains from her cheeks. "Few husbands do."

"As you say. Your financial smooth sailing these past months—it coincided with your lord's dealings with Cavitty?"

She peered hard. "Now you say so, yes. You imply that is why we have been well off?"

"I could not do that, for your husband said his fortunes were recouped by gaming."

Her small frown said that she began to doubt.

"I have heard there was some rancor betwixt the men."

"I do not know of it—though I could understand if there were."

"Indeed, many did not care for Cavitty. So your husband has concluded the business on his country estate. He spoke of nothing that might have took him elsewhere?"

"No."

"By the by: a young woman—Annie, I believe she is called—is employed as underhousemaid in the Cavitty household. She came from this place, she said, two or three years ago. Is this true?"

"Annie . . . ? You must ask my husband. This is his house, which we occupy only part of the year. He hires and dismisses all the servants; though, come to think on it, some were let go at about the time you say, when he determined we did not need so large a staff. Why do you ask?"

"No significant reason. The girl spoke well of your husband, that is all."

"He is a good master."

Generous, too, giving valuable rings to maids. "May I speak to him?"

"O, I do not think, in his state—"

"Yet he may be able to help me in my task. And I may be able to set his mind at ease. Will you tell him I am come? If he refuses, I shall go at once."

She frowned but said she would try and departed in a rustle

of skirts, whilst I spent my time strolling the hall outside the drawing room. This was a customary site for art, but, though my lord was said to be a connoisseur, he displayed precious few pictures save a dozen family portraits brown with age and dull in execution. Yet ghost shapes on the walls said there had been other works. Where now? Passed on through Cavitty's agency? Cavitty's engravings damned Shenstone, but a paradox plagued me: if the artist had helped pass on forged works did he not implicate himself by the satire of my lord, which he had meant to publish?

What had the man been about?

Lady Shenstone returned to say that her husband had agreed to come down. Her expression still wondered if the meeting were wise, but she departed to letters she said she must write whilst I returned to the drawing room.

A moment passed. I heard rapid steps.

The door flew open, and the man we met at Augustus Broome's walked in.

What a change. He had appeared cheerful and confident then; he was sour and suspicious now. He was young, little past thirty, yet he looked older, his gray eyes pinched, his mouth set like iron, a scowl on his brow that warned he would drive out any fool who dared try to extricate him from misery. He wore no wig; his lightish hair hung in tangles, and dark circles rimmed his eyes. He had thrown on a long morning coat that flapped about his ankles.

Stomping to me, he thrust his face in mine. "I know you."

"We have met." I told him where.

"By God, yes! You had a boy with you—a boy with an eye."

"Nick is indeed observant."

"Nick, eh? But what of *you*?" He began to prowl like a cat. "My wife has told me about my diamond—gone! She says in my absence she called upon you to get it back." He thumped his chest. "She should have called upon *me* to retrieve it. Am I not her husband? Am I not its owner?"

"You were out of town, my lord. On pressing business. She did not wish to trouble you. Further, when the gem vanished, Cavitty urged that 'twas only misplaced; in a day or so he would recover it. Do not blame her too much for counting upon his promises, though time seems to have proved the diamond truly lost."

His lips curled bitterly beneath his moustache. "Lost?" He charged toward me. "Damn it, man, someone has stolen it! Cavitty, likely. And then someone killed the wretch to get it, and it is now irretrievably gone."

"Surely you do not wish to believe that?"

"I will not lie to myself."

" 'Tis no lie to admit you do not know the truth. I make no promises, but I am in a small way experienced in discovering what has been hid. Help me to find your diamond—or do you not wish to rescue the thing?"

He made mouths. "Damn it, man, I want it more than anything in the world. I *need* it. It means . . . it is—"

Whence this passion? If his lady and the diamond were thrown in the balance, would she weigh as much in his heart?

He mastered himself. "My wife says you have questions for me. Ask 'em, then, damn it."

"Your wife said you were out of town for a fortnight, yet I met you at Augustus Broome's. Why?"

"A man returns to town."

"He does so for reasons. What were yours?"

"Business."

"What sort?"

"My own."

"You refuse to say? Very well. To Cavitty. Why are you so certain he stole the gem?"

214

"Who else could have?"

"Sev'ral persons could have, servants and others. They had ample opportunity. You have no evidence against the man. Apply logic: it makes no sense he would take it. To steal something which ev'ryone knows is in your possession argues a want of reason."

"Whenever did he show reason? Besides, he would make up some story. He would say his drapery man took it—has he not already hinted just that?"

"Futilely. You have not much regard for him, I see."

"I have not."

"And yet you were at one time friends."

"Ha, the Grand Tour? That was not friendship, 'twas service-for-hire. Cavitty made himself out to be an expert in art, and I believed him and paid him to companion me and teach me what he knew."

"He was not expert, then?"

"He was expert, I concede. He taught me near all I know of art."

"A very great deal?"

Grudgingly: "Much."

"How, for example, to tell a masterwork from a forgery?"

Something flickered deep in Shenstone's eyes. "Why do you ask about forgery?"

"You lessoned me and my boy in it. Have you forgot?"

An ironic laugh. "So I did. You should thank me. Knowing the true from the false is a great necessity."

"So, you are never fooled when you buy a painting?"

"Less often than most, though I am not above error."

"But if Cavitty served you so well, why dislike him—apart from the fact that you believe he stole your diamond?"

"You met him. He was an objectionable man."

"Yet you had business dealings with him."

"My wife told you that?"

"Come, what dealings?"

He shrugged. "The buying and selling of art. I had agents on the continent. They dug up things—paintings, old marble heads, what have you; they shipped 'em to Dover, where I fetched 'em for Cavitty to pass on."

"Could you not have sold 'em on your own?"

"The way of the world, Franklin—it does not do for a lord to appear to depend too much on trade. But I needed Cavitty for other reasons. He was skilled at cleaning (the old stuff is in dev'lish need of it). And putting-together. Rubble is not art."

"Indeed, I hear they make new statues from the leftovers of old ones. And that a clever brush can turn a tatter to a Titian. Your wife has told me you were in straitened circumstances for a time, but you are well-off now. Luck at the gaming tables, she says."

"I game no more."

"Yet surely cards and dice did not make ev'rything right. Your dealings with Cavitty helped too?"

"I made money from 'em, if that is what you mean."

"A great deal?"

"That is none of your affair."

"As you say. I dwell upon Cavitty (forgive me), because if we could learn who murdered him we might recover your gem. You must know some of those with whom he had dealings. DuVerre, the printer. He says you have bought engravings of him."

"Once or twice."

"And Cope, the printseller. Noyce, the drapery man. Any amongst 'em who might've killed him?"

"None can have loved him any better than I."

"But no particular enemy you can name?"

"No."

216

"Or reason?"

"No."

"A pity. You ended your business with Cavitty recently."

His eyes narrowed. "Surely my wife did not tell you that too?"

I lied. "Cavitty himself told me."

"Ha! He was angry about it, I suppose? Called me names?"

"After a fashion. Why did you end it?"

"I no longer needed him."

"A new source of income, eh? Or will you sell the art yourself?"

"I have other means, which—" he turned ashen. "—which . . ." His thought sank away, and all his belligerence seemed to die at the hands of some terrible remembrance. What sent him down?

"Did you know that Cavitty planned a series of prints satirizing you?"

Bleakly: "Did he? His means of getting back, no doubt. I am not surprised. The man was rash. He did not know his own best interest."

"Plainly not, for he is dead." I regarded my lord, hands jammed in the pockets of his gown. Gaunt face. Hollow eyes. From somewhere in the house sounded the cheery tinkle of a spinet, seeming to mock. "I will ask no more for now. I shall bid you good day."

He dragged his hands from his pockets. "You have asked much of me. I have a question for you: how will you pursue this?"

"By fishing; I have lines in the stream. Cavitty's apprentice nibbles, and I may reel him in soon. As to the others in Cranbourne Street . . . you remind me, there is a serving girl, Annie by name. You know her?"

"I have seen a serving girl."

"A pretty one."

"If you will."

"Young."

"Yes."

"She worked for you once."

He blinked. "She never worked for me, sir."

"No?" I gathered my hat and stick. "I am mistaken. Good day . . ."

It was seven P.M. and dark by the time Mr. Franklin ended his story, I scribbling its last words by the light of two candles which Mrs. Stevenson had carried in. Bearing one, we mounted to the gentleman's chamber, he sinking into his chair whilst I set the flickering flame on the table beside him. Its light picked out the steel of his spectacles, which made him look owlish against the shadowy background of books by his bed. Lips pursed, he made small disgruntled "ahems" and "ahas", and I could almost see his mind toying with fragments of fact and rumor, trying 'em here, there, attempting to fit 'em into some whole.

If anyone could do the job, 'twas Mr. Franklin.

Yet I began to doubt the Shenstone Diamond. How could we recover so small a thing, so easily transported? Did its Dutch buyer already have it in hand?

The casement was open, night rustling ominously despite a sharp redolence of spring that stirred my heart. A cry sounded from below; one heard 'em often, after dark.

Mr. Franklin heard. Half-lifting a hand, he listened, but the sound did not repeat. He wore a frown. "Some dog, some poor dog," murmured he.

✵ 21 ✵

IN WHICH a young man is found dead and another is pursued . . .

ames Cavitty leapt from the trestle table upon which he
had been laid. His skin was blue. Blood streamed from his
throat. Thrusting out a finger, he moaned from a mouth as
black as a cave, "I accuse!"

He pointed the finger at me.

Crying out, I sat up in my narrow bed. I was soaked in sweat,
sure what I had dreamt was real, but only night greeted my
gaping eyes, whilst beyond my window London stirred as if
with dark dreams of its own. "Dear God," moaned I. Shudder-
ing, I made myself sink back, curl up, hide beneath the coverlet. I wrestled with sleep.

Thus I was in no easy or rested state when Peter met me
with the coach at half past six next morn. Mist shrouded the
Thames, gulls wheeling in and out of its tendrils. Before
climbing to my seat I peered warily about, but all that greeted
my eyes were some ragged street boys in a circle by water's
edge, very still, like a convocation of judges. A tall man in a
long coat stood amongst 'em, silhouetted by the rising gray
dawn. Something grave about their look chilled me, but I had
no time to ponder it.

I climbed in. Peter set out as London woke to day.

Cully Stringer had gone missing.

This was what I learnt upon arriving in Cranbourne Street. He customarily slept on the third floor in one of the servants' rooms carved out under the eaves, a cell as small and cramped as Annie's, but when he did not arrive in the workshop by seven, Peasgood had sent Biggs to rouse him. I was just hanging up my coat as the little soldier marched down to report Stringer's room empty, the bed unslept in. "Tell that to yer Mr. Franklin," whispered he, rubbing a finger and thumb under my nose. "Ain't it worth sommat?" What else had occurred whilst I was gone? Beckoning Biggs near, I pried from him that the funeral had been at seven, a meager procession. "Stringer kept alookin' about, he jumped at noises." Supper had convened at eight, from which the apprentice excused himself early—and no one had seen him since, not going up the stairs nor coming down; no one had seen him leave the house.

I hated going to the storage room to fetch the picture Signore Mazzoni sent me for, so I brought the painting promptly. As he worked on it the Italian muttered in his native tongue, but his drift was plain: Damn Cully Stringer for running off! I fretted too. Had someone lured Stringer away? Abducted him? Fear had stricken him yesterday. Had he bolted to save his skin?

In his absence I was given the task of applying color to a small dog in the corner of a picture. I laid on glazes as I had seen James Cavitty do, dabbing, judiciously squinting, dabbing; the end was not wholly displeasing. My dog might not be of any breed God had created, but it would never be mistook for a cabbage.

Signore Mazzoni came to look when I was done. "They will never know the difference." He took the picture away.

220

I was occupied by other tasks, but as the morning crawled on and Stringer did not return, I almost missed him. He had threatened me, struck me, even, but I had never truly feared him. Was he not to be pitied, for his sour, pushing nature and sorry lack of skills boded no happy future? Peasgood poked his lugubrious old head in thrice, as if he hoped the apprentice might've crept back so he could carry the news to Mrs. Bone. Felicity slipped in too; I looked up at her peculiar sweet-sour smell. All in black, she stood not three feet from where I varnished a painting, rocking on her turned-in toes, the little jewel of spittle hanging by her mouth, the hectic in her cheeks. I was startled when she suddenly chirped, "Uncle?" like a wounded bird. Her eyes seemed to search. Did she truly miss Cavitty? But she would never see him more; even if Mr. Franklin tracked down his murderer it would not bring him back.

Mrs. Fanny Bone swept in in her mourning weeds. "So there you are. I do not like you in this room." Snatching Felicity to her, she turned to Mazzoni. "Does it go well?" Her eyes hoped against hope.

Opening his hands, the Italian made a gesture as to say, *The apprentice is gone, how should it go?* and Mrs. Bone's mouth drew tight. I pondered. If one or the other, or both in conspiracy, had done murder they would be doubly sorry if they got no gain by it.

'Twas eleven. Mrs. Bone took her daughter from the room. At five past, a patron arrived, and I recognized him at once: the angry merchant who had complained of his portrait.

"Hebthorpe," growled the man just inside the door, as if ready for battle. Mazzoni was all deference, but his visitor still frowned. "I have heard of James Cavitty's death. Too bad, a pity, but I must look after my affairs, and I am come to see if he remedied my picture as he said he would. If not, I must refuse it. And pay nothing, do you hear?"

"Naturally," replied Mazzoni.

Hebthorpe's little eyes narrowed. "Naturally?"

"But, yes. The signore must not pay for what he does not like. See?" The painting was the very one I had brought from storage. Completed but half an hour ago, it sat nearby. Mazzoni's gesture turned Hebthorpe toward it.

The man peered. He wiped at his bristling moustache. "Hum . . ." murmured he, and, "Well . . ." The picture had depicted a smug, pinch-browed example of the rising merchant class, pompous in an elegant new suit of clothes, with a money-grubbing glint in the eyes. Mazzoni had changed all that. Though still elegant, the clothes now suited the man who had been re-cut in a finer mold. The face remained Hebthorpe's, but it had been ennobled, and the pose was subtly altered so that the *nouveau riche* might've been the master of a name for a thousand years. "More like it," murmured the merchant after a calculating moment. For my part, I had mixed feelings. Mazzoni had given the man what he wanted, but in doing so he had drained the life from James Cavitty's satire.

Hebthorpe cleared his throat. "I am glad to see Cavitty did right by me before he died."

"Beg pardon, signore, but it is I who changed the painting."

Hebthorpe turned upon the Italian. "You?"

"*Sì.* I have taken charge of all work now he is gone."

"Have you?" Hebthorpe looked at the painting. "Hem." He looked back. "Well . . . I suppose that is all right. The result suits. But, hear, what name will be on it?" He stabbed a finger like a sword point. "I will not have a murdered man's name! You finished it. Sign yours. I will then own a— What're ye called?"

"Amadeo Mazzoni, at your service, signore."

"Mazzoni, eh? Capital. Look you, I have a brother wants his picture. You could do that too? I shall send him round. Now, when mine dries I want a glossy coat of varnish, a little brown so it looks like the old masters. You can give me that?"

"Whatever you desire."

"As for pay . . . this is not truly a Cavitty, as I contracted—but as it agrees with me I shall make no reduction in what I owe."

"As the signore wishes."

The signore plainly wished just so. He patted Mazzoni's arm. "Send round when I may pick it up. Good day."

When he had sailed off, the Italian gave me a hopeful look. This small triumph might portend larger ones. Did we not need good news in Cranbourne Street?

There remained tasks to be done, and, lacking Cully Stringer, I was put to double labor. I ground colors and mixed colors, Lady Shenstone's portrait looking on. Mazzoni frowned at it now and again. What was to become of it with Cavitty dead? Would Lord Shenstone take it, as Hebthorpe had taken his? The woman's cool, mysteriously troubled eyes seemed a reproach. Was that why Mazzoni never looked at it long?

Noon's approach delivered a constable to our door.

Davitts was the name of this one, a tall, sallow man with grim wide-set eyes and knobby-knuckled hands that moved ceaselessly at his sides. He wore the customary long green watchcoat, and at first sight of him I started, for I knew him.

The strangely solemn circle of boys I had seen by the Thames, the mist, the stillness, the wheeling gulls—he was the man who had stood amongst 'em.

Peasgood showed him in, waiting patiently whilst Davitts

glowered round, as if a bluff manner might make up for the news he carried. Biggs was present, wiping his nose. Signore Mazzoni looked up from his brush and palette.

"Now, then—" Shuffling his feet Constable Davitts first ascertained that a young man of Cully Stringer's description and Cully Stringer's name, had served as apprentice at number 23. He cleared his throat. "Aye? Well, he's dead."

Peasgood emitted a quavering sigh. Biggs stopped wiping his nose. Mazzoni's brush and palette sank to his sides.

"Murdered," went on the constable, inexorable, whilst I struggled to regain my footing in a world which seemed to reel. "Drowned at the foot o' Craven Street." (I clutched my heart.) " 'Tis a distance from here." Davitts squinted round. "Why might he've gone so far?"

I knew.

Greeted by silence, the constable plunged ahead: "Happened last night. His hands was tied behind his back, a rag was stuffed in his mouth. He was tossed on the embankment afterwards, just his head and shoulders wet. They dipped him in by the feet, they did, 'til the old Thames did him in."

I felt sick. Bound and gagged and dangled head down? Rushing water flooding his nose? Guilt at all the anger I had felt against Cully Stringer threatened to tear a cry from me, and I bit my tongue 'til blood came.

Yet the man was not through: "He was in a bad way. The rats'd got at him. Fingers. Eyes. (They like the eyes.) Some street boys found what was left at dawn."

Signore Mazzoni had gone white as chalk, but he was able to ask, *"Per favore . . .* how did you learn that he came from here?"

"Bit o' luck. Some gen'leman lives in Craven Street knew him and said where we could ask after his master. We must find his relations, father and mother, to let 'em know. Did he have a father and mother?"

Yes, a father and a mother who had been persuaded that her son's ugly scribbles were art. A drawing he had done leant against a wall; I stared at it. 'Twas a botched thing.

Yet though Cully Stringer had been no artist, he had lived and breathed and had not deserved to die like this.

Mazzoni told where he believed the parents might be found, and the constable made to go. It was his duty, said he, drawing himself up, to inform the "unfortunate bereaved." "I may be back to ask questions," added he meaningly, but Cully Stringer had been only an apprentice, and when the constable marched out I doubted we would see him more.

The rest of the house must be told; they were. Mrs. Bone sent her regrets through Peasgood, hoping we would all bear up bravely. Biggs chattered as he worked, pale beneath his sticking-up hair. He had hated Stringer, but the death plainly shook him. At luncheon Mrs. Cockle's gaze was as gray as winter as she muttered that perhaps it was not safe to stay on at number 23 after all. "I shall inquire if some other house needs a cook." I sat opposite Annie, her eyes red with weeping. She had liked Stringer no more than Biggs had, but a familiar soul had been snatched from our little community, horribly murdered, and her tears flowed freely.

Back in the painting room Signore Mazzoni stood Biggs and me before him, his big hands opening and closing at his sides. Our work was not to be affected by anything, even so bad a thing as this, said he fiercely. "We will make a success, do you hear?"

We bobbed our heads and, glancing at Biggs, who for once looked cowed, I thought that without Stringer's bullying and Cavitty's capriciousness, the urchin might be whipped into a tolerably useful boy of work.

225

I found Mazzoni's deep-set eyes on me. "I need an apprentice. Perhaps you, eh? We must speak to Sir Bartleby Bart."

I stared. "Th-thank you, sir." Did I dare to be an apprentice in this house?

I needed no more bad news today, but it came. Biggs was sent to the framers at three. I chanced to see him in the street as he returned just before four.

With Bertie Hexham.

I stood near the large front window. 'Twas a hide-and-seek afternoon, the sun flitting amongst clouds. Reflecting numbly on all that had occurred, I gazed out. A shadow darkened Cranbourne Street—and when it lifted, there in the distance, in the direction of Leicester Square, stood Bertie Hexham.

He bent over Biggs. Plainly he had accosted the urchin, and my surprise rapidly turned to alarm. The fop wore his usual finery; lazy-eyed, he poked a finger whilst Biggs cocked an ear. A purse appeared, a glint of coin; then Hexham straightened, glanced about, strode off, whilst Biggs sauntered toward number 23 with his hands in pockets. I sucked dry breath. One more turn of the screw? Who would suffer from it now?

Feeling events careering out of control, I did what I might not otherwise: accosted Biggs myself. Signore Mazzoni had been summoned by Mrs. Bone; I was alone. Hearing Peasgood send Biggs to hearthstone the rear steps, I gave him a moment to get to it, then slipped out the back door. A wind had blown up, rattling leaves. The sky seemed to moan.

Hunkering, Biggs scrubbed in his desultory fashion. I planted my feet beside him. "The man who spoke to you in the street just now, what did he want?"

The urchin looked up in his insolent way. "Wot man?"

Something came over me—no more petty arrogance! no lies!—and, snatching Biggs's collar, I dragged him up so that his feet dangled. He made a little yelp of protest, but I paid no heed. "Don't come the innocent with me!" cried I. "Two murders, do you hear? Two!" I shook him. "Now, tell me about that man!"

He gaped, he wriggled, and almost at once began to jabber: "I dunno. Truly. He didn't say his name. But he said he wanted some'un to spy for him in the house. To look for things. He give me three shillings, more'n your Mr. Franklin ever give, and said there'd be more if I helped him. I said I'd think on it, and he said if I thought too long I'd have to think upside down." To my surprise tears sprang into Biggs's eyes. "Wot'd he mean? The Thames? Not the Thames! Wot'd he mean?"

"Look for what things?" demanded I.

"The . . . the diamond. The Shenstone Diamond."

Staring into Biggs's terror, I released the boy. He scrambled to the foot of the steps to lick his wounds whilst I flushed with shame. He was a child, no more than ten, and the world was cruel enough to a poor, friendless creature without my hurting him more. "Sorry . . ." murmured I, backing up the steps. "But look here, you must not do anything that man says, for he will get his hooks into you. It is not worth your life."

Seeing my chagrin, Biggs wiped defiantly at his cheeks. "Don't you try t' scare me! Yer not master here."

"The man who was master is dead," said I.

Biggs paled.

"Remember, it is not worth your life."

Six P.M., time to return to Craven Street. Hanging my apron beside that of the young man who would never wear his again, I paused outside the front door. The sun hung low in the west, and shadows spread like ink as the street began to clear of costers and mendicants and all the commerce that filled it during

227

day. 'Twas shop-closing time, wending-home time. Coach wheels rattled with a hollow sound, closing shutters made *cracks!* like pistol shots, and eyes did not meet eyes as tardy souls scurried.

Churchbells tolled as I stepped down the stoop to turn toward St. Martin's Lane. I sunk my hands in my pockets. Ten minutes to the Strand, where Peter waited. Walking quickly, I hated the distance I must travel. Two murders. My hackles rose. Was I watched? I had felt so before and, glancing round, I shuddered to discover a figure wrapped in a greatcoat trudging purposefully behind me. He was not the only one at my back—yet when I glanced round, I saw that though other souls peeled off into this door or that, into grogshops or little side streets and mews, this one kept coming. I began to perspire. Dear God, Cully Stringer bound and held under the Thames, then heaved upon the stones like a carcass. Would I be done in too, in some likewise horrid way?

The blackish sky lowered. A cold wind blew grit into my eyes, but still I peered back. My pursuer had kept his distance but closed it now, with purposeful steps. I went faster. The Strand was some distance away, yet achingly visible. Could I reach it, where traffic still plied? Another glance back. My pursuer was terribly near, not a dozen feet at my heels, his face wrapped to the eyes. My heart gave a leap. I set out running. My breath tore from my lungs.

Too late. The man's hand closed upon my shoulder. I tried to pull free but could not, and twisted to fight him, for I should never give in without a struggle.

"Nick, Nick," came Benjamin Franklin's voice, and I saw the warm glow of his eyes beneath his low-pulled hat. "In the midst of danger could I let you walk home alone?"

✣ 22 ✣

IN WHICH Mr. Franklin thinks on murder, John Fielding collars a fop, and a lord consents to tell all . . .

D id *I* murder him, Nick?" murmured Mr. Franklin. "Did I cause poor Stringer's death?" He leant on his bamboo by his bow window gazing out at the smoke of a thousand chimneypots rising to greet the night. No moon or stars twinkled in the thick, smudged dusk. Ordinarily the gentleman was ruddy-faced, but he was gray and grim now. He turned with troubled eyes. "Whyever did I hint to Shenstone that the apprentice might come to me?"

"My lord did him in?"

"I do not know. But I told no other. Shenstone may have had as strong motive to stop his tongue as he did to stop Cavitty's."

"*If* he stopped Cavitty's, sir," said I.

"You are right." Sunk in gloom, he went to his chair. "And indeed Hexham's warning to Biggs, which you told me of, seems to point away from Shenstone. Did Quimp, then, drown Stringer? Could there be some connection betwixt him and my lord? (Quimp's web ensnares many.) In any case, there is a desperation about Shenstone. Determination too, despite his locking himself away; I am not persuaded he is as helpless as he makes out. Does he mean to disguise his aims from his wife—and from Benjamin Franklin?''

With no idea how to answer, I knelt to add coals to the fire. It was a mild spring eve, but after the day's events I could not rid myself of chill. The cry we had heard at night haunted me. Stringer's as he was took? His last before his voice was stilled forever?

Thank God the man in St. Martin's Lane had been Mr. Franklin.

He watched me from his chair. "You cannot go back, you know," said he. " 'Tis a peril. I was foolish to let you set foot there today."

"Yes, sir." Yet though I knew he was right, I felt sad, for I should miss the smell of pigments and oils, the feel of the brush in my hands, the little shipboard of companions with whom I had sailed into such troubled waters. Should I see Annie again? I was troubled at the thought of her. She had given herself to me. How gentle she had been—sad, hopeful, good of heart too, I believed. (How could she be, as she had said, wicked?) I wished no harm to befall her.

As if reading my thoughts, Mr. Franklin said determinedly, "We must prevent more murders from being done, Nick."

"Let us!" was my fervent reply.

I settled upon the hearth by his feet whilst he made a little tent of fingers before his chin. " 'Tis money, Nick, that is the motive—but how does it relate to thievery and murder? We know Cavitty and Shenstone were joined in the business of obtaining and selling art. We know too that they went on the Grand Tour together and visited artists in Italy, Holland, France. They visited forgers as well, acquiring expert knowledge. Did these visits suggest a plan, hatched over the years, in which they trafficked in false pictures? Then: a falling out. Angry and vindictive, Cavitty threatened by his satirical

230

engravings to put 'em both in danger. (DuVerre and others have testified to his rash judgment.) Was that why my lord returned to London, to seek the opportune moment to silence Cavitty?"

"Perhaps Cully Stringer did it for him, and he did in Stringer to shut him up?"

"Is it possible? But Annie—we must think on her. The ring from Shenstone. A 'wicked girl,' she called herself—was she my lord's agent?"

I went cold. "I cannot believe it."

Mr. Franklin peered. "You believe she earned the ring another way?"

I flushed.

"In any case, 'til we know for sure we must suspect Mrs. Bone too, for she had more than one motive."

"And Signore Mazzoni," added I.

"Indeed, *il signore* is ambitious. From what you tell of Hebthorpe, he may make a success." Mr. Franklin gazed out at the night. "Then there is Quimp."

Despite the fire at my back the room suddenly felt like ice.

"Bertie Hexham put Cully Stringer in his pocket; plainly he wishes to put Biggs there too. We know what happened to Stringer; we must fear for Biggs. Can anyone escape Quimp for long? Plainly he is after the gem. Yet though he has formidable means—spies, bribery, terror—why has he failed to get his hands on it? Where is the thing? I am certain we are close to it—or at least close to learning where it has gone. Is Annie a key? And the little copperplate. . . ." Plucking it up, he wrinkled his brow at its soft, reddish sheen. "Does it signify—or is it a jest tossed in our faces?" He flung it upon the table. "John Fielding, Nick. Through him we shall lay hands on Bertie Hexham."

* * *

231

I was pleased to hear Mr. Franklin had a plan, but it was no more talked on that eve, for he was to sup with men of the Royal Society, he said, and in a quarter hour he had vanished to mutton, port, and lively talk. Thus Mrs. Stevenson, Polly, and I were thrown into one another's company again, though this time William joined us at table, in honor of whom our landlady prepared a game pie.

William sat with great ceremony. He turned his condescending eyes upon me. "And how do you do at the artist's?"

"Well enough, sir," replied I guardedly, for even he was not privy to all that occurred in Cranbourne Street. Indeed, none of 'em knew murder had happened.

William stuffed in a forkful of pie. "See you do not get beyond yourself."

I opened my mouth to retort, for I hated such admonitions from him whose father feared his Tory leanings might carry *him* too far! But I bit my tongue, trudging upstairs to lie awake with *Robinson Crusoe* until I heard Mr. Franklin come in at half past eleven. Crossing the landing, I found him in his greatcoat, frowning at a piece of paper.

Wordlessly he passed the paper to me.

I read:

> You discommode me, Franklin. Cease at once or suffer.

There was no name. I looked up. "Quimp, sir?" asked I in alarm.

"Who else? I found it pinned to my coach seat when I left the *Bedford Head*. Peter swore no one had come near the conveyance, so how was it done? But it was." He threw off his coat. "Yet though Quimp is a man of remarkable resources, none has availed him of the missing gem. We must find it first, Nick—but with great care, with very great care."

Next morn dawned brighter than yesterday, both in sunshine and in spirits, for I knew I need not travel to Cranbourne Street. Mr. Franklin sent a note to Mrs. Bone saying that in the circumstances he must keep me home. This would greatly discommode Signore Mazzoni, but it must be done.

Shortly, we took coach to number 4 Bow Street to apprise old John Fielding, Chief Magistrate of Westminster, of our need.

The fat, triple-chinned criminal-chaser heard us out behind his desk in his office with the faded, foxed racing prints on the walls. "Cavitty dead. And now his 'prentice murdered too. Drowned near your doorstep to boot? Damnable business!"

"Stringer must have come to tell me what he knew," said Mr. Franklin. "—perhaps even who stabbed Cavitty."

"And was followed and done in to stop him. (I have Constable Davitts's report.) But why do you want Bertie Hexham snatched?"

"To ask questions of him. Not to put too fine a point on it, to have *you*, sir, ram the fear of English law in him."

Fielding grunted in satisfaction. "I may be blind, but I know the voices of a thousand criminals and could hang nine hundred by a word. Hexham is amongst those I watch. He has kept on the right side of the law—if only just—since you brought his father to justice, but no matter; tho' I have cutpurses and counterfeiters aplenty to deal with, I shall do as you wish."

And so Bertie Hexham was brought in. It took but a word to Joshua Brogden to send out two strong specimens of "Mr. Fielding's People" to snatch him from his morning coffee at the *Thistle* and within half an hour to stand him before us in the Justice Room, where King George's portrait glowered down. Fielding had put on his official long white wig and his official robe and his official hang-'em scowl and sat like Jove in his official chair whilst Hexham gaped and gulped on the other side of the bar. Mr. Franklin stood on the magistrate's right-hand side, I next him, the large chamber, lit by its glass dome, cleared of ev'ryone, so we might have our object to ourselves. 'Twas no joy to see the ferret-eyed young man again. In more prosperous days he had been a noted rake, priding himself on his shiny black boots and fashionable attire; yet though his clothes were still in fashion, his boots showed a touch of wear, as if 'twas now a struggle to keep up appearances. His sleek figure had begun to run to fat, and his curling sneer ran like water on his lips. "Hear, now!" barked he plaintively, whilst he twisted his hat in his hands. "Hear, now, I say, hear, now!"

"Hear what, you dog?" growled Fielding. His sightless eyes squinted. "You know I can hang you, don't you? Better, I'll tie your hands behind your back and fish with you in the Thames? Food for rats, eh?" A long and terrible pause. "Now, you know Mr. Benjamin Franklin. You *do* know him, don't you?—speak up!"

A squeaking "Yes."

"He has some questions to put, which you will answer or find yourself remanded to the Fleet before you can say 'Ty-burn Tree.' Do you hear me, sir?"

"I d-do."

Fielding sank back. "He is yours."

Mr. Franklin pressed his fingers hard against the bench. "You work for a man named Quimp, do you not?" asked he.

"Dear God." Hexham's knees wobbled.

"Answer me, sir!"

"We . . . we are never to say his name."

234

"Why not?"

"B-because he does not like it spread about. Because if he hears report we have even thought on saying it, he . . . he—" Hexham choked on the words.

"He will see you do not awake next morn, eh? I well know his way. But you *do* work for him, and your present job is to obtain the Shenstone Diamond from number 23 Cranbourne Street, is it not?"

"Please never tell him I said it was."

"You bribed the apprentice, Cully Stringer, into helping you discover what had become of the gem?"

"Y-yes."

"He failed."

"He did not find it, if that is what you mean. Could not, he said."

"And so you killed him."

Hexham's eyes grew to balls. "I did not! I never! I only reported to my master what he said. The truth. That Stringer threatened to go to you."

Mr. Franklin's lips compressed. "And so your 'master' had him watched and followed and drowned; he snuffed out the life of a boy."

"You are an accessory, sir," put in Fielding, shooting out a finger.

A spot of damp appeared on Hexham's trousers, and he went so pale he looked green.

"You claim you never touched Stringer," pursued Mr. Franklin, "but I know a man you *did* murder: Cavitty himself."

"No!"

Striding round the bench, Mr. Franklin thrust his face into Hexham's. "Your master looked to place his hands on the most famous diamond in Europe. Not that he cared for the thing,

235

only for what it might bring. Did he already have a buyer? A Dutchman, perhaps? Cavitty had to know where it had gone, you reasoned. So when Stringer failed, you caught the artist alone and tried to make him tell of it, but when he would not—or could not—you stabbed him with his graver."

Hexham fell to his knees. "Please, please, I swear to God I did not!"

Mr. Franklin turned away. "Quimp himself did, then. Or some other of his vile minions."

Hexham plucked at Mr. Franklin's coat. "No."

The gentleman turned. "How may you be sure?"

"B-because I saw his face when I told him Cavitty was dead. He hides his face, but he did not hide it then. He was furious. 'Now I may never get the gem!' he cried."

Mr. Franklin gazed at the groveling man. "You are a lost soul, sir." He flashed his eyes at the bench. "Question him hard, Mr. Fielding, to learn whatever may lead to Quimp; some day the felon must fall. Come, Nick, to fresher air."

Out in the coach, moving off into the noise and bustle of London, Mr. Franklin plucked at a brow. " 'Tis Hexham I went to learn from—yet something Fielding said has most provoked my brain. Is it possible . . . ?" Shaking his head as if to clear a fog, he looked at me. "I am inclined to believe Hexham. But if Quimp did not do in Cavitty, who did? In any case I have not yet told you of last night. Amongst the many good fellows of the Royal Society was an acquaintance of Lord Shenstone, newly returned from France, Mr. Hawker. This Hawker let fall that he had seen Shenstone in Dover three days ago—glimpsed him, that is, for when Shenstone saw him he darted into a small quayside hostelry as if he wished not to be seen. It is time for bold moves, Nick. 'Tis time to beard the lion in his den."

*　*　*

"I know of your travels to Dover, sir," said Mr. Franklin to Lord Shenstone some forty minutes later in his drawing room in St. James's Street, "and am come to seek the reason why." Light slanted in long bars through the three tall windows. Mr. Franklin stood in his plain brown suit, his round face grave, his gaze intent. 'Twas bold indeed to speak thus, but Mr. Franklin never feared boldness. Too, it had the element of surprise; Shenstone could not guess that we had very little else in our bag.

My lord wore a suit of fine blue stuff, but his hair hung lank and unkempt to his shoulders, and he looked gaunter than I remembered, though a spark of spirit smoldered behind his squarish gray gaze. He smirked at me. "So. The boy with an eye. Had I some paintings I should show 'em you, to test your powers. Cherish him, Franklin. Cherish anyone who sees truth."

"I cherish him. I trust him, too. He is my confidant, and you may say in front of him anything you might before any close-mouthed friend."

"I believe I may. I have talked at greater length to my wife about you, sir. She told me what she learnt of you before she sought your aid. She told me what you have accomplished so far. Too, I have sent inquiries about town. In short, I believe I may trust you, and so I shall tell you—and your closemouthed, sharp-eyed boy—what I have told no other soul."

"A tale of forgery?" proposed Mr. Franklin.

"You are shrewd. Yes. The forgery of the Shenstone Diamond."

❧ 23 ❧

IN WHICH a lord tells a secret, and
Mr. Franklin sifts truth from lies . . .

I started, but if Lord Shenstone's announcement surprised Mr. Franklin he showed no trace, his inquiring brown eyes remaining coolly fixed upon his lordship, who bade us sit. We did, on a brocade sofa, whilst he lowered himself onto the spindle-legged chair opposite.

My mind raced. Forgery of the gem?

"You traveled to Dover to sell the Shenstone Diamond, then," said Mr. Franklin.

"I did. To complete negotiations with a Dutchman."

"You chose well. The Dutch are knowledgable in gems. Good at forging 'em too?"

"I had a Florentine for that."

"A man you met on the Grand Tour?"

"A man I learnt of then, yes. An artist. Superbly skilled."

"You traveled to Dover twice during the fortnight you said you were away on estate matters, the first time to meet your Dutchman. To assure one another that matters would be soon settled? The second, then . . . to meet your Florentine?"

"His agent. You had me followed *both* times? Damn your impudence." But there was no anger behind the words. Shenstone rose. "You may as well see this." Going to the broad white mantel, he took from it an ormolu box.

Carrying it near, he released a hidden catch to reveal a false bottom, from which the Shenstone Diamond dropped into his hand.

I gasped. It had been striking as it was depicted upon Lady Shenstone's breast in Cavitty's painting, but the real thing was a wonder, its ornate setting a gold-wrought bed on which a many-faceted oval luxuriated in glints of blue and white. Its very size impressed. No wonder men had murdered for it before Shenstone's grandfather bought it. I stole a glance at the present lord. Had someone murdered for it now?

Mr. Franklin lifted his quizzing glass; through it he coolly addressed the gem. "Hum," said he, sinking back. "Remarkable—for a forgery. The Florentine gave you good value."

I was amazed. Not the real gem?

His lordship smiled bitterly. "I challenge any expert to tell the difference without his picks and his chemicals."

I stared at the thing, hardly able to believe it was false.

"So you meant secretly to sell the real diamond and replace it with the false," said Mr. Franklin, "so that no one—perhaps not even your wife—would know you had given it up."

" 'Twas a good plan, sir."

"And might have succeeded had the real gem not disappeared."

Shenstone dropped the false gem upon a table betwixt us. "It has plunged me to despair."

And to desperate acts? wondered I.

"Come, all is not lost," urged Mr. Franklin. "Tell your tale from the start."

Shenstone's expression was pained. "I doubt even your powers can save me, but—" He drew a hand across his brow. "Very well. Much you know. The diamond, which has been in my family many years, has grown synonymous with my name. 'There goes Shenstone, he owns the gem,' men say, and I take pride in that; it sets me apart. You also know that my grandfather nearly bankrupted himself to buy the thing. (I curse his wife her greed!) Since that day the Shenstones have had their ups and downs—yet lately, in the past few years, mostly down, falling into greater and greater debt. My gaming did not help. (I have foresworn it, but giving up a vice does not cure the ills it has engendered.) My wife brought a dowry with her; it alleviated my worries for a time—it paid some bills—but soon 'twas gone, and I was back where I had begun. My Oxfordshire house and lands sink to ruin out of neglect. I might sell 'em— but then where would I be? After paying off a dunning world, I would be a gentleman with no land and no fortune; and that, sir, is a gross and ugly thing, the butt of jokes. Yet, I had one great asset, the Shenstone Diamond, worth thousands—but, curse my pride, I could not sell it.

"And yet I must. It had brought my family near ruin, it could restore it. And so I began inquiries on the continent— but discreetly. (I wanted no one to know how needy I had become.) Many nibbled at the bait, but few offered what I asked; they wished to make a great noise of the sale, which would never do.

"And then came the Dutchman, little-known amongst the general but with a great reputation amongst the gem-cutters of Amsterdam. He would buy the diamond, he said, under circumstances which were better than I had ever dreamt, for he wished to buy it in secret, never letting anyone know."

"But why should he do that?"

"The diamond is large. He planned to recut it into three smaller yet still-sizable gems. Properly mounted—and with invented provenances to give 'em an air (they might be royal gems of Cathay, for all their buyers would know)—three would bring him far better profit than one."

"Clever Dutchman. You settled upon this arrangement six months ago."

"How do you know the date?"

"You came into money then. You told your wife 'twas luck at gaming. In truth, the Dutchman had paid you something on account. Yet you did not hand over the gem, for you had first to obtain its copy. Until you had that, you dared not relinquish your prize."

"You are dev'lish clever, Franklin. Yes. My mind leapt to my Florentine, for 'twas rumored that many a jewel of the grand courts of Europe, supposed genuine, was really by his hand. What a chance!—to sell the gem, to reap all its profit, yet to appear in the eyes of the world still to possess it."

"Appearance is a very great thing in men's eyes. The forged gem must have cost you much."

"Half all the Dutchman gave on account."

"But worth it. When the false diamond, *this* diamond," Mr. Franklin tapped the thing, "was placed in your hands by the Florentine at Dover, you could at last deliver the real gem. Does your Dutchman know you cannot fulfill your promise?"

Shenstone was grim. "I sent him word. Reply has just come. He demands back all he paid. With interest. If I do not return it within a fortnight, he will expose me."

There was a silence. "You might still fulfill your agreement," said Mr. Franklin.

Shenstone peered. "Do not trifle with a doomed man's hopes!"

"The diamond is somewhere; it has not flown to the moon. I believe 'tis still in London."

A feverish light flickered in the man's eyes. "Where?"

241

"Tell me, did you meet Cavitty the night before he was murdered?"

"How could I? I was in Dover to see the Florentine, to receive the forged gem. Your spies have already told you that."

"You had no appointment to meet him?"

"No."

"Might your wife have met him? Or thought to?"

"What? She felt the greatest distaste for how he had treated her. She would never do such a thing."

"As you say. You recall my inquiry about the serving girl who works in Cranbourne Street? You still say she was never employed here?"

"Never. I have thought on her and recall her well, for I once helped her escape the clutches of Cavitty's apprentice (he had caught her in a room I chanced to enter; I do not like such depredations), and I tell you, she was never employed by me. My diamond. How will you recover it?"

"By questions. I must put another to you. It touches on your honor, but I must ask it nonetheless: have you forged anything else? With Cavitty's collusion? In your mutual dealings, did he invent works which you, as a known connoisseur amongst your circle, recommended as genuine?"

My lord licked dry lips; his eyes seemed to peer into his soul. "Never," said he. "—but, O, the temptation was great. . . ."

"Are we to believe him, Nick?" asked Mr. Franklin as our coach drove from his door five minutes later.

I thought on our last moment: his little son, honey-haired, scampering into the chamber to climb upon his father's lap. Dandling him, my lord had gazed into his face with a heart-rending mixture of affection and sorrow. Can I save us, can I save you? he seemed to ask. The boy was the future Lord

Shenstone. Was he to be reduced to beggary? Though I longed to say yes to Mr. Franklin, the preserving of a place in society was a great motive to wickedness, and I replied, "I do not know." Our coach rocked and swayed. Other thoughts crowded in. "Sir, had you guessed what my lord would reveal?"

"I saw its possibility—but I confess I came to St. James's Street with no certainty. Yet forgery has been a theme all along, and the moment my lord spoke of a counterfeit gem, all fell into place: Joseph de Medina's story of a sale of the diamond must be true—though the man who sought to pass it on was not its thief, but Shenstone himself. And that painting of his wife is one more copy of the thing before he must give it up. Do you believe what he told about Annie?"

"That he saved her from Stringer?"

"That she never worked for him."

I thought. "He spoke convincingly."

"As a good liar must. But does he persuade? Does he prove *her* a liar?" Mr. Franklin squinted out our window where Cockspur Street bent into Charing Cross. The equestrian statue of Charles I loomed heroically. "The source of Shenstone's windfall may be answered—but where did Cavitty come by his? Shenstone says there was no forgery of art, yet . . ." He thumped the roof of our carriage. "Faster, Peter, to Craven Street."

In his chamber twenty minutes later he once more picked up the small copperplate from the table by his chair.

It too had been a theme.

"A palimpsest, Nick," said he. "Damn me, it cannot be caprice that someone effaced what was here." With a finger he began to trace the faint hints. He snorted, he hummed, he clucked his tongue.

243

Then, with a sudden "Aha!" he cried, "Forgery, forgery, forgery!"

I stared.

His eyes twinkled, and his spectacles threatened to fly off in his agitation. "Why did I not see it sooner? Have I not done the same, with my own hand? O, Ben, you fool! A gem, no; nor reputation—'twas not for either that James Cavitty was murdered."

Mrs. Stevenson chanced just then to appear in the half-open chamber door; her lodger's wild look made her start. "Dear sir . . . !"

He waved an arm. "Nay, good woman, no luncheon now. Come, Nick, to John Fielding." He pulled me with him. "Afterward: one final call, and a murderer shall be in our hands."

An hour and a quarter later, at three-thirty by the large hunter watch which Mr. Franklin plucked from his waistcoat pocket, Peter drew up before Phillippe duVerre's engraving shop in Princes Street. It was elegant indeed, set amongst other fine shops in a genial company where the *ton* bought their wares. On this pleasant spring afternoon, sunlight splashed down, ladies under parasols surveying the goods in windows whilst their servants trailed with the packages their mistresses had purchased. Ornate chairs came and went, and gentlemen strolled in brass-buttoned coats and gilt-trimmed tricorns. We entered to the tinkling of a bell. The front room of the shop well set off the engravings on its walls. Three or four patrons browsed, but as duVerre expected Mr. Franklin (he had sent word he came), the Frenchman informed them that he must close his doors for a while, and off they went.

"No need to send 'em away," demurred Mr. Franklin.

DuVerre wore his tight-fitting suit of clothes. He made a

small bow. "It will allow us to talk the easier, monsieur." He frowned at me. "But I know this boy."

"He is in my employ."

"Does he not work at Cavitty's?"

"*Has* worked there. Sent by me to spy." Mr. Franklin meaningly tapped his nose. "To see if he might discover what became of Lord Shenstone's diamond."

A small furrow, like the cut of a knife, sliced the Frenchman's brow. "There is more to you than I thought, monsieur." Shutting the door, he pulled down over its glass a long parchment shade. "The afternoon sun is not healthy for prints."

"Nor for honest conversation?" Mr. Franklin gazed about. "But what a fine shop you have. And in such an excellent part of town. Pray, what is the ground rent? A pretty sum, I guess— though 'tis none of my business."

As he said this, I glanced through the door which led into the printing room, a large chamber containing two engraving presses and benches on which various tools of the craft were laid out. Prints hung to dry, and the odor of strong black ink prevailed. I caught the stink of acid too, which wrinkled my nose. A burly man worked one of the presses, his forearms rippling as he turned the handle, his legs like two strong trees. He seemed intent on his task, yet I felt certain from the tilt of his head that he hearkened to ev'ry word we said.

He glared at me. Shivering, I turned quickly back to the gentlemen.

"And did your boy find Lord Shenstone's missing gem?" duVerre was inquiring.

"No. He discovered more interesting news."

"I am glad if it was of interest to you. But, come: to your purpose. I am puzzled. Your note said you had urgent business with Phillippe duVerre. What can that be?"

"The reason you fled France."

"I did not 'flee' France, monsieur."

"But you did. If only I had thought to inquire of John Fielding sooner. He knows much. He knows of you. He informed me that you came to these shores to escape a charge that would have put you in the hands of the law. A charge of forgery."

DuVerre drew himself up. His gray eyes flashed. "Preposterous. Forgery of what?"

"*Louis d'or.* You were a counterfeiter, monsieur."

There was a long silence in which I heard only the soft creak of the press. DuVerre emitted a slow breath. "I have honored you, monsieur," said he evenly. "I have welcomed you to my shop. I have answered your questions. But I can no longer honor a man who listens to rumors."

Mr. Franklin shook his head. "A fool listens to rumors, a wise man winnows truth. I have winnowed to find the kernel. You were a counterfeiter in France. You had expertise in metals, you forged false coin. But paper money—how much quicker and easier to forge that!" Pulling from his coat pocket the small copperplate, he held it out. "You have counterfeited in England too."

For a long moment duVerre seemed incapable of lifting his gaze from the plate.

Mr. Franklin gestured. "Come, sir, it is time to confess. This copper—the size of a bank note. You wished to lead me astray by suggesting it had been a book illustration, as it might well have been; and, indeed, I believed it was for a time. But my inquiries told me that Cavitty had not been working on any such thing. Was it a plate he had done some months ago? But what, then, was it doing in the acid? Chief Justice Fielding, whom you will soon know better than you desire, inadvertently led me to the truth. He grumbled often about the counterfeiters of London; I paid scant attention, but at last I harkened. You, monsieur, and James Cavitty—"

"This is madness! What has Cavitty to do with—?"

"He made the plates, for he is as skilled with the graver as any man who incises the notes by law. You are equally expert in your craft. You were their printer. Fielding has shown me money which must have resulted from your collaboration—remarkable! How did you come to your plan? No matter. He needed funds to raise himself in the estimation of the gentry. You needed the same to set up shop in the heart of fashionable London. You found one another, you hatched your scheme. Cavitty could secretly make the plates, but he dared not turn 'em out in his shop; there were too many people about. But here, with your shade pulled, you could print hundreds of pounds unbeknownst to anyone except your man."

DuVerre stood stiff as a stick. His fine gray eyes glazed with venom. "You are clever, monsieur. I gave you that when you first came to my shop. I give it you now."

"Not so clever. I should have come to truth sooner, but I was misled by the idea of forged paintings. Too, you were expert at throwing sand in my eyes. It must have wrung you to learn that Cavitty had a notebook in his pocket when you murdered him, in which he had writ down his intention of meeting you that eve. And here came I, nosy Ben Franklin, to confront you with this book. But you diverted me. (You improvise well.) You had already planted a clue to incriminate Lord Shenstone: the plate of the *Follies* you dropped in the acid. You knew he and Cavitty had had a falling out. Further, you knew that others had seen enough of their enmity to testify against him. Now Cavitty was engraving a series of prints to make my lord the butt of jests. Shenstone was fiercely jealous of his name. Might he not have murdered the artist? And so, when you

247

poured acid and dropped in the copperplate of the latest counterfeit bank note, you slid the lampoon of Shenstone on top. The inspiration of the moment, monsieur? Or had you planned it?"

"Inspiration," gave duVerre betwixt his teeth.

"Inspiration, too, when I called, to agree that Cavitty was meant to meet you that eve but had gone to Lord Shenstone instead? Shenstone was not then in town, I have sure proof of that. Yet you cast your seed well, and for a time Ben Franklin pecked at it."

"Damn Cavitty," breathed duVerre.

A movement caught my notice. The man in the next room had stopped pulling the press. He stood louring.

Mr. Franklin tutted. "Was murder necessary? Did Cavitty have to die?"

"The fool wanted to go on printing the bank notes!" burst out duVerre. "We had taken great care spending them, buying goods here and there under false names, which we then resold to obtain genuine money. Thus, when I took this establishment, no crime could be laid to me. Cavitty was careful too—at first. But then he grew lax. He began to pay for his pigments and frames with the bad notes; he even gave some to his sister, for expenses. Worse, in his rush to resettle in Leicester Square he meant to pass on some to the house agent too. I learnt of this from his own lips. I reasoned with him: 'You will lead the law to your door!' But he pooh-poohed my fears. He must take the chance, he said; he could not wait to move. I was in agonies. I knew if ever he were caught he would tell who had printed the notes. (There was no honor betwixt us.)

"And so I asked him to visit me the night before he was to settle with the agent. I only meant to reason with him. I begged him to put off his move until it was safe. I argued that we must give over counterfeiting. Did we not have what we

248

wanted? 'You have what *you* want,' said he. 'And so do you,' said I, but he was willful, rash, greedy. He wanted to go on printing money, as a surety. Too, he had begun to fret about the Shenstone Diamond—what if it were held that the thing had been lost through his negligence and some judgment were made against him? This had nothing to do with me. I had my shop, I had no need to go on. But he had a hold on me, for he knew my crime. He had engraved a new plate, and I must come with him that very hour to obtain it. I should bring it back, I should print more false notes whilst he watched. I stared at him. I saw that he was fixed on the mad idea. I saw that he would drag us both down, and all our planning would be for naught, and I should be what I had been in my last days in France." DuVerre pled: "I never wanted more than to ply my trade! I am proud of my skills—I was one of the best printers of copper in Paris and am the best in London. O, curse the man, curse the man!" He shook all over.

"I went back with him in the dead of night. We came to his painting room, creeping so as not to be heard. By candlelight he drew the plate from a secret place behind his engraving table. I looked at it. 'Twas good; he was amazingly skilled. If I printed it, it would fool many innocent eyes—for a time. But a terror filled me. Fury, too. And so, when he turned his back to wrap the plate in paper I snatched the graver from his bench and plunged it into his neck."

DuVerre looked away. "He clutched his throat. *Mon dieu*, how many times since have I seen those brown, bulging eyes, which I loathed, staring at me before the blood spurted and he dropped to the floor stone dead. I fell back. I thought I should faint. Never had I done such a thing, and for many moments I leant upon the workbench. But once one begins one must go on—how one must!—and so I dragged him into his storage room, to be discovered as late as possible, and came back and poured acid and dropped in the counterfeit plate and watched the lines begin to go. When I saw this well in progress, I dropped in the plate of the *Follies*, too. Let Shenstone, whose gem had urged Cavitty to his rashness, be suspect. I crept out home."

"Leaving the door unlatched behind you."

"Did I? Ah."

"And you know nothing of the missing diamond?"

"Nothing, curse it too."

Something flickered in Mr. Franklin's eyes. "As for the third *particeps criminis*, he is amongst us now."

Startled, I turned to discover the burly man from the printing room almost at my elbow. He stood half a foot taller than Mr. Franklin and weighed three stone more. How he had sneaked in so quietly I did not know, but I felt great trepidation for he glowered fiercely.

The man's brows were a thick, black line. Turning a look upon duVerre, he barked something in French, yet he had some English, for he ended with a little spray of spittle: "Kill them. . . ."

DuVerre gestured, "Monsieur Daste," in a macabre parody of politeness. "He came with me from Le Havre. He is excellent with his hands. See how strong they are? They helped to print the counterfeit notes. We cannot let you live, says he." His lean head tilted. "Might we pay you to keep silent?" A weary smile. "But that would not answer. You cannot be bought."

"You have cheated honest men. You have murdered, too. 'Tis the law you must pay."

DuVerre's smile died. He slid a hand along his throat; 'twas the hangman's noose if he were taken. It might not be in his nature to murder (Mr. Franklin had said that no man was a murderer 'til he committed the crime), but I saw resolve stiffen his features. Chance, kings, and desperate men. The Frenchman was desperate, his eyes narrowed, and I drew nearer Mr. Franklin.

I felt the gentleman's fingers close upon my shoulder—and then I was tumbling away from him, for he had pushed me hard. Command had glinted in duVerre's eyes, and Monsieur Daste had lunged, a graver gleaming in the hand which had been hidden behind his back. With a grunt he lashed out—but Mr. Franklin had left his bamboo stick at home in favor of his hard polished oak, and with ready dexterity, he swung this stick upward, catching the onrushing man square betwixt the legs. There was an audible thud, and something died in the man's eyes, a mewling cry escaped him, and he stumbled. He tried to fend with the graver, but with this same stick Mr. Franklin struck his right arm a cracking blow which must have numbed it to the shoulder, for it flopped as if broke, and the graver flew from helpless fingers. His other hand clutched his groin as he fell upon the floor.

DuVerre was quick. In one long stride he had me by the collar, jerking. The writhing man lay betwixt us and Mr. Franklin. Wrapping an arm about my throat duVerre dragged me backward into the printing room.

I struggled, but he had a choking grip. Mr. Franklin followed. DuVerre's bottles of acid sat on a wooden shelf by his workbench. He snatched one up as Mr. Franklin came through the door. He bit off its cork.

"I shall burn the boy," said he tightening his arm.

Mr. Franklin halted. He held out a hand. "Stop, sir. Think. What can it gain you?"

I could hardly breathe, yet I smelt the pungent stink of aquafortis. My finger had been painfully burnt with only diluted acid. How might undiluted niter sear my flesh?

I could hear the Frenchman's ragged breathing near my ear.

"Damn you, damn you, damn you!" tore from him, a raging litany. For a moment we made a tableau, unmoving. Would he truly pour the acid?

But, no. I heard a sound at our backs. DuVerre heard it too, for he stiffened. And then I heard a scuffling and was tossed about as someone struggled with the Frenchman, a gruff voice barking, "Here, now, let go the boy. We have you. Let him go." I felt other hands at my throat, releasing me. Then I stumbled into Mr. Franklin's arms.

He held me as I caught my breath. "Are you well, Nick? He did not harm you?"

"I . . . I am unharmed, sir."

Rarely did I hear him reproach John Fielding, but he did so now: "You are tardy, sir!"

The blind magistrate stood in the rear door of the premises. Two of his men held duVerre. One pried the acid bottle from the Frenchman's clutching fingers.

"Yet I am here, and all's well." Fielding stumped forward. "These sharp ears listened in the alley at the window, as you advised. They heard ev'ry word, whilst my picklock prised the back door—but slow. Damn it, Burridge, have you lost your touch? Hark, the other Frenchie seeks to 'scape, a creeping fellow. Quick, Fletcher, show him the Blind Beak does not let 'em go once he's got 'em in his net."

🌿 24 🌿

IN WHICH *a lost thing comes to light . . .*

T was still a fine spring afternoon, hardly past four, when we emerged from Phillippe duVerre's printing shop. I gazed about. Sunlight flickered above slate rooftops whilst finely dressed ladies and gentlemen strode the cobbles, and an elegant coach passed near. A woman twirled her parasol, her little dog, in the arms of a turbaned blackamoor, madly biting at fleas—the world unchanged. I was still shaken—I shuddered to think what the acid would have done to my face—but fresh air steadied me, and when Mr. Franklin inquired gravely, "Are you certain you are well, Nick?" I replied, "I am."

Our dun brown coach stood some way off beside two gold-embossed carriages, Peter in its box. Turning toward it (we had played our parts; we could go home) we glanced round at the sound of scuffing boots. DuVerre and his man were being led by two strong constables to a large black rig by his shop; both were manacled. Monsieur Daste stumbled, his heavy features twisted in pain; he did not look round. DuVerre turned. Wrists bound by irons, he peered bewilderedly, his wig askew. He seemed to measure Mr. Franklin: How did you defeat me?

How did I lose all I believed I had won? His gaze grazed me, his mouth twisted. Would he truly have flung acid upon me? I could not meet his stare, and my eyes fell to his feet, shod in fine soft leather, and for a moment I seemed to see 'em kick as the Tyburn hangman broke his neck.

I swallowed. Phillippe duVerre turned his back. Mr. Franklin and I got into our coach.

Peter flicked the reins, and we set out. DuVerre would hang for murder. For counterfeiting as well, proof of that being firmly in John Fielding's possession; for a search of the upstairs rooms had discovered near three hundred pounds in false notes hidden under a pile of fine lace handkerchiefs. (DuVerre could be careless, too.) By comparison James Cavitty had had a fortunate death, for the Frenchman must taste defeat for months before the London mob jeered him to his end. Would the ballad-mongers write a song on him?

I turned to Mr. Franklin. "DuVerre murdered Cavitty—but who did in Cully Stringer?"

"Quimp—one of his men, rather. (Our old enemy takes care never to dirty his hands.) 'Twas surely Stringer who left the door unlatched that second time, so Quimp's men might creep in to see if more brutal methods could discover what the apprentice had not. When they failed to find the diamond, Hexham put the screws to Stringer. In terror the poor lad sought me; that sealed his doom. And truly Quimp is not done yet. We are pursued."

Alarmed, I poked out my head. A closed black coach rattled twenty yards behind us, its driver a muffled shape.

"I glimpsed it in Princes Street," said Mr. Franklin when I pulled in my head. "It has followed us since we left. Lacking the diamond, Quimp must wonder what I know of it—ha! He pursues openly, for we are meant to tremble; our flesh must crawl. I cannot say I am unaffected, but I am damned if I will stop when the end is so close at hand."

"The end, sir?"

He bent near. "The diamond, Nick."

I stared. "You know where it is, who has it?"

"Come, do not you? Think."

A quarter of an hour later we pulled up in front of number 23 Cranbourne Street. I had thought I should never enter the benighted house again, but I did, by the front door, with Benjamin Franklin.

I gazed about the entryway. Truly near a fortnight since I first stood here with Sir Bartleby Bart? Much had changed but not Felicity, for her odd little face once more peered through the stair rail like some changeling or elf. Did her look say she knew me?

Peasgood had let us in. He seemed inured to surprises, for he did not appear took aback. He spoke with cautious hope: "No more bad news, sir?" A thin, pained smile. "Bring us some good?"

Mr. Franklin clapped his shoulder. "If the discovery of a murderer is good, then I bring you good news."

"We are to learn who struck down Master?"

"You may inform your mistress—and the household—that 'twas the Frenchman duVerre."

"The Frenchman . . . ! Dear me."

"He is in custody now, likely to hang."

"But why should he do such a terrible thing?"

It was a delicate matter who was to be informed that James Cavitty had been a counterfeiter. "I shall speak to Mrs. Bone about that," Mr. Franklin replied.

"Very good, sir. But poor Cully Stringer—did the Frenchman strike him down too?"

"No. His vile murderer is not took and, alas, is not likely to be. Nonetheless the curse is lifted from this house. No one need fear any longer."

Peasgood gave his tired smile, "We are all glad to hear it." Bowing, he went to speak to Mrs. Bone, who descended ten minutes later in her black weeds. I went with her and Mr. Franklin into the display room, where with great delicacy he told her what her brother had been about.

She pressed white knuckles to her mouth. "I knew there was something . . . I knew it . . . !"

"Your brother has paid for his crime."

"Poor James!" Her eyes pled "I did not hate him. I hated his rashness, but I knew he was a good painter, and when I watched him tell the truth about some pompous fool I often saw the justice in it though I could never say so. If only I had told him, just once . . . but I had to hold the house together. I had to save the roof over our heads."

"You loved him, I see."

Tears squeezed from her eyes. "My only brother . . ."

"I have spoken to John Fielding. He is Chief Magistrate for Westminster and will do what he can to keep your brother's crime from public knowledge. The Frenchman may wish to trumpet it, but I believe Fielding can persuade him not to. Likely he cannot keep the noose from the man's neck, but he may offer some mitigation if the Frenchman will say he himself engraved the plates. As for a motive for the murder—well, there are plenty of possibilities; Fielding shall serve up a convincing one. If the Crown has its man, it is not overnice about motive."

*   *   *

Annie.

We met her in her small, mean chamber under the eaves, Mr. Franklin scraping his balding head on its sloping roof, my elbow near knocking the basin and ewer from their stand. I looked about. There lay the narrow bed on which the housemaid and I had made love. And there stood she herself by the closed door, pulling at one of the frayed strands of hair that had escaped from her cap. All in the household had known we went up. Mrs. Cockle's fish-eyes had itched to know our business.

Annie gave me one of her wan smiles. *All's up?* it seemed to say. *I knew 'twould be and don't blame you one whit.* She was a girl who dreamt beyond her station, whilst ev'ry moment of her life cried out that those dreams could never come true, and I still felt chagrined that I had been unable to tell her who I was.

Mr. Franklin stood before her. Kind-eyed, he lifted her chin. "You know who I am, child?"

Her lips trembled. "Y-yes, sir. Mr. Franklin, who found out who murdered Master."

"I seek to find out more, but I mean you no harm. Will you believe me?"

"O, I believe you are a good man, sir!"

"And good men must ask for truth?"

"They must."

"And good girls must give it if they can?"

A little shrug. She was resigned.

"Very well. You never worked for Lord Shenstone, did you?"

She stared at her toes. "No, sir."

"You should have liked to. My lord was gentle, handsome. And he was kind to you—on one occasion especially, when Cully Stringer attempted to take advantage of you. You thought on him. You longed to be in his household, and your desire found voice when you told Nick you had been a maid in St. James's Street. You did not plan to lie?"

Her eyes lifted. "O, never, sir!"

"We all say things which are not true. But once out, your story needed polish, and so you produced a ring which you told Nick my lord had given to you when you left his service."

Annie twisted her hands. "I am so wicked!"

"Not wicked. May I see the ring?"

She pulled it from her apron pocket. Mr. Franklin turned it in his fingers. " 'Tis pretty. Not greatly valuable, however. Where did you obtain it."

She faltered. "Must I tell? V-very well, I . . . I stole it from Mrs. Bone."

Ah, thought I.

"And other things as well?" pursued Mr. Franklin.

"Only a thimble, and . . . and—"

"Odds and ends?"

"Which I never thought she'd miss. I had so little of my own. Those things made me feel . . . made me—"

He touched her arm. "You need not explain. 'Twas not a terrible crime; most of what you stole was of little account— save for one thing."

She cried out wildly: "I never meant to take it!"

"The diamond, then."

"Yes." Tears spilt upon her cheeks. "I saw the drapery man bring it back. I saw Master put it in his drawer. Later that day I was alone in the painting room, tidying. I only wished to see it, hold it. It was Lord Shenstone's, that was one reason. And it was so pretty. And I should never have a chance again in my life to touch such a thing. And so I got the drawer out (the lock was weak) and opened the box and took the diamond in my hand. How cold it was to the touch, but how warm it looked! I thought to pin it on, just for a moment. What would it feel like to be a lady—his lady—and wear such a thing? I fastened the catch to my bodice. I walked about like the grand dames do. And then I heard a noise: someone in the entryway! I tore at my bodice, but the clasp had become stuck. I was affrighted, and in my fear I shut the box and flung it in the drawer and dashed out through the storage room and up the servants' stairs. Once in my room I undid the clasp. But I was terrified. The Shenstone Diamond! It lay in my lap. What to do? But before I could replace it, it began to be whispered all over the house that 'twas gone, and Master was mad to find it. If he caught me putting it back, he would toss me out in the street. (I know what happens to girls like that.) Still I wanted to put it back, but there was almost always someone in the painting room; the house had become watchful, eyes ev'rywhere." She glanced at me. "I . . . I did not know what to do."

"And so you kept the Shenstone Diamond."

"Kept it safe."

Mr. Franklin patted her hand. "Yes."

I thought. If she had not hid it Cully Stringer might still be alive. But then Quimp would have got the gem and Lord Shenstone would be ruined. How to weigh these in the balance? In any case Annie's crime was an innocent one.

"You must give me the diamond," said Mr. Franklin, holding out his hand.

She nodded. Turning, she lifted the thin pallet on which she rested each night. There at its foot, in an easily accessible place, ripe for depredations, lay her hoard: the thimble, a tiny porcelain dog, some amber buttons, two bits of lace, and under the lace, the Shenstone Diamond. She drew it forth. 'Twas near five o' the afternoon, the sun declining, but even in the dim rays which penetrated Annie's small garret window the treasure shone: glistening gold with an adamantine heart.

Mr. Franklin weighed it in his palm—"At last . . ."—and I thought for a moment that he would rather crush the thing under his heel than drop it in his pocket. What trouble it had caused!

But he had promised Lady Shenstone. And her lord. "I thank you, Annie." He handed the gem to me. "Keep it, Nick, awhile."

And so another adventure with Mr. Benjamin Franklin came to an end. Mr. Franklin gathered up the rest of the hoard which Annie had stolen. "Nick and I shall find opportunity before we depart to leave it about the house, here and there, under seat cushions and in back of drawers, to be found later." He adjured Annie to steal no more.

She burst into tears: "No more . . . no more . . . !" Whether her light fingers would never again lift any baubles we could not be sure, but I hoped she had learnt her lesson.

"Neither Nick nor I will reveal who had the Shenstone Diamond," concluded Mr. Franklin. Going down, he contrived to leave me alone with her for a moment, dusk gathering beyond her tiny window. We hardly knew how to look at one another.

"I s'pose you will not be back," said she, twisting her fingers.

"No," said I.

She flew to me then and kissed me. 'Twas a kiss of thank you rather than a lover's farewell, and I knew that we both set out on different paths. Backing out, I near stumbled upon the narrow stair, looking my last upon the pretty girl who had first taken me to bed. The round cheeks, the flyaway hair, the applewine breath. I should not forget her.

Spring sent green shoots all over London two weeks later, as Mr. Franklin and I drew up before the Shenstone manse.

'Twas eleven A.M., blue sky above. We had not seen my lord and his lady since we restored the true diamond to 'em. They had been together with their boy when they received it, and I had noted, in her look at my lord, and his at her—then theirs at their son, inheritor of the Shenstone name—that they were determined to set their lives aright. There would be more honesty betwixt 'em, firmer management of monies, no more gaming.

Mr. Franklin had beamed.

Now we joined more than a dozen of London's gentry—earls, viscounts, marchionesses—to see James Cavitty's portrait of Lady Shenstone. Signore Mazzoni had completed the remaining touches, my lord had paid him all that was due, and now, varnished and elegantly framed, the work hung on display. Murmurs of approbation abounded in the long hall: "What excellent work (a pity the artist is dead) . . ." "What lambent blues . . ." "What penetrating reds . . ." "How beautiful is Lady Shenstone, how lifelike the diamond . . ." Mr. Franklin and I exchanged a glance, for just two nights ago he had attended a concert by Handel at which my lady had for the first time worn the false diamond (the other was in the hands of the Dutchman). He had reported how ev'ry voice exclaimed at the exquisiteness of the gem.

Afterward we drove to Cranbourne Street. "So I may show you something, Nick." Mr. Franklin led me to the door of number 23; and there, where had been affixed the brass plaque with James Cavitty's name, was a shiny new plaque: *Signore Amadeo Mazzoni, Painter.* The gentleman winked. "All will be well with him. Shenstone tells ev'ryone the Italian had a significant hand in his wife's portrait; that is sure to bring him custom. I myself have sent round three or four men. And Jimmy Ralph has dug up a likely young fellow to serve as his

261

apprentice. Mazzoni deserves success. As for Felicity, I do not doubt she shall have a new father."

Yet all was not well, for the following afternoon Mr. Franklin received in the post a cutting from an Amsterdam newspaper. We could but guess who had sent it. As he could not read Dutch he had an acquaintance translate it, and we both paled as we learned that it told of the murder by strangulation of one Jan Vanderdonck, a gem-cutter, who had just placed on the market three remarkable diamonds reputed to be from a royal cache of ancient China.

Vanderdonck had been discovered dead at his workbench, eyes bulging, tongue black in his mouth.

All three diamonds were nowhere to be found.

"Dear God," breathed Mr. Franklin.

But this proved not the last bitter morsel, for another note came as dusk settled over London. It was slipped under Mrs. Stevenson's door; she herself brought it up.

Breaking the seal, Mr. Franklin read, then passed the paper to me:

> Franklin,
>
> I thought to punish you for thwarting my plans, but you and Shenstone have not been so clever as you think. Did you enjoy the newspaper cutting I sent? Indeed, I owe you thanks, for I now have more than I hoped: three "royal" gems, which shall bring me much profit. So I sheathe my knife. (It was out, sir, it was out.) Watch your step in future.
>
> Yours, most sincerely

It was not signed.

"Poor Dutchman," said said Mr. Franklin. "Poor London."

He peered into the fire; and I read in the licking flames that all was not over betwixt Benjamin Franklin and Quimp.

But the gentleman could never remain glum for long. Rousing himself, he reached under his chair. "For you, lad." He handed me a book.

I examined it. *The Practice of Painting and Perspective,* by Thomas Bardwell. "Thank you, sir," said I.

"Recently published. Jimmy Ralph says it is excellent. Study it, as I know you will. You began to learn at Cavitty's. We must do more for you in that line. A drawing master, perhaps?" He slapped his chair arms. "But now—" Rising, he led me to the workshop behind his bedchamber, which contained the *apparati* whereby he investigated Nature. In one corner, by the window, was a shelf upon which he had begun to place mementos of his pursuit of crime: the Bible whose hidden papers had led to the murderer of Ebenezer Inch; the flask of Opliss Popliss drops which had poisoned Roderick Fairbrass; the Wedgewood chess set David Garrick had given him for ridding Drury Lane of threats. Pulling from his coat pocket the small copperplate, Mr. Franklin placed it amongst the rest. "Reminders, Nick," said he.

We went down to supper. In the cosy room off the kitchen I found our little family waiting by white damask and flickering candles: Mrs. Stevenson, Polly, William with his customary hauteur. At first I could not understand their watchful expressions. Then I saw the drawing on the wall: mine—of the marble hand.

It was framed, under glass. Mr. Franklin rose and fell on his heels. "Mrs. Bone asked what she might offer in return for my help. There was but one thing I desired."

" 'Tis very good, Handy," drawled William, great praise from him who thought I took far too much of his father's time.

"Good, indeed," murmured Mrs. Stevenson and Polly.

My eyes fixed upon Mr. Franklin. "Thank you again, sir," said I.

"O, tut." He clapped my shoulder.

We sat, I pleased to eat the roast beef of old England beside the best and wisest man whom I have known.